Fire Maidens: Paris

Billionaires & Bodyguards
Book 1

by Anna Lowe

Twin Moon Press

Copyright © 2019 Anna Lowe

All rights reserved.

Editing by Lisa A. Hollett

Covert art by Kim Killion

Contents

Contents	i
Other books in this series	iii
Free Books	v
Chapter One	1
Chapter Two	9
Chapter Three	17
Chapter Four	23
Chapter Five	31
Chapter Six	41
Chapter Seven	53
Chapter Eight	61
Chapter Nine	69
Chapter Ten	81
Chapter Eleven	93
Chapter Twelve	103

Chapter Thirteen	115
Chapter Fourteen	127
Chapter Fifteen	133
Chapter Sixteen	143
Chapter Seventeen	151
Chapter Eighteen	161
Chapter Nineteen	171
Chapter Twenty	181
Chapter Twenty-One	189
Chapter Twenty-Two	195
Chapter Twenty-Three	207
Chapter Twenty-Four	219
Chapter Twenty-Five	231
Epilogue	247
Sneak Peek: Fire Maidens: London	255
Books by Anna Lowe	257
About the Author	265

Other books in this series

Fire Maidens - Billionaires & Bodyguards

Fire Maidens: Paris (Book 1)

Fire Maidens: London (Book 2)

Fire Maidens: Rome (Book 3)

Fire Maidens: Portugal (Book 4)

Fire Maidens: Ireland (Book 5)

visit www.annalowebooks.com

Free Books

Get your free e-books now!

Sign up for my newsletter at *annalowebooks.com* to get three free books!

- *Desert Wolf*: Friend or Foe (Book 1.1 in the Twin Moon Ranch series)

- *Off the Charts* (the prequel to the Serendipity Adventure series)

- *Perfection* (the prequel to the Blue Moon Saloon series)

Chapter One

There's no such thing as vampires. No such thing as vampires...

It didn't matter how often Natalie whispered those words to herself. One look at the man at the table by the window made her blood run cold. His teeth were perfectly normal, and yet she kept imagining them extending into fangs. But that was crazy, right?

"Are you going to check on him, or am I?" the woman behind the serving counter asked.

Natalie steeled her nerves, pasted on a stiff smile, and walked over to the new "guest," as the homeless people at the soup kitchen were called. Usually, she loved interacting with guests. Each had his or her own story, their own unique character. Plus, they were patient with her imperfect French, and she'd gained incredible insights into life in Paris from volunteering there. In some ways, it was a lot like the soup kitchen she'd volunteered at back home in Philadelphia.

But vampires? No thanks.

She glanced at the man by the window. Wasn't it time to get over her overactive imagination and help the poor man?

The thing was, he didn't seem the least bit poor. Not with that tailored suit, sophisticated cologne, and manicured nails. But there was no telling who was down on his luck in Paris these days, and this section of the Latin Quarter was a real mix.

She walked over, trying to quell her nerves. Then she pasted on a smile and welcomed him in French. "Good evening. How are you?"

Usually, it was easy to offer the warm smile and few minutes of chitchat that many of the guests craved. But with this man...

He took her in with cold, appraising eyes that seemed intent on sucking the heat right out of her body... or her blood.

Cut that out, she ordered herself.

Often, the biggest trick at *Solidarité du Coeur* was guessing whether a guest was struggling to get by, truly homeless, or a freeloader, like the occasional backpacker who came through. But with this man, Natalie's mind kept sliding over to a different question: human or vampire?

Not that she had any real evidence to go on — just the nightmares that had been plaguing her lately. The kind that ripped her out of bed in a cold sweat and left her jumping at shadows afterward. That, and the sensation of being followed she'd experienced all day, as if she were a moving target, slipping in and out of an assassin's sights.

"I'd love a warm drink," the man said.

His lips barely moved, but his eyes strayed to her wrists where the veins showed.

"Sure." Natalie rushed back to the bar, wishing she'd worn something more conservative than a tight-fitting black top. Say, a turtleneck or an oversized sweater.

The crowd at one side of the soup kitchen exploded into cheers and jeers at a soccer game on TV. Most looked jubilant, and a few waved blue-and-red scarves, while others hissed.

"PSG one, Arsenal zero," the announcer crowed as Natalie squeezed past.

It had taken her weeks to figure out that those letters denoted the city's premier soccer squad, and another week to grasp how important the Champions League was. Then again, everything had been new to her when she'd first come to Paris.

She detoured to several more tables, collecting empty bread baskets and taking drink orders. But all the while, she felt hot, piercing eyes on her back. When she glanced over, the creepy guest didn't so much as look away. He watched her with unblinking eyes. Each table seated ten, but no one sat anywhere near him.

Finally, she worked up the nerve to carry over a pot of tea, hoping he'd drink quickly and move on.

"*Merci, ma belle,*" the creep said, locking his long, slender fingers around the mug before she set it down.

The crystal she wore around her neck — a pretty trinket she'd found in a flea market along the Seine — swung away from her chest as she moved, and the man's eyes moved with it. Or was he staring at her chest?

When she jerked away, one of his nails nicked her palm, and he murmured, *"Excusez-moi."*

"No problem," Natalie said, hurrying away.

But he'd drawn blood, dammit. Just a bead, but still. Did the guy file his nails into points or something?

She glanced back and nearly froze. The creep was licking the blood off his finger. Or, wait. Was he innocently licking a drop of spilled cream?

Innocent, my ass, her inner radar said.

"Olivier." One of the other volunteers shot the man a dark look. "I swear he has no business here. But you never know. Sometimes the best dressed are the ones who've lost everything."

Natalie wasn't so sure, but she wasn't about to bring up vampires, no matter how foreboding her dreams had become. Some in a good way, like the dreams that had made her move to Paris in the first place. Those dreams had been sunny and warm, with long walks along riverbanks and cobblestoned streets. Dreams so detailed and lifelike, they felt like scenes she'd already lived.

Other dreams were weirdly empowering, like dreams of flying — and not just flying around the rooms of her childhood home as she had imagined as a kid. These strange new dreams had her swooping over a lavender-lined landscape by night with the wind whistling in her ears. In them, the world was hushed, and the moon shone orange and extra large, making her feel as if she could glide for hours.

Lately, though, her dreams had grown darker and more chilling. Shadows followed her down dim alleys, and when she tried to run — or fly — she felt stuck in place. Sinister men stepped out of nowhere, flashing fangs. Their fingers closed over her throat, and she felt powerless to move. Then they would lean in with their jaws opened wide...

She shivered. Most of the time, moving to Paris seemed like the best decision of her life. She felt freer, happier, and more independent than she'd ever been. But occasionally, a creep like Olivier would come along and make her wonder about the difference between premonitions and harmless dreams.

"*Merde*," a guest blurted, riveted to the TV screen.

Yeah, *shit* was the word, and not just for a missed free kick. Natalie straightened her shoulders, reminding herself she could manage everything on her own. That was part of her coming to Paris, too. A new life. A new start. A new everything.

"Any chance for a refill?" another guest asked, holding up his bowl.

As she stepped over, the front door opened, letting in a gust of fresh night air. Curtains stirred, and the guests all glanced up at the sound of huge boots clomping confidently down the stairs from street level.

Natalie looked too, and for a moment, time stood still. Her breath caught, and her pulse skipped as the security man backed away, revealing the newcomer's face.

It's him! It's him! part of her cheered.

It was ridiculous, reacting to a near-stranger that way. But, hell. In three years of dating a guy named Dean in Philly, she'd never gotten as excited as she got around Mr. Tall, Dark, and distinctly Parisian. Not even when Dean would come over — late, usually, because she had never been as important to him as his job — and not on weekends, no matter how much time she put into planning a nice time. Not even in bed, if she had to admit as much.

But one look — one breath — in the presence of this stranger had a way of making her feel reborn.

Hi, she wanted to murmur, although he was a good thirty feet away.

His scowl broke long enough for him to smile at her. A brief but bright smile, as if he'd located the sun in a world of constant storms. His eyes sparkled, and though his lips didn't move, she imagined a low *Hi* rumble through her mind.

The wind had whisked a few leaves in after him, and they swirled around his ankles, as happy and free as Natalie felt. Boy, was he handsome — handsome enough to pull off that musketeer beard and mustache, like a man intent on swashbuckling his way into her heart. But then one of the volunteers pranced over, calling, "Tristan!"

His face went dull, and when he turned to the woman, the upward curl of his lips was forced.

"Marie," he murmured, kissing her on each cheek.

Natalie turned away. Was that special smile just wistful thinking on her part? She barely knew the man, and they'd never exchanged more than a few words. Yet every time Tristan entered, it felt as though he was only there for her. Every time he left, part of her mourned. And as for the dreams he inspired...

Natalie puffed a breath upward, cooling herself off.

"*Mademoiselle, du sucre, s'il vous plaît?*" *Some sugar, please?* a guest called, pulling her back to work.

Still, her mind stayed with Tristan. Rumors abounded about him. Some said he was an undercover *gendarme*, keeping an eye out for trouble. Others said he was a bounty hunter searching for deadbeats who owed money to criminals in Paris's shady underworld. Some insisted he was an agent with the *DGSI* — the French equivalent of the FBI. Marie insisted he was an ultra-rich benefactor checking up on one of his pet projects. And in a way, all those theories fit. The man exuded authority, power, and a mysterious *je ne sais quoi* that put him a class above everyone else.

Natalie glanced back, and miracle of miracles, Tristan's eyes met hers. Like she was the real beauty there and not curvy Marie, who tossed back her sleek hair and giggled in one smooth, practiced move.

Every head in the soup kitchen turned to admire Marie's figure, but Tristan's eyes didn't stray from Natalie's.

Hi, she breathed all over again.

His gaze was soft and concerned, and his chest — a broad expanse that stretched the fabric of the black shirt under his jacket — rose and fell in a deep breath. But the next time he inhaled—

His nostrils flared, and his head whipped around. He scanned the area, then pinned his gaze squarely on Olivier, the creep by the window.

You, Tristan's accusing gaze declared.

You, Oliver might as well have replied. His brow furrowed, and his nails scratched at the wooden tabletop. The air grew charged as the men stared each other down.

"Miss? Some sugar? Please?"

Natalie blinked at the guest before her. "Oh, sorry. I'll be right back."

As she hurried to the kitchen, Tristan and Olivier sized each other up like a couple of gorillas about to thump their chests. Tristan was a good six feet tall, but he seemed to grow even taller as he stared the other man down. Olivier, though slighter in build, was taller. He had a sinister aura, and his pale skin appeared to give off an effervescent glow.

Natalie glanced around. Did no one else pick up on the testosterone-laced vibes filling the room?

But even Madame Monet — the stout matron with a knack for squelching petty disagreements before they exploded into all-out fights — didn't so much as give the two men a second glance.

"*Goooooal!*" the television announcer hollered, and everyone leaped to their feet. Everyone but Tristan and Olivier, who continued to stare each other down.

In the jubilation that followed the goal, Natalie lost sight of the two men. She shook herself back into action. It didn't matter what the score was or who had walked in. Her job was to work the soup kitchen floor, and she'd been neglecting her guests. For the next few minutes, she bustled back and forth, clearing dishes and serving tea with biscuits. But when she turned away from wiping down one table—

Oof! She bumped into a brick wall. Or rather, into someone built as solidly as a brick wall.

"*Excusez-moi,*" she murmured, looking up — way up — into eyes the color of a stormy sky. Tristan?

It was a whole new angle on him. Usually, he stood in a corner, quietly refusing food or drink while he surveyed the area. Now, she spotted all the details she'd never noticed from afar. The tiny scar on one cheek where no stubble grew. The length of his eyelashes. The curls of brown hair that reached to just beneath his ears. The depths of his pure eyes, as blue as the sea...

For a moment, she lost track of time, and Tristan seemed equally mesmerized. Then he frowned, grabbed her elbow, and spoke in French.

"You have to leave. Now."

His voice was deep. Growly. So full of authority, Natalie nearly nodded.

Then she caught herself. "Wait. What?"

In one deft movement, he turned her toward the kitchen, using just enough force to make his urgency clear.

"Leave. Now. Trust me," he said, making the strands of her hair move. "You have to go."

"But..."

She'd spent many a lonely night entertaining fantasies about the mysterious cop/millionaire/secret agent, but none of them had gone anything like this. Still, when she turned to face him, she saw what had entranced her from the very start: those deep, sincere eyes. Eyes that promised, *You can trust me.*

"You have to go," he insisted, switching to English.

His accent was almost North American, but every once in a while, a vowel would slip, and a French accent came through. Who was he, exactly? Where was he from? And why did he want her to run out on the job now?

She motioned toward tables that needed clearing, about to protest. Then she spotted Olivier jumping to his feet, staring at her with an expression that said, *Don't you dare move.*

It was an order accompanied by a burning, unrelenting glare. *Literally* burning, Natalie realized, when she saw two red points of light spark where his irises should have been.

Help. Call the police. He's a monster, she wanted to scream. But no one seemed perturbed — not even Marie, who passed between them. Could she not see the man's eyes glow?

"Quick, while we still have time," Tristan said, hustling her through the kitchen's swinging door.

"Hey!" Madame Monet called, but it was too late.

Natalie squinted through the kitchen's cloud of steam. Dishes clattered, oil splattered, and volunteer cooks called to each other over the usual kitchen din. Tristan kept hold of Natalie's elbow — gently enough not to pinch, yet firmly enough to hurry her along. In no time, they reached the back door, which was partially blocked by a stack of wooden pallets.

She balked. "This is crazy. Let me go."

She spun, staring Tristan down. The height difference made her tilt her head way back, but when her eyes locked on his...

You can trust him, a little voice whispered. *You* must *trust him.*

Her lips moved in protest, but no words came. Just a little squeak that made his face soften.

Then the swinging door burst open, and Olivier appeared.

"Hey!" one of the cooks yelled. "You can't come back here."

Olivier — pale, creepy Olivier, who seemed twice as sinister as before — ignored the protest and stalked forward.

You, his eyes promised Natalie. *You are mine.*

Natalie watched in horror as Olivier's lips peeled back, exposing long, pointy canines. The only thing that kept her from screaming was the steady grip of Tristan's hand on her arm, propelling her toward the door.

"That way," he grunted. "If you want to live, get moving. Now."

Chapter Two

Tristan shoved the door open, pushed Natalie into the rear alley, and knocked over the stack of wooden pallets to block the space behind them. That might not delay the vampire for long, but every minute counted. He kept his right hand on his mate's elbow as they—

Whoa. What had his inner dragon just said?

Mate, the beast hissed in his mind.

His legs nearly froze in midstride, while his mind spun.

For weeks, he'd been ending his Thursday patrols of the Latin Quarter at the soup kitchen, telling himself he was being thorough. But who was he kidding? It had nothing to do with security. It was all about *her.* The woman with the long, coppery hair and brilliant sapphire eyes. The one who moved shyly, like she had no idea how beautiful she was.

Natalie, his dragon breathed.

They'd never made contact before, so he hadn't realized until he'd touched her arm. Then, wham! The embers that glowed in his dragon soul burst into an all-out bonfire.

Mate, his dragon murmured. *She's my mate.*

Of course, he'd grown up hearing about destined mates. That when you met The One, you just knew, and your life would never be the same. But, hell. Now?

As he hustled Natalie onward, the cool nighttime air whipped her hair, setting off a thousand fantasies in his mind. Nice fantasies, like leaning in close and sniffing her lavender scent. Dirty fantasies too, like seeing those long, silky strands sway as she moved over him, both of them naked and in bed. A big bed with a sturdy frame that wouldn't so much as squeak when he and she—

He sucked in a sharp breath and cursed his dragon. *Would you cut that out?*

Having a ferocious, animal side had its advantages, but there were drawbacks, too. Like having to suppress caveman urges at the least opportune times. Women weren't objects to be possessed like jewels, and they were capable of a hell of a lot more than sex. He knew that firsthand. Men started wars, while women picked up the pieces and plowed on. Women pulled their families through the roughest, toughest times. When the power company turned off the heat in the dead of winter, when there was no money to buy shoes, when deadbeat dads took off, leaving nothing — women found a way.

A scrap of newspaper drifted down the alley, and something fluttered overhead. Tristan looked up just in time to see a twisted figure launch itself into the inky sky.

"Please tell me that wasn't a vampire," Natalie whispered.

He scowled. No, that was a gargoyle. One that had led Olivier to Natalie, perhaps.

Tristan blinked and looked around. Gargoyles posed no threat — not to a dragon shifter like him. But vampires...

Along the alley, lumps of cobblestones shone in the dim light of a single lamppost. Puddles formed in the depressions between stones, each glinting with...water? Urine? Spilled beer? He wrinkled his nose. Judging by the scent, it was a mixture of all three.

"*That* was a vampire." He motioned back toward the soup kitchen. "We need to get you out of here."

He hated that his words came out all snippy and cold, when all he wanted was to reassure her. Hold her. Keep her safe. But somehow, he couldn't get it out the way he meant, what with his mind spinning so quickly.

Save mate. Kill vampire. Report to the big boss — who would not be pleased.

Shit. What a mess. He'd been hired by the Guardians of Paris to report wayward vampires, but not to engage any. That could set off a whole new wave of conflict between shifters and vampires, throwing Europe into another Dark Age.

Not that humans would be aware of anything but the instability that ensued. Humans, who were totally ignorant of shifters, believed *they* ran things. In truth, humans tended to make a mess of things. Over centuries, powerful shifter clans had watched over the cities, maintaining peace among the supernaturals who could wreak havoc on unsuspecting humans. Wolves ran Rome, lions kept an eye on London, and dragons oversaw law and order in Paris. At least, they tried. But if the fragile truce between shifters and vampires wavered...

Tristan sniffed the air, trying to tease out each scent. Paris had its share of resident vampires who had proven they could play by the rules. No stalking humans, no murdering. Just catch-and-release blood-sucking that didn't result in permanent harm. Some vampires found human consorts — willing playthings who enjoyed the lifestyle. It turned Tristan's stomach, but hell. As a dragon shifter, he devoured the occasional deer or boar, so who was he to judge?

But the power of the Guardians was waning, and the threat of evil elements was on the rise. Rogue wolf shifters tired of prowling the woods came to cities for new adventures. Malcontent dragons plotted to snatch power. Unruly vampires wandered in, sucking their victims dry of blood.

"A vampire? Are you serious?" Natalie stared at him through those startled doe eyes. Deep, intelligent eyes that went with her earnest face. Clearly, she was new to Paris. Why had she come? When? What did she have planned?

"Dead serious," he murmured in reply.

Natalie paled, and he cursed himself. Could he say nothing right?

He looked around. His top priority was to keep Natalie safe. Second on the list was not revealing his dragon side, which would be tricky with a vampire to fight. Third was figuring out some way to explain to his boss why he'd engaged a vampire rather than reporting it.

"That way." He pointed left, focusing on priority number one — keeping his mate safe.

But as soon as he faced that end of the alley — the one with the shortest distance to the main road — two tall figures swept into view.

"Oh God," Natalie grabbed Tristan's arm. "More vampires?"

He tested the air and found it devoid of anything but stale alley scents. Yep, those were vampires, all right — creatures distinguished by the absence of scent other than a faint whiff of ammonia. No wonder the bastards practically bathed in cologne.

Pricks of red light showed in the vampires' eyes, a sign that they were on the hunt.

"Stay close," Tristan grunted.

Natalie followed him into an about-face, and he marveled at her composure. Vampires had a magical aura that could stop an average human in his or her tracks. As a shifter, Tristan was immune, but few humans were strong enough to resist. And yet, there went Natalie, scurrying ahead of him, getting away on her own.

And not a second too soon. She had barely retraced her steps past the back door of the soup kitchen when it flew open, and Olivier hurtled out.

"Stop," the vampire ordered, using a deep, authoritative tone laced with magic.

But Natalie just huffed and hurried on. "Like hell, I am."

Another vampire appeared before them, cutting off their only avenue of escape. Which left Tristan with four vampires after his mate — and only one of him. How was he going to pull that off without revealing his dragon?

The soup kitchen staff threw a few halfhearted protests after Olivier, but even they had the good sense to yank the door shut. A moment later, the heavy grind of a bolt sounded, and the alley went deathly still.

Natalie backed away from the fourth vampire, bumping into Tristan's chest. When he looped an arm around her, she put a hand on his forearm. And, wow. Though Tristan was totally focused on the threat before them, a corner of his mind registered that he would remember that moment for the rest of his life. The trust. The perfect fit of her body against his. The gesture that said, *Your fate is mine.*

But, damn. He had to think fast, with one vampire before him and three more behind.

"When I say run, go. Run for your life."

He kept his whisper so low, he wasn't sure Natalie could hear. But her chin dipped slightly, and her body tensed in the prelude to a sprint.

Kill, his inner dragon growled, focusing on the vampire before them.

Oh, he planned to, all right. But he had Natalie to consider first.

"My dear, what are you doing? You can't trust him," Olivier purred in a hypnotizing voice. "You can only trust us."

Natalie snorted, and Olivier's brow furrowed. Clearly, the vampire was used to enthralling humans, but Natalie seemed immune.

The other vampires murmured to one another, and their eyes fell to her chest — or rather, her necklace. Tristan couldn't see it, but he could sense a low, pulsing power and see a hint of a golden glow.

"Close your eyes," he whispered.

One curt shake of her head said, *Are you nuts?*

"Close your eyes," he insisted.

He doubted she would, though, and there was no time to waste. So he slapped a hand over her eyes and leaned to one side, opening his mouth on a huge inhale.

The vampire's eyes went wide with an expression that said, *Oh shit.*

Oh shit, was right. Or rather, *Oh sh—,* because an instant later, Tristan hit the vampire with a long plume of fire. Nothing as big or as powerful as he could summon in dragon form, but enough to make the bastard duck and roll aside.

"Run." Tristan pushed Natalie forward.

She took off past the fallen vampire, and for three steps, Tristan followed. Then he spun and held his ground, listening to her footsteps race down the alley.

Mate, his dragon whimpered. *Need to keep her close.*

But *close* didn't work with four vampires around, so he let her go, mourning the whole time. If the woman had any sense, she would disappear in the maze of streets, then catch the next plane home, wherever that was. How would he ever find her again?

"Step aside," Olivier ordered. "She's mine."

Tristan stood firm. "You step aside. Find someone else's blood to suck."

The vampire sneered. "You think blood like that comes along every day? Royal blood? With it, I would have the power to—"

Another of the vampires cut him off with a cough. Olivier shot him a dark look and motioned after Natalie. "She's mine."

Tristan shook his head, resisting the urge to lick his chapped lips. They weren't made for spitting fire, and it showed. But that was nothing compared to the pain he was about to inflict on the vampires. With a sweeping gesture, he flicked the claws of his right hand free. A partial shift took concentration, but a few claws were all he could afford to reveal right now.

"She's mine," he retorted, leaping at the nearest vampire.

He'd meant to hiss the words, but they came out in more of a roar. A trickle of fire escaped his lips, and his jump was a couple feet higher than he'd expected. His arm moved so fast, it blurred, and a moment later, a vampire's head thumped to the ground. Tristan stared as the body sank in on itself and crumbled into dry ashes scattered by the next gust of wind.

"Didier," Olivier mourned.

Tristan turned, glaring. Didier could burn in hell, as could the other three.

The red points in their eyes intensified, and Olivier growled, "Kill him."

An instant later, three very pissed-off vampires pounced. Tristan had caught the first one by surprise, but these three were better prepared. Their nails were sharp as razors, and the lightest contact cut deep. Fangs flashed at him from every direction, and it was all he could do to fend them off.

Snippets of every shifter fight he'd ever been in raced through his mind, but that experience didn't apply to vampires. Their sheer speed was one thing, the three-sided attack another. And while his claws found their mark often, the vampires struck too. Soon, his body burned from half a dozen wounds. Deep slashes that bled and bled, as all vampire-inflicted wounds did. A long gash made his left arm ache, and blood dripped into his right eye from a cut on his forehead.

Let me out, his dragon insisted. *Let me finish them.*

Tristan considered. Shifting into full dragon form was his last resort. But, heck — he was getting close to that point. Shifters healed quickly, but they weren't immortal. One misstep, and the vampires could wrestle him to the ground. The three of them would suck his blood until he was dry and lifeless. Worse, they'd chase down Natalie soon after.

Tristan gritted his teeth. No way.

Summoning his last reserves, he shoved the nearest vampire back. In one long, arcing gesture, he slashed a claw across one vampire's chest and over to the other's cheek. Then he staggered back, sure it was time to shift. His vision was starting to blur, and his ears rang.

But two of the vampires whirled, and it struck Tristan that he might not be imagining that ringing sound.

"*Merde. Voilà les gendarmes,*" one of the vampires cursed, looking up in the direction of police sirens.

Tristan exhaled. It wasn't often a shifter welcomed cops to the scene of a fight — too many prying human eyes, too many questions raised. But in this case, he wouldn't mind.

Two vampires backed away, dragging the third.

"I am not finished with you," Olivier spat as he went. "And as for the woman, I swear, she shall be mine."

A moment later, they disappeared around the corner. Tristan stumbled back against a brick wall. The world tilted sideways, and he slumped to the ground, panting. Crap, was he tired.

Police, his dragon warned. *Get moving.*

His eyes slid shut. *Just one minute.*

We don't have a minute.

In his mind, he could see the consequences all too clearly. If he didn't get out of there fast, the mess he was in would grow by a factor of about ten. He'd lose his job. Worse, he'd never get another offer. He'd become one of those shifters who drifted from place to place, unable to settle in a comfortable lair of his own, which meant he could forget about winning over his mate.

Plus, there was just enough vampire poison raging through his body to finish him off for good. If he didn't move quickly, it would take hold, and then...

Get moving, his dragon insisted. *Now.*

But no matter how clear the directive was in his mind, his body just wouldn't cooperate.

"Just one more minute," he mumbled. Then everything went cloudy, and he drifted into a dark void.

Chapter Three

Natalie stood at the street corner, clutching a wall for support. Her eyes darted everywhere. Had the vampires circled the block? Were they coming for her?

But the scene on the street was just another Parisian evening. A pleasant weekday night with a hint of spring — enough to draw a few people out despite the late hour. The street was lit with a row of antique lampposts, and signs beckoned customers into restaurants and bistros. A waiter bustled in and out of a sidewalk café, and couples sauntered by, holding hands. In a tree-lined park at the end of the block, leaves whispered in the breeze, and above them, a whole galaxy of stars shone bright.

It was a nice night. No, a beautiful night. The kind a girl would drop everything and move to Paris for. But behind her...

She glanced back into the alley, ready to bolt at the first sign of a vampire. Her eyes darted upward, too, because something had hovered overhead earlier — a twisted, half human, half monster with wings. Now, the sky was clear, and the terrifying sounds of the fight had died down.

Died? Every muscle in her body tensed at the eerie silence.

The red lights of the subway glowed at the end of the block — one of the old-fashioned stations with Art Nouveau drips and curls around the letters spelling *Metropolitain* — a style that had always reminded her of vampires. But now, that looked like her best escape route. She could jump on a subway car and shuttle to the other side of the city. Heck, she could head straight to the airport and book herself a seat on the first flight home.

Olivier's word words echoed through her mind. *You think blood like that comes along every day? Royal blood?*

What had that been about? And what about that out-of-nowhere burst of fire?

She had every reason to flee, but the ominous silence of the alley called to her, as did the memory of Tristan's earnest expression. *We need to get you out of here.*

Was he lying in the alley, bleeding? Worse, were the vampires bent over him, sucking his blood?

For a full minute, she stood shaking. Then she forced herself to inch back toward the alley. With every hesitant step forward, the sounds and lights of the main street faded, plunging her into a dark, dank world. Stooping, she grabbed a discarded vodka bottle and smashed the end against the cobblestones. The sound of shattering glass made her wince, and something rushed through the litter at the edge of the alley. A rat?

Trembling, she inched forward, holding her makeshift weapon. It took her a solid minute to work up the nerve to peek around the corner of the alley — a minute that felt like an hour. But when she saw Tristan slumped against a wall, alone, she dropped the bottle and rushed to his side.

"Tristan! Tristan?" She crouched beside him, her heart hammering. "Are you all right?"

He mumbled incoherently, and she shook his shoulder. Well, she tried to. But his muscles were the size of boulders — too wide and solid to get her hand around.

"Oh God. Are you all right?"

His lips were chapped, and blood leaked from a dozen wounds. When he stirred and raised his head, images from a zombie movie rushed through her mind, and she half expected to see horrible, bloodshot eyes and a foaming mouth. But, no. His eyes were a clear, startling blue — like the summer sky — and she exhaled.

"Tristan..."

He dipped his head and groaned.

"Police..."

His eyes slid shut, drawing Natalie's gaze down. So much blood — too much.

"You'll be okay," she said, trying to convince herself. "The police will be here soon."

But Tristan groaned and slid his heels along the ground, trying to stand.

"Wait, you're hurt."

He rolled to all fours. "We have to go."

Still, he stopped and hung his head, too injured to go on.

She wanted to run a hand over his back, but there was blood there, too. The jacket he'd discarded earlier was lying on the ground, and she threw it gingerly over his shoulders.

"Just wait. The police are coming."

He rocked back to sit on his heels, grimacing. "You want to explain the vampires to the police, or do you want me to?"

She bit her lip. "But your wounds..."

"Will heal." He extended an arm — a long, muscled arm, like that of an Olympic swimmer. "Help me up. We need to get out of here."

We. It was the second or third time he'd said it, and the word warmed her. *We* meant she didn't have to face this nightmare alone.

As the sirens grew louder, she looped Tristan's arm over her shoulders and heaved. For one hopeless moment, she didn't think she could help him off the ground. But her necklace fell free of her shirt and swung between them, glittering with golden light, and she tried again. Tristan scuffled and slowly rose to his feet, where he wobbled uncertainly, staring at the necklace.

Brakes squealed, and car doors thumped. The flash of police lights illuminated the end of the alley with bursts of blue and red.

"That way," Tristan muttered, tilting his head in the opposite direction.

How Natalie got him all the way to the street, she had no clue. But somehow, she did, half guiding, half dragging him along.

"Metro," he said through clenched teeth. "Keep an eye out for vampires."

Which made every shadow loom and every passerby look like a cold-blooded killer. On the other hand, everyone gave her and Tristan a wide berth, as if *they* were the suspicious ones.

"B line toward Orly," Tristan murmured as she helped him down the steps to the Metro. "Just a few stops."

Natalie wanted to protest that *lots* of stops would be better, but she was too busy getting him through the turnstile — a tricky operation since there wasn't space for two. Luckily, there was no attendant on duty to stop them, just an older couple who shot her disapproving looks.

"Give me a break," she muttered.

As far as she knew, vampire was *vampire* in French, and she was tempted to explain. But they'd just think she was crazy — or worse, drunk, as Tristan appeared with his stumbling step and stooped shoulders. At least the drunk look kept people at arm's length, and his jacket covered most of his wounds.

"Are you okay?" she whispered, helping him into a corner seat on the train.

He slumped. "Been worse."

Worse than after a vampire attack? He was kidding, right?

"Where did you get that?" He jutted his chin toward her necklace.

"This?" She cupped the citrine crystal in one hand. "At one of those vendors along the Seine."

Tristan didn't look convinced, but then again, he probably wasn't seeing — or thinking — straight. His chin dipped, and he seemed to drift away again, but when a garbled announcement sounded, his head jerked up. "Next stop is ours."

Ours. Natalie hesitated. Where was he taking her?

Then it struck her that she was the one taking him, and she relaxed a little. Plus, she was convinced he meant her no harm. His eyes were too sincere, his touch too careful. And heck, he'd saved her from vampires, right?

So she helped him up at the next stop — a feat that seemed even harder than before — and stepped out onto the platform.

"That way," he said, leaning on her.

A vaulted roof stretched overhead, and the exit seemed miles away. But there was an escalator to street level — thank goodness — and when they exited, Natalie sucked in a lungful of fresh air. A tidy row of trees lined the boulevard, and more swayed gently behind a gated park across the street. She squinted, getting her bearings. The Luxembourg Gardens? Boulevard Saint-Michel? A swanky address, indeed. Did Tristan live there?

"Number 71C," he mumbled.

Wow. Apparently, he did. Not only that, but 71C turned out to be a gorgeous, century-old building right across from the park. One with a doorman and everything. The gray-haired gent pulled the double doors open and didn't bat an eye as Tristan staggered in. He didn't look twice at Natalie either, which gave her pause. Was the doorman that unflappable, or did Tristan regularly stumble in with a lady on his arm?

"Monsieur Chevalier," the doorman greeted Tristan in a tone that gave nothing away. "Mademoiselle."

"*Merci*," she mumbled, making for the elevator.

Luckily, the doorman helped with that, too, because it was one of those antique elevators you had to pull a gate across and lock down. Gears turned, and the elevator rose with a grinding lurch.

"*Bonne nuit,*" the doorman called.

Natalie clutched at the handrail. So far, her *nuit* hadn't been all too *bonne*. But unless Tristan took her to a dark, creepy apartment, things could hardly get worse.

Chapter Four

The elevator rattled along, and Natalie fully expected it to break down between floors. But it chugged up and up, taking her all the way to—

The penthouse? She looked Tristan over. Really?

"This is it," he said, fumbling with the latch.

"Are you sure?"

He didn't answer, but his key fit the door, and it turned smoothly. There was a second lock, and a third, and he cursed over each. Finally, he pushed the door open with a weary sigh. "Home."

He said it the way a soldier might after a long tour of duty, and she wondered why. But then she spotted a pair of glittering eyes and jumped back, ready to scream.

"That's Bijou," Tristan sighed. "He came with the place."

Natalie stuck a hand against her thumping heart. A cat. It was just a cat. A slim, black feline who arched and hissed at Tristan. Tristan cursed back in French and weaved down a narrow hallway. Natalie helped him along until they reached a huge, arched doorway, where she couldn't help but pause.

Wow.

That was the penthouse, all right. A span of four gilded rooms formed the front of the apartment, with floor-to-ceiling windows framing views of the Luxembourg Gardens. She could see the palace, the tidy tulip beds, and even the pool where kids sailed model boats by day. Beyond the park, the lights of Paris stretched in every direction, some in neat rows, others curved. A dark, serpentine line marked the course of the river Seine, and when Tristan leaned left—

"Wow," she breathed, staring at the Eiffel Tower.

But Tristan nearly toppled over, and she rushed to help him to the next room. All four were connected by wide, graceful archways, giving the place an open feel. But the apartment echoed with every step she took, and her reflection ghosted through a series of mirrors that reflected the dim light from outside. The bedroom was the last in the row of four, and when they got there, Tristan collapsed onto the unmade sheets of a huge four-poster bed.

Natalie bent over him, wringing her hands. "What should I do? Can I get you something?"

His deep voice was muffled by the sheets. "Nothing. I just need some rest."

Carefully, she peeled back his jacket, afraid it might stick to his wounds. But any blood on his shirt had already dried, and the gash across his back didn't look quite as bad as before.

"I should clean the wounds..."

He shook his head, then groaned, and his voice grew fainter. "Don't do anything. It'll be fine."

She bit her fingernail. Should she help or leave him be? What exactly was the protocol for dealing with vampire cuts?

"I could look for some bandages." She motioned vaguely. There had to be a twenty-four-hour drugstore somewhere, right?

He clutched the sheets. "Not safe out there. Not now. Stay here."

Staying here meant staying the night, and her heart pounded as she looked around. The tiny place she rented was all the way out in the seventeenth *arrondissement*, and the thought of traveling across Paris alone terrified her now. On the other hand, she could hardly spend the night with a perfect stranger.

"But your wounds... They won't make you turn into a vampire, will they?"

He gave a shaky chuckle. "No."

"Are you sure?"

"I'm sure." His voice grew weaker with every word. "I promise I'll explain... tomorrow."

Natalie stood, totally at a loss. Should she clean his wounds? Run for her life?

She settled for touching his shoulder and murmuring, "Are you sure you're all right?"

Tristan barely dipped his chin. Was that a nod?

"Thank you," she whispered. "For everything."

He flapped a hand as if vampire attacks were an everyday occurrence in his life.

She stepped back. "I'll be close if you need me." She cocked her head, and even though Tristan looked out for the count by then, she whispered, *"Bonne nuit."*

Something brushed against her leg, and she jumped. But it was only Bijou blinking up at her with huge, green eyes. The cat opened its mouth to meow, revealing laughably thin fangs.

Natalie bent to pet it. "Nice kitty..."

To her surprise, the cat was friendly — to her, if not to Tristan. And boy, was it comforting to run her hands over that soft fur. Soon, the cat's eyes closed in sheer pleasure, and Tristan's did in sleep. Natalie crouched, holding her breath, watching him.

Strangely, it all felt very *déjà vu*. As if she spent every night in a fancy Paris apartment watching a wounded warrior sleep. As if she'd known Tristan for ages and belonged at his side. Watching over him... Watching over Paris, even. She closed her eyes, letting her senses drift away.

And *zoom*! Just like that, she was flying like a dragon — in her imagination, at least. High in the air, with Paris laid out before her in a dazzling pattern of lights. Swooping over the streets, she would keep a keen eye below. Vampires would take one look at her and flee, and the City of Lights could truly slumber in peace.

She sighed then sniffed. Was it the rose-laced scent of the sheets that seemed so familiar? She could have sworn she recognized the chevron pattern of the hardwood floors and the vines shaped into the fine plaster ceilings. Even Bijou felt like an old friend.

Then a car horn tooted in the street below, and she puffed out a breath, ruffling Bijou's fur. Who was she kidding? She'd helped an injured stranger home, not moved in with him.

Still, she remained at his side for a good half hour. Watching. Thinking. Wondering. Tristan's breath was like a metronome, and it eased her ragged nerves to see his chest rise and fall in a steady rhythm. Other than the hum of cars on the street, Paris seemed totally at peace.

Except Bijou, who meowed and stepped away in a hint. Natalie followed the cat through the echoing apartment. The place was stunning, but there wasn't a stick of furniture apart from the bed at one end and a red velvet couch all the way at the other. No paintings. No carpets. No chairs or tables. It was as if Tristan had just moved in — or was about to move out. She couldn't tell which.

He came with the place, he'd said of Bijou.

That suggested Tristan had recently moved in, she supposed. But still. So many mysteries remained...

Meow, the cat called, urging her along.

Natalie sighed, tagging along. The only thing that made sense to her was the cat's name. Bijou — *jewel* — was fitting, given those luminous eyes that kept turning back to check if she was following him into the kitchen at the back.

Natalie clicked on a light and looked at the empty bowl that stood on a gleaming tile floor. "You hungry, kitty?"

Bijou meowed as if to say, *Mais oui — but of course.* He wound around her legs, a soft figure over the strict pattern of black-and-white tiles on the floor.

The first cabinet Natalie tried was empty. The second had a single pack of spaghetti. The third held a set of gleaming cutlery — solid silver, from the look of it. The fourth practically overflowed with packages of snack food — mountains of it. Enough to feed a dozen hikers for a week in the woods. At the fourth cabinet—

She smiled. "Jackpot."

Stacks of aluminum cat food tins filled the entire space. Apparently, Bijou ate better than his master. Or did Tristan dine out?

Natalie grabbed several tins and turned them in the light.

"You want *poulet, boeuf,* or *saumon*?"

Bijou meowed.

Whether that meant chicken, beef, or salmon, Natalie wasn't sure, but she went with chicken, and Bijou gobbled it up. While he did, she ran warm water over a kitchen towel, returned to the central room at the front, and gazed out over the city. Then she tiptoed over to Tristan. The poor guy was out like a light, but he couldn't be comfortable. So she eased his shoes off and dabbed gently at his injuries with the damp cloth. Every bit of exposed skin was smeared with blood. But once she cleaned that off, his wounds were minimal — or they'd already healed, which was strange. Very strange. On the other hand, her whole evening had been strange. And since he didn't seem on the brink of death, she left it at that.

Then she paced through the apartment. Every room had a view of the Eiffel Tower, Sacré-Coeur, and the Louvre. Views you saw in postcards but never in real life — not unless you had millions to spend.

She glanced back at Tristan. Had he inherited the place? Was he borrowing it from a friend? And, wait. Did the man patrol Paris every night looking for vampires?

Quietly, she peeked from room to room. The apartment was sparkling clean but totally empty — even the single closet she peeked into. The bathroom could have housed a family of four, but all it contained were the basics for one — a toothbrush, toothpaste, and a shaving kit. No perfume, no second toothbrush, Natalie noted with some satisfaction. Apparently, there wasn't a woman in Tristan's life. Not at the moment, at least. Then again, a man like him probably didn't suffer long dry spells between hot dates with rail-thin, supermodel types. She frowned into a mirror, plucking at her wrinkled shirt and ragged hair.

The entry hallway had a narrow table where he'd thrown his keys beside a jar that gleamed with coins — a miniature treasure trove of copper, silver, and gold.

She wandered the apartment a few more times, wondering what to do. It was late — very late — and since she wasn't going home...

"Do you mind if I, um..." she whispered, slipping Tristan's jacket away from where it lay under his arm. Then she covered him with a blanket and stood at the bedside, whispering, "Good night."

Good night, she imagined Tristan saying, though the silence of the apartment was undisturbed.

Finally, she took his jacket, walked to the velvet couch at the far end of the apartment, and sank down onto it. The couch was set at ninety degrees to a fireplace — a mirror of the hearth at Tristan's end — and angled to face the lights of Paris. Natalie lay down and curled up, soaking in the view. The city looked peaceful, but somewhere out there, vampires roamed.

Shivering, she pulled the jacket around her shoulders. It smelled of leather, smoke, whiskey... and Tristan. She snuggled inside it, trying to block out fear so she could sleep.

Moments later, she opened her eyes, sensing someone watching her. But it was just Bijou, gazing up from the floor.

"You want to join me?" she whispered.

Bijou jumped up, landing smoothly in the space between Natalie's knees and arms. Then he curled up, rearranged his paws and tail just so, and settled in.

Natalie smiled. If only it were that easy to curl up with a friend. Unconsciously, she glanced over at Tristan and all the space in that huge bed. Then she forced her eyes back to the design molded into the plaster ceiling.

Go to sleep. Relax. Tristan wasn't far, and she was safe. Or so she hoped.

But a short time later, her mind filled with ugly visions. Men with fangs reached for her, calling her name. Tristan groaned, still covered in blood. She watched her own hands fend off vampires and heard her screams filling the night. And those weren't even nightmares, because she was still awake. Were they visions of the future, or was she imagining things?

She curled up tightly, trying not to shake. Counting seconds, minutes, and what felt like hours. Praying for dawn and salvation. But Olivier's voice cackled in her nightmares, and she kept nodding off then waking in a cold sweat. Bijou had moved over to the windows and was sitting silhouetted by the lights of Paris, not moving except for precise lashes of his tail. She watched for a while, telling herself he was a sentinel. Eventually, she fell asleep again, and in her dreams, she ran. On and on, running for her life. But no matter how fast she went, she couldn't outrun the vampire's voice. The one that kept insisting, *You are mine.*

Not yours, she wanted to scream, but no sound came.

You are mine, princess, a voice taunted in her mind. *And soon, I will find you. I promise I will.*

Chapter Five

Tristan woke slowly, not sure where he was. He flexed his hands, finding silk sheets... a soft mattress... a pillow. Home? He sniffed, catching the scent of floral laundry detergent and pine cleaner.

He groaned. Being home was good, but if the housekeeper, Madame Colette, had come in to clean around him with her usual mercenary vigor, he might as well head back to that alley. The housekeeper was thorough, but he had the sneaking suspicion she'd like to scrub him right out of the apartment along with whatever filth he'd tracked in.

Then it hit him. *Solidarité du Coeur* — the soup kitchen. Alley. Vampires.

Natalie, his dragon cried.

He sat up quickly — too quickly — and jumped to his feet. He wobbled there for a moment, waiting for his head to stop spinning. Beams of golden light streamed through the windows of the long, lonely apartment, but his world didn't brighten until he spotted Natalie curled up on the couch, all the way over in the last room of the four spanning the front of the building.

My mate. Must keep her safe, his dragon puffed.

Sometimes, he really did feel like a big, mighty dragon. But occasionally, life had a way of making him feel awfully small — like now. Because if the shaky memories filtering back into his conscious served, Natalie was the one who'd kept him safe and helped him get home.

His dragon mourned. *And now she's huddled up as far away as possible.*

His spirits sank, and the wounds that crisscrossed his body all throbbed at the same time. Thanks to accelerated shifter healing, they might not show, but all he felt was pain — throughout his body and deep in his heart. Which was crazy, because he'd never given much thought to finding his mate. Older shifters talked about a smack of realization, a bolt of lightning to the heart. But fate didn't bless everyone with that kind of luck — especially not guys like him, who were more skilled in fighting than the mysterious art of love. His mother had warned him about that a thousand times.

You're just like your father, the poor woman would sigh. *Promise me you'll stick to what you were born for. Promise you won't go breaking a nice girl's heart.*

He scowled. He had only the vaguest memories of his father, a dragon who came and went with every passing whim. Each time his father had come home, the man had sworn to do better. And each time, he failed more miserably than before.

We don't have to be him, Tristan's dragon whispered.

Tristan stood still, rubbing his stiff arm. Yeah, well. Did he dare find out the hard way?

Natalie stirred, and he hurried forward, then stopped. The last thing she needed was a stranger rushing her like the vampires of the previous night. She needed rest.

Rest, his dragon agreed. *Nice and cozy. Right there under our coat.*

He looked closer, and indeed, she was cuddled up under his coat, bundling it around her shoulders and under her chin as if...

As if she likes it, his dragon hummed.

Tristan's pulse skipped. Her hair curled around her face in gorgeous coppery locks, and though her eyes were closed, he could picture the rich sapphire of her eyes. She looked at peace, and he found his breaths slowing. Calming in a way he'd never felt before.

Sleep, my mate, his dragon side cooed. *We'll keep you safe.*

He wanted to slide in beside her and hold her hand, but he didn't dare move. The breeze from the open window stirred the curtains, carrying a mix of rich morning scents to his nose.

Then he frowned. If Natalie needed sleep, he needed a shower. Badly.

So he padded to the bathroom and stayed there a long time, luxuriating in the kind of hot, steamy shower he hadn't taken in years. The kind that didn't exist in the military. The kind you didn't take when you got home either, because you'd forgotten life could be that good.

That shower, like Natalie's touch the night before, worked on him like a drug. Standing with his eyes closed, he let water cascade over aching muscles and joints. It was only the water turning cold that finally prompted him to step out and towel off. The mirror was all steamed up, which was probably for the better. He pulled on a change of clothes, still stiff but not as robotic as before.

We need to take more showers, his dragon said, picturing blue skies and tropical waterfalls... swaying palm trees... golden arcs of sand...

He sighed. From what he'd heard, some of the men he'd worked with in the military — Silas Llewellyn, Connor Hoving, and their shifter brethren — had landed sweet security jobs in Hawaii. Now *that* was the way to retire.

But then the buttery scent of fresh croissants wafted in from the street below, and he shook his head. Much as the tropics appealed, Paris had been calling to him for some time. No city really compared. If Silas, Connor, and the others had found their place in the world, he was happy for them. As for him... He streaked a hand across the mirror and looked at his own blurry reflection. He still had to earn that right.

He stood a little straighter, finger-combed his hair, and stepped into the hallway, where he paused at the sound of a soft voice.

"Come on, kitty. Sweet kitty..."

He smiled. Apparently, Natalie was up, and she hadn't discovered what a spitfire Bijou was. It was funny to hear English, too — but nice. A blast from his past.

"Sweet kitty. Bijou..."

Tristan smiled. Some American accents struck him as squeaky, while others were too sweet. Natalie's was a melody pitched perfectly to his ears.

He padded around the corner then stopped, fascinated. Her hair glinted in the morning light, calling to him in a way no treasure ever had. Her eyes shone with lust for life — brighter than any jewel he'd ever seen. And her voice made him want to close his eyes and purr. No wonder Bijou liked her so much.

"You want *poulet* or *boeuf*?" she asked Bijou in the same tone she used to offer homeless people tea or coffee.

"Sounds a little heavy for breakfast, don't you think?" he couldn't resist interjecting.

Natalie spun, blushing. Bijou hissed.

Tristan stuck up his hands. "Sorry. Didn't mean to sneak up on you."

He truly hadn't, and he truly did feel badly about it. But, damn, was that blush cute.

Natalie shook her head. "It is your home."

For a long, quiet minute, Tristan just stood there, drinking her in while his dragon crooned about love, mates, and forever — as if the beast had any clue about that kind of thing.

I do know, the beast insisted, still wallowing in bliss.

The thing was, his human side felt it too. A warm, fluttering happiness, like a hundred butterflies flying around his heart. A blur that pushed the outside world far, far away, along with all his worries and responsibilities. A sensation of his lungs filling more easily and his body warming, just from having her nearby.

Natalie stared back, eyes wide and full of wonder. Did she feel it too?

A magical sensation filled the space around them. Without thinking, Tristan reached out to take her hand...

Their fingers had barely brushed when Bijou meowed and butted Natalie's shin. The little brat might as well have banged a fist on a table and growled, *Feed me.*

"Oh, sorry." Natalie spun, blushing all over again. "Poor kitty." She knelt and opened the cat food.

Bijou shot Tristan a smug look. The cat was just a cat, not a shifter of some kind. But, damn. There were times Tristan swore the little monster was possessed.

"Look, Bijou. Beef." Natalie spooned the food into the bowl. "Yummy."

Tristan normally turned up his nose at the overly juicy, artificial smell that filled the kitchen. But Natalie made cat food sound delicious, and Bijou looked smugger than ever before.

She likes me, the cat said with a flick of his black tail. Then he lowered his head and nibbled daintily at the food.

The thing was, Tristan had leaned in, and when Natalie stood, she would have fit right into his arms. As it was, it took everything he had to keep them locked at his sides. Which was a damn shame, but at least she didn't skitter away. She just stood there, nice and close, making him marvel at the lavender in her scent. Why did it seem so familiar?

Provence, he realized. One of the many places his mother had dragged him to live as a kid — one of the few he'd enjoyed. Detroit had come next, and that hadn't smelled half as nice as the south of France. Neither had Lyon, where they'd moved afterward, nor New Jersey, where they'd continued on to in his mother's constant, gypsylike search for the perfect place.

This is perfect, his dragon said. *Our mate is perfect. Perfect for us, at least.*

"I'm Natalie. Natalie Brewer," she murmured, as if destiny were prompting her to get to know her mate.

But humans didn't know about mates, and only a rare few were tuned in enough to recognize their life partner from any other Joe who wandered along.

"Tristan Chevalier."

The pale morning light caught in the hollows under her eyes, and she looked more vulnerable than before.

"Thank you." She gulped. "Thank you so much. You saved me last night."

"You saved me."

Her lips twisted. "All I did was get you on the Metro."

He wished he could explain why it felt like so much more. She'd essentially lifted his sad, battered soul, dusted him off, and set him on a whole new direction in life.

But then she covered her mouth and reached out as if he might keel over. "Oh God. Your injuries. Are you all right?"

"I'm fine."

"But you were hurt. Really hurt."

He shrugged, wondering how much to admit. "I heal quickly."

"That quickly?"

He pursed his lips. "It wasn't as bad as it looked. Sorry to scare you."

"But... but..." She frowned. "Were those really vampires, or am I going crazy?"

And just like that, it all came back. His job. Strict orders to report on vampire activity without getting involved. Instead, he'd killed one vampire and sent three others packing.

Oops, his dragon murmured, not all too earnestly.

"They really were vampires." He hated to scare her, but she had to know what she was up against. The problem was, that explanation would overlap with who he was, and he wasn't ready to go there yet. "But you're safe now."

Her eyes shone — so bright, he could have taken it for a supernatural shifter glow. But her scent was pure human — heavenly, but still human — so it must have been a trick of the light.

"Safe for how long?"

Forever, he wanted to say. But, hell. Even if she was his destined mate, there were no guarantees. History was full of tragic, star-crossed lovers.

So, we fight for her. We make our own history, his dragon growled.

He reached for her hands, and that time, Bijou didn't interfere. They stood facing each other, knowing so little about each other, yet so much passed back and forth without a word. Trust. Hope. Humility. A zing went through his veins, and his gaze dropped to the soft, pearly lips he longed to kiss.

Maybe someday, we can. Maybe someday, we will, his dragon breathed.

Most of the time, *someday* was right up there with *sometime* and *somewhere* for guys like him — all of them over the rainbow, an impossible dream. But looking into Natalie's eyes — holding those warm hands, so perfect in his — he nearly believed. Enough to lean closer and reach for her lips. Natalie leaned too, and he held his breath.

But the doorbell rang with a heart-stopping buzz, and they jumped apart.

"Um... you expecting someone?" Natalie murmured, tense.

He sniffed the air and groaned. "Madame Colette."

Natalie's eyebrows shot up. "Madame who?"

He nodded wearily. "The housekeeper."

The lock turned, and the door rattled on its hinges as Madame Colette came up against the dead bolt. He was tempted to keep it that way, but a moment later, the woman started hammering on the door.

Natalie looked around the empty apartment. "Housekeeper?"

Tristan heaved a sigh. "She came with the place." Bracing himself for a verbal onslaught, he slid the bolt and opened the door. "Madame Colette. *Bonjour.*"

He'd caught the diminutive sixtysomething in mid-knock, and her fist would have whopped his chest if he hadn't pivoted back.

"Monsieur Chevalier," she cried, laying right into him. "It is ten o'clock — and a weekday — if you didn't notice. Every respectable man in Paris has been up for hours." All that came out in a single blast of rapid-fire French, delivered as only Madame Colette could. "If I'm to do my job — and I assure you, I will — you must open the door immediately. I'm sure the neighbors don't appreciate the racket—"

Tristan nearly muttered, *So don't knock so loud.* Then again, there were no neighbors. Not on his floor. And anyway, Madame Colette was inhaling sharply, ready for her next volley.

A volley that never came, because she spotted Natalie and froze.

"And who is this?"

Her voice was as severe as the bun her gray hair was winched back in, and a frown cut deeply into her face.

Tristan folded his arms and bristled. Madame Colette could be as bitchy to him as she wanted. Lord knew, there was no stopping her. But he'd be damned if he let the woman get on Natalie's case.

Bijou appeared, purring, and leaped right into Natalie's arms. Natalie ran her chin over the cat's soft fur, offered a hand to the housekeeper, and introduced herself in slightly accented French.

"Natalie Brewer. It's a pleasure, madame."

She even went as far as giving a half curtsy, and Tristan exhaled. Apparently, Natalie had been in Paris long enough to know how to handle blustery older women with bees in their bonnets.

Madame Colette continued her inspection, unimpressed. Natalie stood her ground, sticking to her smile. A bright, happy one that didn't hint at the nightmare she'd survived. What other trials had she been through that she hid?

Finally, with a stern look at Bijou, Madame Colette shook Natalie's hand. Just for a microsecond, but more than she'd ever offered Tristan.

"Hmpf," the housekeeper grunted, sweeping past them and into the kitchen — where she halted in her tracks.

Natalie winced. "I fed Bijou. Just one packet. I hope it's all right."

Madame Colette hmpfed again and set off on a close inspection of the apartment. Tristan watched her go. Madame Colette might be a housekeeper, but he had the sneaking suspicion she was there to snoop for his employers — the shifters who had offered him the apartment and the security job. The one that had sounded so simple and straightforward until last night.

Natalie looked about to whisper something when Madame Colette reappeared with a look of sheer horror.

"The couch? You demanded that your guest sleep on the couch?"

Tristan pursed his lips. Should he admit to passing out on his bed first? Probably not.

"It was fine. I slept like a baby," Natalie said, coming to his rescue again.

Madame Colette ignored her and stuck a finger in Tristan's face. "Monsieur Chevalier, I believed it beyond the realm of possibility that even a man with as poor an understanding of etiquette as you could be so rude as to relegate a guest to the couch. Alas, I fear I am wrong."

Alas, I had a run-in with some vampires, he nearly said. But Natalie didn't need the reminder, so he kept his mouth shut.

"It really was fine," Natalie insisted.

"It could not possibly have been fine," Madame Colette declared as if she'd been the one on the couch.

"No, really..." Natalie tried, then stopped when her stomach growled.

Madame Colette froze. "No bed... No shower... No breakfast? Monsieur Chevalier—"

You are an utter failure, he could have filled in. *You are corrupting this young woman — and probably Bijou as well. How you ever hope to become a permanent hire, I cannot imagine.*

Madame Colette didn't say as much, but her flashing eyes enunciated every word.

Lucky for him, the Guardians of Paris valued traits other than old-world manners. Like strength. Tenacity. A sharp shifter nose and mastery of hand-to-hand combat. Not that any of that would impress Madame Colette.

"I was about to get some breakfast," he swore.

For the next five minutes, Madame Colette went on scolding him. Natalie kept insisting everything was wonderful, and Tristan kept counting to ten, trying not to blow up. Then Madame Colette huffed, shooed Natalie toward the shower, and headed out the door, declaring she would take care of breakfast herself.

The door slammed behind her, and the apartment fell into blissful silence.

"Wow," Natalie murmured, peeking out of the bathroom.

"Wow," Tristan sighed.

Chapter Six

"So. Vampires..." Natalie said firmly.

It was half an hour later, and they were on the rooftop terrace, lingering over breakfast at a table for two — a luxury Tristan never knew the apartment offered until Madame Colette had ordered him to pull it out from a corner.

I think Madame likes Natalie, his dragon sighed.

That, or Madame felt sorry for Natalie for getting stuck with him. The housekeeper had put on quite a spread, with a basket of fresh rolls, buttery croissants, and his favorite, a rolled pastry called *pain au chocolate.* Not only that, but Madame Colette had brewed coffee that smelled richer than the stuff she deemed good enough for him — and served it with milk so creamy, he licked it off his lips. There was jam too, a bowl of fruit... even cloth napkins.

He dipped his croissant in his coffee and considered. Madame liked Natalie. Bijou liked Natalie. No one liked him, but hey. He didn't need friends, just a job.

Need Natalie, his dragon whispered.

With every passing minute, that felt more and more true.

He looked out over the rooftops, stalling. Wishing that, for once, he could just relax and take in the stunning view. So far, he'd only been on the roof in dragon form, too busy taking off or landing to soak in the rich atmosphere of Paris. Even now, he felt more at work than at rest.

"Tristan." Natalie tapped his hand. "Vampires?"

Her tone said she didn't just want to know — she *needed* to know.

"Vampires..." he started, trying to decide where to begin. Suddenly, the coffee tasted bitter, the croissant stale. "Paris used to be overrun with them..."

Downstairs, dishes clattered. Was Madame Colette cleaning or hinting for him not to reveal the details of how dragons had come to dominate the city centuries ago?

Tristan heaved an inner sigh. Did she really think so little of him?

His dragon snorted. *Yes.*

He cleared his throat and picked up again. "There are only a few vampires left in Paris these days."

Natalie stared into her coffee and muttered, "Not few enough." Then she looked up, a little pale. "Do they drink blood like the stories say?"

"Some just drink a little. Others bleed you dry."

Natalie blanched, and he winced at his word choice.

"Me?" she squeaked.

"Not you," he said immediately. "Not if I can help it. But it would help if I understood what drew them to you. You, in particular, I mean."

"I wish I knew."

"What were you doing at *Solidarité du Coeur* anyway?"

She gave him a stern look. "I love volunteering there. It's important work."

He stuck up his hands. It *was* important work. In a way, it paralleled what he did — protecting the city and its people. But Olivier hadn't given the impression of simply stumbling into that soup kitchen. He and the others had hunted Natalie down. Why?

"What were you doing there?" Natalie asked.

Tristan hemmed and hawed. Now would be a good time to tell her about his true nature. *I'm a dragon shifter, hired by the Guardians to keep an eye out for trouble.* But he didn't want to dump everything on Natalie at once.

"I work for a security conglomerate. Kind of like...what is that called? Neighborhood watch."

Her eyebrows shot up. "Some neighborhood watch."

Okay, so she wasn't buying that, but he wasn't quite ready to explain. Instead, he pressed on about her.

Yes. His dragon nodded eagerly. *More about her.*

"I work at Paddy's Irish Pub, plus a few hours in an English bookstore."

That didn't explain the vampires either, not with Olivier's words echoing through his mind.

You think blood like that comes along every day? Royal blood?

"What about your family? Any ties to Europe?"

"Yes, but that was generations ago. My great-grandmother emigrated from France to Quebec, then to the US. Would that make me tastier or something?" She frowned. "Wait. How do you know so much about vampires?"

He squeezed his lips together. That was the tricky part.

"There are lots of supernaturals around."

Bad way to begin, he realized when Natalie blanched.

"Supernaturals? Lots?"

He hurried to correct himself. "I mean, it seems like a lot once you know they exist. Really, there are only a few. Most humans go their whole lives without realizing they're there."

She stared. "How do you know?"

Because I'm a dragon shifter didn't seem like the best place to start, so he dodged the question. "I was hired to keep an eye out for vampires. It's my job."

Downstairs, a wet mop slapped the floor. Madame Colette was hinting again. Still, she was cleaning, so that was a plus.

Meanwhile, Natalie stared at Tristan. "Your job? Your actual job? Do you go around with cloves of garlic?"

He smiled, though she didn't. "No garlic. My job is to report on any vampires who cause trouble, not to go after them." That part was entirely true, though he frowned at the reminder of how pissed off his boss would be.

"And who exactly hired you to do this job?"

He waved around. "The people who own this apartment."

"It's not yours?"

That made him cackle out loud. "Me, owning a place like this? Maybe in my dreams."

You got that right, the pause in the steady swipe of Madame mopping agreed.

Tristan shook his head. He'd never been rich and never would be. Still, the place was a huge step up from where he'd started when he'd first come to Paris. He and several other former military shifters who'd had been hired by the Guardians had bunked in much rougher digs at first. Since then, some had been promoted, some posted to other locations, others laid off. Tristan felt like a pawn being moved over a chessboard he could only see a few squares of. The Guardians were a secretive bunch, and in the beginning, that hadn't bothered him much. A job was a job, and as long as he worked for the good guys, he was fine with that. But now...

His eyes drifted to Natalie, and his dragon growled. *Not just a job anymore.*

No, it wasn't. But how exactly did Natalie figure in? Was she just another pawn, like him?

More like the queen, his dragon growled. *And we will make her our mate someday.*

If she agrees, he shot back.

His dragon might think the world still worked as it had centuries before, with a knight claiming the hand of the woman he saved. But things had changed in the twenty-first century, and a good thing, too. He didn't want a mate who had no choice in her partner. He wanted her to want him too.

Downstairs, the mop slapped against the marble floor of the hallway, and he could practically hear Madame laughing. *Why would a nice girl like Natalie want you?*

He frowned into his coffee. Why, indeed?

Natalie stared over the crests of the trees gracing the Jardin du Luxembourg. "I started feeling it yesterday afternoon, not long after I took a walk. I stopped for a crêpe, and everything was fine. But then I started imagining someone was following me." She frowned. "I guess I wasn't imagining."

Tristan thought that one over. Few humans sensed vampires until it was too late. But Natalie had?

"My dream was to live in Paris. But vampires..." She shivered. "Why would vampires be after me? I'm not special in any way."

I beg to differ, his dragon sniffed.

Aloud, he muttered, "I don't know."

Most of his life, he'd dealt with shifters. Wolves were stubborn as anything. Bear shifters were mostly easygoing but dangerously possessive around their mates. Lions were obsessed with looking good, and dragons came in two flavors — snobby blue bloods and plain old commoners like him.

But vampires? He'd never dealt with any before this latest assignment. The fact that four had come after Natalie at the same time didn't bode well.

"Is there anything special in your family? Ancient nobility, perhaps?"

The mopping downstairs slowed as Madame Colette listened in.

Natalie snorted. "Hardly. Just normal folks living modest lives."

Tristan took another bite of croissant. *Normal* didn't fit what the vampire had said.

"Did you ever have any trouble before?"

"With vampires? Are you kidding?"

"I mean at home. You're from America, *oui?* What brought you to Paris?"

He half expected to hear one of the usual expat reasons. *For the art... For the culture... I wanted to find myself...*

But Natalie just stared out into the distance and whispered one word. "Dean."

Tristan tensed. Whoever Dean was, he already hated the guy.

Natalie smiled faintly. "Dean was supposed to bring me to Paris, but he never did. So, I came on my own."

Tristan tilted his head, and she looked at him, then sighed.

"It's a long story. Do you really want to hear it?"

No, his dragon muttered. *Not if it includes a shithead named Dean.*

"Yes," he said.

"I work — worked — in the human resources department of a big consulting company at home. A job I took to follow Dean, whom I met just as I was finishing college." Her tone soured. "He liked having everything on his terms, and for some reason, I always tagged along. Don't ask what I saw in him. I'm still not sure." She pushed her plate away with a frown. "The job turned out okay, especially when I got to work in community outreach — you know, supporting fundraisers, organizing office charity runs..."

Tristan nodded, though he didn't actually know. Community service in his military unit was mostly a matter of limiting collateral damage.

Natalie had lit up at the mention of her work, but then she clouded again. "Dean refused to talk about getting serious, and I was okay with that. But then he proposed, totally out of the blue. We'd gone out to dinner, and he ordered expensive champagne. Then he said he'd just been offered a year-long project in Paris, and he wanted me to go with him. I was so excited. I've dreamed about Paris ever since I was a kid. I minored in French and everything."

That explained some things, but not others. Tristan tapped the table quietly, waiting for her to go on.

"I asked the company about transferring me here too, but there was no opening for me. Dean said not to worry — he'd take care of everything. He said I should take the time off. Enjoy Paris." She stared in the direction of the Eiffel Tower. "I loved the idea, but it came out of nowhere, and I wasn't even that sure what we had was... Well, the real thing."

Her gaze drifted over to Tristan, and when their eyes met, another zing ricocheted through his veins. His body warmed, and he leaned forward, tempted to cup her cheek. *No, that wasn't the real thing. But I think this is.*

Natalie gulped, turned pink, and looked away. "Anyway... As excited as I was about Paris, I wasn't sure about leaving my job. Professionally, it was a great opportunity for Dean, but not for me. When I got cold feet, Dean did an about-face. He said we needed more time to work things out." She shook her head bitterly. "As I found out, what he needed was time to figure out Plan B. Which he did. Her name was Mary, and she worked in accounting."

Tristan's jaw dropped. "He didn't care who he was with?"

Natalie laughed humorlessly. "Apparently not. From what I heard afterward, it's easier to make senior partner if you've done a stint abroad — and if you're married." She made a face. "You know — showing what a nice, stable guy you are. Anyway, I guess Dean figured he could kill two birds with one stone."

Tristan balled his hands into fists. "You're no stone."

Natalie shot him a smile that made his world light up for a few heartbeats, at least. Then she frowned, and Tristan wanted to kill Dean all over again.

"Apparently, Dean was more interested in making senior partner than he was in me. But it did get me thinking. What was I waiting for? I'd dreamed about Paris for so long but never made that come true. I was always compromising for someone. In college, I was all set to do a semester abroad, but my parents split up, and my mother said she couldn't handle me being so far away. Then I started working, and the dream slipped further and further away. Instead of moving to Paris, I made a trip here. A one-week trip, three years ago — just long enough to fall in love with the city before going back to Philly. *Philly*," she muttered.

Then she leveled a fierce stare at the chimney of the neighboring building. "The good thing was, I started asking myself why I needed a guy to realize my dream. I might have gone on thinking about it forever. But then Notre Dame burned..."

Tristan tilted his head. The cathedral fire had ousted dozens of gargoyle shifters from their ancestral home, and it had caused many supernaturals to turn bitter toward humans for setting off the accidental fire in the first place. He would never forget the night he'd stood, dumbstruck, along with so many other Parisians. But what did it have to do with Natalie?

She shrugged. "I know it sounds crazy, but somehow, that's what finally made me act. It made me think I could miss other treasures I'd never truly appreciated before. I even felt..."

He leaned closer. "What?"

She knotted her fingers and twisted them shyly. "It's silly, really. But I felt like I needed to help. Not with the cathedral, maybe, but in other ways. It just seemed like what I had to do."

Somewhere in the back of Tristan's mind, a voice whispered, *Fire Maiden.*

The voice of destiny, echoing an old legend he didn't know much about. Only that they were the ancestors of a mighty dragon queen who protected Europe's great cities. Why did it come to his mind now?

Natalie flashed a weak smile. "So, here I am. My father calls it my premature midlife crisis. But you know what? I love it. I love doing things on my own terms." She motioned around. "I earn a quarter of what I used to and pay three times the rent for a tiny place. But I love it. I love living my dream."

Tristan found himself grinning. "Good for you. Dean's loss, by the way. And poor whatshername — Mary."

Natalie laughed — a real one for a change. "Yes, poor Mary. That big project Dean was gunning for fell through. He never made it to Paris in the end, but they did get married."

"Did he make senior partner?"

A naughty glint showed in Natalie's eye. "Nope. Not yet, at least." Then her face fell. "Of course, my dream of Paris didn't include vampires..."

Tristan put a hand over hers. "We'll figure it out. We'll keep you safe."

She bit her lip. "You've already done enough."

He shook his head. "Three of them are still out there."

"Three?" Her face went white. "You... killed one?"

He shifted in his seat, having experienced this before — the moment when a nice, normal person who lived a nice, normal life realized he was capable of killing. It almost didn't matter that the deceased was one of the bad guys, or that Tristan only killed when he absolutely had to. He could practically see horror creep into her mind.

It was him or me, Tristan wanted to explain. *Actually, him or you. Easy decision.*

The coffee cup trembled in her hand, and she set it down with a clatter. Tristan braced himself for her to stand, thank him for breakfast, and hurry the hell away.

But when Natalie spoke again, it was a whisper, and she didn't make a move to leave. "I'm sorry. I'm so sorry." She covered her face with her hands. "This is my fault. I dragged you into this."

Relief flooded him. She wasn't mad. She didn't blame him. But, wait. Why blame herself?

He squeezed her hand. "You didn't do anything. They're the bad guys, Natalie."

She looked on the verge of tears, and Tristan burned to hug her. To hold her, protect her, and never, ever let her go.

"I have these dreams..." she said in a shaky whisper. "Where a vampire grabs me..."

He shook his head quickly. "It won't happen. Not with me around."

She forced a weak smile but shook her head. "But what if? I keep picturing the same thing. The vampire grabs me, and I can't get away."

Tristan fought the urge to let out his claws and flex in anger. God, he hated vampires. But she was right. What if?

So he stood and motioned for her to do the same. "Show me." Dammit, his voice was all croaky. "I mean, if you don't mind."

She rose uncertainly, then gulped and turned her back to him. "He grabs me from behind and pins my arms."

Slowly, Tristan looped his arms around her. She trembled, and damn — he did too.

He cleared his throat, trying to concentrate. "Like this?"

Just like that, his dragon purred.

Natalie nodded. "Yes, but tighter. So tight, I can't even move."

Tristan had never been so caught between fear, arousal, and anger. Gradually, he tightened his grip, reminding his dragon this was about life and death, not about him and her.

But it was hard. The top of her head was at about chin height, and he longed to cuddle her close. Then he'd nuzzle her cheek, brush his lips over her jawline, and—

Downstairs, something banged, and he snapped upright. Another reminder from Madame Colette.

"You can get out of every hold, no matter how tight," he said quickly. "Just remember not to panic."

And not to get aroused, he ordered his dragon.

"Okay," Natalie whispered.

He considered the options. What would work for someone her size?

"Three steps. Snap, jab, elbow," he said, deciding quickly. "Number one, snap your arms up."

He showed her, and she mimicked him in halting movements. They would have to work on that for sure.

Definitely needs more practice, his dragon hummed.

"Really snap up, hard. It won't break you free, but it will give you a little space. Then, step two. Jut your elbows into his ribs."

Two points gently pressed into his abdomen, and he resisted the urge to pick her up and carry her to bed.

"Harder," he insisted.

"Are you sure?"

He hid a smile. "I'm sure. Just jab." If his abs couldn't take it, he'd have to quit his line of work.

She did, though not nearly hard enough.

Oh, this is fun, his dragon crooned. *We could teach her lots of moves.*

Not fun, he retorted. *Life and death.*

Madame Colette backed that up with the firm snap of a rag.

"You have to put everything into the jab. Then comes three — whirl and throw an elbow at his face." He forced himself away from Natalie long enough to demonstrate the move.

Natalie stared at his arms. "Then what?"

He shrugged. "Then you run."

She looked dubious, and he would have given anything to add, *Then you douse him with dragon fire. Problem solved.*

But she wasn't a dragon, so running was her best option. He'd just have to make sure never to leave her alone long enough for vampires to attack.

No problem, his dragon agreed. *We'll stay nice and close.*

"Try it," he said, nestling her back into a bear hug. "One..."

Her hands snapped up a little faster than the first time.

"Two..."

She jabbed his ribs, and though it wasn't much more than a tickle, there was potential there.

"Three."

She whirled, practically baring her teeth, and rammed an elbow at his face. He ducked. Whoa. For a nice girl, Natalie sure was fast — and fierce.

"*C' est ça,*" he said. "Perfect."

Natalie grinned, and that nearly bowled him over, too. One little smile with the power to go right to his heart. He'd like to see more of that smile. He'd like to be the one who inspired it, too. Maybe they could go to a café sometime and chat. Or take a walk through the Tuileries or along the Seine. Paris had lots of nice walks and even some canals...

And just like that, his mind flew to his favorite Paris haunts. All the viewpoints, all the cafés. For the next minute, he and Natalie grinned at each other, feeling the way you ought to when you were young, in Paris, and in love.

But then he remembered how they'd gotten to that moment, and the magic faded. Natalie's face clouded, and she looked down, forlorn.

One, two, three? Tristan's gut churned. Obviously, it wasn't as simple as that.

"Anyway," he said quickly. "That's just for emergencies. The thing is to avoid vampires in the first place."

"I know." She wiped her cheek. "But what if they hunt me down? What if there's more than one?"

Her words tore at his heart, because he didn't know.

We'll hunt those bastards down, his dragon snarled. *Kill every vampire. Keep her safe.*

He fought the urge away. It was one of those blustery, from-the-gut ideas that was all action and no plan. And while he'd gotten away with that in the past, it wouldn't work now. Not when an innocent woman's life was on the line.

"I'm not sure," he admitted. Her face fell, so he hurried to add, "Do you trust me?"

She went very still, and he held his breath. He wouldn't blame her for saying, *Of course not.* But maybe, just maybe, she felt the same special connection he did.

Her eyes clouded, and her fingers plucked nervously at her shirt. But a moment later, her gaze warmed, and she nodded.

"I trust you."

A lump formed in his throat — one he had to gulp away before replying. "Good. I know someone who can help."

She leaned forward eagerly. "Who?"

He took a deep breath. The oldest, most venerable dragon he'd ever met. The most senior of Paris's shifter Guardians. Alaric, the powerful dragon who had hired him to help keep Paris safe.

"The Guardians of Paris. The good guys," Tristan said. Then he murmured to himself, too low for Natalie to hear. "I think."

Chapter Seven

"This way."

Natalie looked on uncertainly as Tristan opened a door at the back of the kitchen's massive pantry and gestured her through. She peered down into the darkness. Why didn't they exit the building the way they had come in?

"Back door," he said. "So no one sees us leave. Just in case."

Natalie bit her lip. The winding staircase was dark and creepy. But with vampires on the loose in Paris...

She forced herself to nod. "After you."

He grinned, and her whole world lit up. The man didn't smile often, but he did for her.

Then she chastised herself. She was a grown woman, not a giddy teen. And yet Tristan made her imagination race and her body heat. Did she have some kind of rescuer complex when it came to him?

That was it, she decided. He'd saved her the previous night, so it was natural for her to feel warm, safe, and protected. Right?

Except it went beyond that. Everything Tristan did made her feel like a treasure, not an imposition. A queen, not just plain old her. When she talked, he listened. When she was silent, he appeared worried, like maybe she wasn't all right. And when he gazed into her eyes...

Heat trickled through her veins, and Tristan's face flushed. Was he thinking the same thing?

She chastised herself. It wasn't normal for two strangers to set off so many sparks so quickly. Then again, nothing about the situation was normal, was it?

His Adam's apple bobbed, and he turned to the stairs. Natalie gripped the railing and steeled herself to follow.

The spiral staircase was a riveted metal design that reminded her of the Eiffel Tower. But instead of rising gracefully upward, it plunged into an abyss. Her footsteps echoed through the darkness, and the structure rattled as she and Tristan wound around and around. Thank goodness for the occasional platform that gave her a break from the dizzying spiral. No other apartments connected to the stairwell, only Tristan's. Light fixtures were few and far between, casting sections of the stairwell in long black shadows. The sole skylight became a weak dot of light above, as distant as a star in another galaxy. A star you'd wish upon to escape to another place.

Tristan glanced back. "*Ça va?* All good?"

She nodded quickly. As long as he was there, yes.

"Eight stories altogether, right?" she whispered, trying to judge how far they'd come.

"Eight to ground level." Tristan's answer echoed in the darkness.

But when they reached a door with a tiny window that looked onto the building's foyer, Tristan continued downward instead. The air grew damp and heavy, the narrow space that much creepier.

"Almost there," Tristan murmured, offering his hand.

The words weren't as comforting as his firm grip, and Natalie hung on tightly as they rotated through another few levels. Tristan had called a friend to fetch some clothes from her apartment and drop them with the doorman, but the thin peasant blouse and tan slacks were better suited for spring. Which it might be outside, but this dim, dank world reminded her of the last days of autumn, when days grew short and dark, and leaves wilted and died.

Finally, the stairs ended, and they emerged onto a long, narrow tunnel.

"Do you use the back door often?" she asked.

It was a joke, but Tristan's reply was dead serious. "Only when I have to."

Apparently, even big, dangerous guys like him had places they didn't stray into by choice.

Soon after, they reached a fork, and Tristan kept left.

"Where does that go?" she asked as he whisked her past the passage on the right.

He towed her firmly onward. "The catacombs."

A cold lick of air brushed her cheek — a ghostly kiss from the netherworld. She hurried after Tristan, picturing towers of human bones stacked into elaborate designs, with femurs forming crosses and skulls staring out in ghostly silence. The catacombs were a maze of ancient tunnels dug several stories below Paris, filled with bones cleared out from the city's overfull cemeteries. She'd been meaning to visit, but now, she wasn't so sure.

"Aren't the catacombs open to the public?"

"Not that part." The grim note in his tone told her to banish the thought from her mind.

Up to that point, the lights in the tunnel had been weak and gloomy, like lonely sentinels abandoned at their posts. But eventually, the lights grew brighter, conquering the darkness rather than barely keeping it at bay. Natalie made a mental note: *Left tunnel good. Right tunnel bad.* Just in case.

Next, they came to a huge steel door, where Tristan stopped and listened before pushing through. The room they stepped into was tangled with ducts and wires. That led to another door, which opened to a stairway climbing upward. A short time later, they emerged into an alley.

Natalie gulped as if that were the freshest, cleanest air she'd ever breathed. Overhead, the sky was blue and sunny, just as it had been at the breakfast that felt a million miles and years away. Even Tristan seemed to breathe more freely. When he led her onto the bustling main street, he straightened his collar and deadpanned, "Ah, Paris."

She laughed. "You're not fond of tunnels either?"

He shook his head. "I hate them, like all drag—" He cut himself off with a hasty cough and motioned around. "I prefer being in the open air."

She could relate, although the upward sweep of his hand was funny, almost as if he preferred ballooning or gliding. And who could blame him? It was a beautiful day. Gorgeous, even.

"I prefer it too," she said, taking in the refreshingly ordinary scene.

It was just another normal spring day in Paris — but that meant magnificent. The streets were lined with trees, the air brisk, and storefronts decorated just so. One displayed clothing that looked too fashionable to wear, and every woman on the street looked just as chic. The scent of freshly baked *baguettes* wafted from a bakery — the kind of bread you could nibble on as a snack, it was that good. Another shop displayed gold watches, while the next sold secondhand books. All in all, a microcosm of everything Natalie loved about Paris. She closed her eyes to absorb all the impressions, trusting Tristan to guide her along.

"How long have you been in Paris?" he asked.

She opened her eyes, surprised to find him studying her.

"Just six weeks." Then she laughed. "There was a time when I'd called myself spoiled for saying 'just' to six weeks in Paris. But now, I never want to leave."

She paused, reconsidering. With vampires around, did that still ring true?

Yes and no, she decided. She wasn't ready to risk her life. Still, the prospect of leaving Paris made her want to dig in her heels and declare, *No. I'll never leave.*

Tristan was looking at her — intently, as if trying to read her mind — so she cleared her throat and spoke quickly. "And you? Been in Paris long?"

"On and off for my whole life."

She waited, eager for more, and gradually, as they walked, Tristan opened up.

"My parents are from Belgium, but I was born here. I moved away at age three, returned when I was six, and left — again — when I was ten..."

Soon, she lost count of how often he'd had to pick up and start over, due to his mother, a deadbeat father, and something about... destiny? He'd made dozens of moves, including several stints in North America.

"California... Michigan... Toronto... Places that had just gotten to feel like home when it was time to move again."

He said it like it was nothing, but his eyes were wistful. There was a protective spark too — one that flashed whenever he mentioned his mother. Whether she had been on the run from an abusive partner or simply a flaky free spirit, Natalie couldn't tell. But Tristan's demeanor was consistent with how he'd stepped in to help her when the vampires appeared.

Even now, his body formed a solid wall at her side, and he glared at any man who strayed close. He kept his hand wrapped around hers, and their sides brushed as they walked. It was nice. Cozy. Comforting — and not just due to the threat of vampires.

She glanced around, but there was no one suspicious on the street. "Can vampires go out in the daytime?"

"Yes. Forget everything in the movies."

"But they really do suck blood?" Her voice rose with hope. Maybe what Tristan had said earlier was wrong.

His lips turned down. "Yes."

Her veins ran cold, and she forced herself to change the subject.

"What did you do when you grew up?"

"I joined the Foreign Legion."

Her jaw dropped. The French Foreign Legion?

He flashed a grim smile. "It was that or the Marines. I thought the Foreign Legion sounded more glamorous." His expression said, *Little did I know*, and he sighed. "Anyway, I did my ten years. A few months ago, I wrapped that up and returned to Paris."

His words were casual, but his intonation said he wasn't planning to move anytime soon.

Never, his eyes insisted.

Exactly the way she felt. She might not have been born or raised in Paris, but it felt as if she'd been born *for* Paris. The grand avenues, the winding side streets, the sweeping curves of the river — it all felt like home. All the times she'd been out wandering, she never lost her bearings, and while most of the sights took her breath away, they seemed strangely familiar, too. In college, she'd decorated her room with posters of Paris and watched French films. She'd experimented with French recipes and read everything she could, from *Babar* to Victor Hugo and even *Les Fleurs du mal*. Paris felt like home in ways she couldn't explain.

"Where are we going?"

Tristan gestured north. "To the other side of town."

She had so many questions. About him. About the Guardians he'd mentioned. About vampires — and other supernaturals. But she was afraid of the answers, so she stuck to silence. Tristan fell into a pensive silence as well.

Eventually, they rounded a corner and descended to a subway station. Not the closest to his apartment, Natalie noticed, as if he'd needed the walk as much as she. But soon, they were riding the number twelve northbound. As the metro car rattled along, Natalie imagined where they were going. *Guardians* sounded ancient. Important. Imposing. They would have to be if they kept order among supernaturals like vampires. She pictured a villa in a classy neighborhood with a leafy park not too far from the Opera. How rich were they if they could afford to lend out apartments like Tristan's penthouse?

But the subway chugged through station after station, and Tristan didn't make a move to exit. Not until—

"Pigalle?" she blurted when he stood.

The metro doors slid open, and Tristan led her out. Down the platform, through the turnstile, and up to street level at another one of those gorgeous Art Nouveau stops.

"Pigalle." He sighed.

Natalie blinked, looking around. Not a villa in sight, nor a leafy park. The building directly in front of her was adorned with red lights that flashed in the midmorning sunlight. *Sex! Sex! Sex!*

The next building sported a huge red sign: *Sexodrome*. The place beside that was labeled *The Love Shop*.

Natalie shot Tristan a pointed look, but he glumly led her onward. "I'm told the neighborhood isn't what it used to be."

Over the next three blocks, Natalie counted twenty-six sex shops, all offering a startling range of toys, gadgets, and garments. She walked briskly, so busy looking-but-not-looking that she nearly bumped into Tristan when he stopped short.

A young, fair-haired man approached them, and Natalie tensed, suddenly on guard.

"Liam," Tristan said as they thumped each other on the back like a couple of... a couple of...

Soldiers. The word popped into Natalie's mind. Soldiers who'd faced impossible odds and survived, forming a bond closer than brothers. She watched them closely. Soldiers fit, for sure. Not just their chiseled, *ready for anything* physiques, but the way their eyes roved their surroundings even as they greeted each other.

"Tristan. You look like hell, man." Liam laughed.

His accent was English, his grin broad and genuine, as if every day was brilliant and life was great.

"This is Natalie," Tristan said, giving her name that lyrical French flair she loved.

When Liam leaned in to shake her hand, Tristan growled under his breath, and his friend's eyes went wide.

"Nice to meet you," Liam murmured, settling for a quick shake. Then he glanced between her and Tristan, and his golden-brown eyes said, *Interesting. Very interesting.*

Natalie nearly fluttered her hands and insisted, *It's not like that.* But somehow, she couldn't get the words out.

"Nice to meet you," she murmured.

Tristan turned slightly, putting his shoulder between her and Liam in a not so subtle signal to his friend. "For once in your life, you're on time."

Liam shook his head. "This is actually the second time in my life." Then he grinned at Natalie and whispered, "Don't tell anyone."

She smiled. Liam had an infectious charm. The kind of guy who could keep your spirits high no matter the circumstances. He was big, too — as tall as Tristan, and even broader in the shoulders. Still, she wondered when he and Tristan had agreed to meet. Tristan had made exactly one phone call before leaving the apartment and that was to the Guardians, whoever they were.

Tristan tilted his head, and Liam went ahead, coordinating their movements with the wordless precision of soldiers who'd completed dangerous missions around the globe. Natalie followed them with a gulp. Was she on a dangerous mission now too?

The sidewalks were full of tourists, but even those intent on gawking at the shops or taking selfies scrambled out of the way. Between Liam's leonine grace and Tristan's powerful, *Don't fuck with me* stride, they made an imposing pair, indeed. Natalie hurried along, still gripping Tristan's hand.

Liam must have caught her looking at the shops, because he pointed across the street. "That's my favorite one. Pussy's." Then he winced as if he realized how that sounded. "*Pussy's* as in possessive, not plural. Like a cat. And I meant my favorite name, not my favorite sex shop. Oh, bugger. I mean..."

Tristan rolled his eyes. "Liam?"

"Yeah?"

"Shut up."

"Right," Liam agreed.

Natalie giggled. Liam certainly helped to keep her mood light. Apparently, he wasn't one to remain silent for long. After a few seconds, he piped up again.

"So." He thumped Tristan on the back and asked Natalie cheerily, "Has this dragon shown decent manners so far?"

Natalie halted in her tracks. Dragon?

Tristan stopped too, shooting Liam a murderous look.

Realization dawned over Liam's face. "Wait. You didn't tell her?"

Tristan stuck out his jaw.

The blood drained from Natalie's face. "Didn't tell me what?"

Chapter Eight

Tristan and Liam exchanged awkward glances while one word echoed through Natalie's mind. *Dragon.* Liam had definitely said dragon. Had he been kidding?

No, he hadn't, judging by the way he shrank back from Tristan's furious face.

"Didn't tell me...what?" she demanded, going from fearful to angry.

The nearest three pedestrians turned at her near-shout. Tristan took her arm, bustling her into a side street, where he stopped and glared at Liam. Finally, he kicked the ground and explained. "I mentioned supernaturals..."

Natalie tossed up her hands. "You *mentioned* a lot of things."

Tristan frowned at the ground, then met her eyes, looking more like a schoolboy than a big, tough, secret-service type.

"I told you about vampires. But there are other supernaturals, like shapeshifters."

She looked from one man to the other. Were they nuts?

"Like werewolves," he explained. "But we come in all kinds."

She froze. "We?"

Liam smiled, and Natalie's eyes went wide.

Tristan nodded slowly. "We."

Her knees trembled, and her jaw went slack. He wasn't pulling her leg, was he?

"Bears...lions...gargoyles," Tristan said in a detached, impersonal way.

Natalie glanced up, startled. "Wait. Gargoyles? As in, stone statues that come alive?"

Liam shook his head. "They're always alive. They just hide it well."

Was he kidding?

Something assured her he wasn't. Not at all.

She turned to Tristan. "Is that what we saw last night? A gargoyle?"

He nodded silently, then spoke, looking pained. "Shifters have two forms — human and animal, or stone and winged creature, in the case of gargoyles."

She stared. He wasn't kidding. At all.

Then a stray thought hit her, and she put her hand over her mouth, shocked. "Did they have anything to do with the fire at Notre Dame?"

Tristan shook his head quickly. "On the contrary, they tried to stop it. But they were too late."

"There is a rival dragon clan, though," Liam chimed in. "The Lombardis. They didn't start the fire, but they did write a nastygram saying they wished—"

Tristan smacked his arm, and Liam blurted, "Hey!"

Natalie clenched her hands tightly. Rival dragons? Gargoyles? Vampires? She pointed one shaky finger at Liam.

"What about you?"

He thumped his chest and replied oh-so-casually. "Lion."

Tristan looked like he wanted to cover his face with his hands.

Natalie had no idea what to think. It was crazy to believe Liam, but something about his blond, windblown hair and golden eyes could pass for a lion's.

Then she turned to Tristan. God, she'd spent the night at his place!

"You too?" she whispered as her mind galloped away.

The night Tristan had fought the vampires in the alley, there had been a roar of fire, but he hadn't had a flamethrower. His lips had been chapped, too. Could he really turn into a... a...

"Dragon," Tristan whispered.

Her heart thumped, and her knees trembled. Of course, the notion shocked her. But at the same time, it fit. Those broad shoulders, those intent eyes. The power that practically crackled every time he moved.

Still, she couldn't quite process the news. "Dragon?"

Liam leaned in with a grin. "He can breathe fire and everything."

Tristan clenched his jaw. "Not helpful, idiot."

"Right. Sorry."

Natalie looked from one to the other. Their words ought to have made her protest, but somehow, it all made sense. "That time in the alley... The fire..."

Tristan nodded slowly. "I couldn't shift in the open, but I had to do something."

She ran a finger over her lips, picturing how chapped his had been.

"You can fly? You can breathe fire?"

"Great party trick," Liam chipped in.

Tristan smacked his arm.

Natalie tilted her head. "You're tricking me, right?"

"I would never trick you." Tristan's eyes glowed, and his voice was so earnest, there was no doubting his conviction.

"Prove it," she finally declared, sounding braver than she felt.

Tristan's jaw tightened, and she was sure he was about to protest. But a moment later, he pulled her into the shade of a tree. The space around him shimmered, and the arm he held out began to change.

"Uh, Tristan..." Liam warned. "Here? Now?"

"Here. Now," Tristan muttered.

Natalie stared as his fingers extended. The skin around them stretched, forming webbing, while his fingernails grew sharper, longer, and darker. His face began to change too, with his ears pulling into points and his jaw lengthening.

Then, as smoothly as he'd started, he reversed the process and stood quietly, waiting for her to react.

She gulped. Surely, she should run... scream... insist on seeing how the trick worked. But as surely as she knew she belonged in Paris, she knew it was all real. That didn't keep her knees from trembling, though.

She forced herself to nod. "What else can you do?"

"We heal quickly. Not much else."

Changing shapes, flying, and breathing fire seemed like plenty to her. But just in case...

"No burning down houses? No pillaging villages?"

"Not in the last few centuries." Liam laughed. "But I'm told my great-grandfather Toby once—"

Tristan cut him off with a thump to the arm, then faced Natalie. "Listen, there are good and bad shifters, just like there are good and bad people. Most of us just want to live and let live. And some of us..."

She waited, holding her breath.

Tristan and Liam exchanged cryptic glances.

"Some of us work hard to maintain peace," he finally finished.

A protest jumped to the tip of her tongue. How could fire-breathing dragons be peaceful? Then again, it did fit Tristan's actions, his military service... His whole aura, really.

So, wow. She'd spent the night in a dragon shifter's apartment. Which meant...

"Madame Colette?" she asked in a shaky voice.

Tristan sighed. "Eagle shifter. They're very bossy."

"What about Bijou?"

Tristan snorted. "Just a cat."

Natalie exhaled. If he'd just told her she'd spent the night cuddled up beside a shifter, she would have flipped.

Liam motioned ahead. "We should get going."

Natalie hesitated, as did Tristan, watching her with eyes that pleaded, *Please trust me. I want to help you.*

The crystal around her neck warmed, and a deep, authoritative voice whispered in her mind. *You can trust him. You must trust him.*

Natalie gathered all her courage and stuck a finger at Tristan's chest. "From now on, no secrets. You got that?"

He nodded solemnly. But then a pained expression crossed his face. "Then I guess I should tell you the people we're about to meet are shifters, too."

She forced herself to breathe evenly. "Shifters who can help me?"

"Yes. At least, I think so."

"You think so?"

"They're the Guardians of Paris. If they can't help..." He trailed off.

No one can, Natalie filled in.

But Tristan took her hand, giving her a shot of confidence. "If they can't help, I'll figure something else out. I promise."

Liam waved them onward. "Come on already."

Natalie wavered. What she really wanted was to go home, hide under the bedcovers, and pretend none of this was happening. But she needed help, and she knew it. Plus, everything Tristan said — and did — clicked like long-lost memories coming back to light.

She took one halting step forward, then another, slowly gaining confidence. She had a fire-breathing dragon on her side, right?

Then she snorted. Yeah. What could possibly go wrong?

"Who are the Guardians?" she whispered.

"Shifters who protect the city."

"From what?"

"From other supernaturals. By the end of the Middle Ages, the human world was a mess, and shifters were completely disorganized. Things only improved when shifters gradually took control of major cities and committed themselves to maintaining law and order. Wolves in Rome, dragons in Paris, lions in London..."

Liam glanced back with a wink.

"But the Guardians' ability to maintain peace waxes and wanes," Tristan continued, shaking his head sadly. "The Thirty Years' War, the Great War, World War II... Whenever infighting among shifters builds, trouble in the human world does too. For the past few decades, the Guardians have kept the peace, but that has been slipping. We're seeing more troublesome vampires, more rogue shifters — that kind of thing. That is paralleled by developments in the human world — terrorism, rioting, xenophobia — you name it. Sometimes, we fight the rise of evil directly..."

Natalie pictured him and Liam in army fatigues, marching through desolate landscapes in far corners of the world.

"Generally, shifters don't meddle directly in human affairs. They focus on their own issues, and the stabilizing effect trickles down to the human world. Lately, that has been harder and harder. There's a legend..." He trailed off.

Liam snickered. "You believe that?"

Natalie looked between them. What legend?

Tristan glanced at her, then at the sky. "Sometimes, I don't know what to believe. All I know is, the less stable the shifter world, the more human conflict escalates. That's why the Guardians brought us in."

"Who's us?" Natalie asked.

Tristan jerked a thumb at himself and then at Liam. "Me. Him. Other members of our unit have returned to their home cities, too. It's the same problem everywhere — not only in Paris."

A somber silence set in, and Natalie tried to make sense of it all. Guardians... legends... real-world problems...

Meanwhile, they continued walking, and the bustle of the red-light district gave way to the kind of upscale, tree-lined side street Natalie had originally imagined. Flowerpots dotted the house fronts, and neat rows of cobblestones marched up an incline. The next section of the side street was higher, narrower, and fancier. Beautiful villas lined both sides, all with wrought-iron gates and floor-to-ceiling windows framed by colorful shutters.

A nice neighborhood. A classy neighborhood. One that oozed old money, power, and connections.

"I should warn you," Liam murmured to Tristan. "Jacqueline will be there."

Tristan's step hitched, but a moment later, he strode on, squaring his shoulders.

"I tried heading her off..." Liam continued.

"How hard did you try?" Tristan's voice was cold and tight.

"Hey, I'm not the fool who dated her. That was all you, man."

Natalie's heart sank, and her hand slipped away from Tristan's. When he glanced over, she avoided his eyes. Whoever Jacqueline was, Natalie had no reason to feel jealous. No reason at all.

Tristan searched her face, but she kept her gaze straight ahead. The street was rapidly coming to a dead end. At the head of the lane was a villa with a concave facade. It stood at the peak of the hill, half hidden behind a stand of tall trees. Dark curtains were drawn over the windows, and an imposing gate cut off access from the street.

Natalie's mind spun. What exactly had she stumbled into?

Before Liam had a chance to ring the bell beside the gate, one of the front doors opened, and a slight man emerged. Tristan stepped forward to speak to him while Natalie hung back. The curtains of a second-floor window stirred, making her tense further.

"Who's Jaqueline?" she whispered to Liam.

He pressed his lips together and murmured cryptically, "You'll see."

Chapter Nine

"Mademoiselle." The butler bowed deeply, inviting her in.

Natalie stepped forward hesitantly, feeling like a lamb being led to slaughter as she followed the butler down a long hallway lined with somber portraits in gilded frames. Every step she took seemed to be followed by dozens of wary eyes. She peeked from side to side. The faces peering out from the portraits were all human, but the backgrounds were full of other creatures. Howling wolves, lumbering bears, strutting lions... Even dragons swooping and breathing fire.

Supernaturals... We come in all kinds, Tristan had said.

A shiver went down her spine. "Are you sure these are friends and not enemies?"

"I've often wondered myself," Liam murmured.

Tristan shot him a dark look. "Friends. The kind you don't want to piss off."

Natalie bit her lip.

The hallway opened on to a grand space four stories high. Sunlight poured in from a huge glass dome, and marble statues lined the balconies above. The ground floor walls were hung with landscapes and *Mona Lisa* style portraits that appeared centuries old. Natalie turned in a slow circle, soaking it all in.

Tristan shot her a look that said, *I told you the penthouse was nothing.*

That might be, but she preferred his apartment. The view was better, for one thing, and even unfurnished, it was cozier than this huge, cold place.

Footsteps tapped down one of the twin staircases that curled around the lofty space, and Natalie whirled. Those sharp clicks came from a woman's heels, producing authoritative taps that echoed from the marble stairs. A tall, slim woman descended, sliding one hand gracefully down the banister. Her flowing red gown was cut low at the front and high in the thigh, revealing a hell of a lot of creamy skin. Long, dangly silver earrings glinted in the light, as did the woman's teeth when she flashed a cruel smile.

"Jacqueline," Tristan muttered.

"Jacqueline!" Liam called out a little too sweetly.

Natalie looked from one man to the other. They'd been on guard the moment they entered the building, but that vigilant air had just spiked by a factor of ten.

Jacqueline floated down the last few steps and made a beeline for Tristan, but Liam quickly stepped forward. Giving his friend some breathing room, perhaps?

"You look lovelier than ever." Liam's tone might have been a little forced, but Jacqueline was stunning, with high, Audrey Hepburn cheeks and shiny black hair styled into a tight, *Breakfast at Tiffany's* bun.

Jacqueline barely turned her head, letting Liam do all the work in their oh-so-French three-kiss greeting. But when she strode toward Tristan, her eyes held a predatory gleam, and she planted three firm kisses on his cheeks. They nearly hit his lips, but Tristan dodged her each time.

"Ah, Tristan," Jacqueline cooed the way a woman might after a round of satisfying sex. "So good to see you again."

The words were spoken in smooth, delicate French, but they made Natalie sick. Had Jacqueline ever slept with Tristan? Was she trying to woo back her ex-lover?

Tristan stepped back and crossed his arms, bristling. Jacqueline pursed her lips the way a centerfold model would.

"Poor Tristan. Always so sad, so serious."

Natalie considered. Serious, yes. But sad? He hadn't been exactly exuberant that morning, but when he had smiled, it was like the sun coming out. Had Jacqueline never seen that smile?

The thought gave Natalie a boost, though Jacqueline destroyed that a moment later with a cutting look.

"Oh my. Is this she?" Jacqueline cackled to Tristan.

Natalie ground her teeth. Tristan's eyes blazed, but Liam spoke first.

"Jacqueline, meet Natalie. Natalie, meet Jacqueline."

Jacqueline's hand was cold and hard, just like her smile. Natalie made damn sure to answer in her best French.

"Pleasure to meet you. How do you do?"

Jacqueline laughed and replied in English. "The pleasure's all mine."

Her eyes swept up and down Natalie's body. While she didn't say anything, her expression dripped disdain. *Those clothes... That hair... And those shoes. What were you thinking?*

Natalie held her chin high. No, she wasn't put together as elegantly as Jacqueline. Whoever had picked up clothes from her apartment didn't have great fashion sense, but she'd been grateful all the same.

Grateful. Did Jacqueline even know the meaning of that word?

A pair of huge oak doors creaked open, and Jacqueline tilted her head. "Ah. They're ready for you. Good luck." She let a split second tick by. "You'll need it."

Tristan growled under his breath, but Jacqueline seemed amused.

Natalie took a deep breath. Jacqueline was one thing. The three older men waiting for her at the doors were another. One had a hooked nose, beady eyes, and a slightly hunched back.

Gargoyle, she remembered Tristan saying.

The second was a tall warrior — what Tristan might look like in another forty years. Handsome in an uncompromisingly grizzled way and fit enough to whip a much younger man's hide. His eyes were steady, his beard white with age, and his cheek was sliced by a jagged scar.

Her mind tried *dragon* then discarded the idea. Was he a wolf shifter? A bear?

"Miss Brewer?" he called in a voice like aged whiskey. "Come in."

Natalie hesitated, glancing at the tall, pale man who stood beside the two. If these were the good guys, she would hate to meet the bad guys. Still, she had no choice but to comply.

A younger man stepped out from behind the three, and while he was handsome, his smile was far too practiced, his styled hair a little too groomed.

"Miss Brewer. Delighted to make your acquaintance." He took her hand — really *took* it before she had any choice in the matter — and lifted it to his lips for a kiss.

"Allow me to introduce myself." He gave a little bow. "I am—"

"Marcel," Tristan muttered, practically shoving the man aside.

Obviously, there was some kind of rivalry there. They were both about the same age, the same height...

Natalie chilled. Were both dragon shifters?

She skittered onward. Then the third man spoke in a voice so smooth and silky, she balked. "Yes, do come in, Miss Brewer."

The words were hypnotic, but his eyes were piercing, and his hungry gaze was aimed at her throat. A vampire?

"That's Morfram," Tristan whispered in her ear.

When the man stepped closer, cold air crept in around Natalie's body, and a horrifying scene played out in her mind. She saw a vampire back her up against a wall, and somehow, her limbs were powerless to resist. Then she tilted back her head, giving the vampire access to her neck. He closed in slowly, bared his fangs, and—

Gasping, she lurched away from Morfram and bumped into Tristan. "You said we could trust these people."

Tristan's eyes blazed. "We can. We have to. There's no one else."

"But he's a vampire!"

Tristan took her arm and stepped around, blocking the others from view. Confusing the hell out of her, dammit, because he was doing that *protector* thing again. Was he on her side, or was he turning her over to vampires?

"Yes, Morfram is a vampire. An ally in good standing for centuries."

Natalie frowned. Centuries? How long did vampires live?

"The big guy is Hugo, a wolf shifter, and the other one is Albiorix, a gargoyle."

She peeked around Tristan's thick arm. *Gargoyle* fit the first man's short, wizened body. And as for Hugo — his honest eyes were those of a loyal canine's. She pictured a huge wolf, staring at her over a flickering bonfire in a wintery campfire.

"But... but..."

"They are the good guys," Liam promised, coming up beside Tristan. The two of them formed a solid wall that should have made her feel boxed in. Instead, she felt safe and secure, huddled in her own private place.

But then Liam ruined the effect completely by adding, "Of course, *good* is relative..."

"Relatively good?" she all but shrieked.

Liam leaned closer. "I wouldn't trust Marcel further than I could throw him, but the others—"

"Dammit, Liam..." Tristan growled.

A low chuckle sounded, and Tristan turned, annoyed.

"At least he's being truthful, Miss Brewer," Hugo, the wolf, said. "Good and bad depend on what side you're on. I can assure you we mean you no harm. Not even Morfram here." He thumped a huge hand on the vampire's shoulder and squeezed. "Right, Morfram?"

The vampire winced and slid away. "Right."

Hugo's huge, scarred hands hinted at a violent past. The sharp lines of his white, buzz-cut hair and sculpted goatee point of a beard added to the edgy, dangerous impression he made. Still, something about him reminded Natalie of her favorite grandfather — the one who'd always been there for her through thick and thin.

So Hugo, she could imagine trusting. But a vampire? She eyed Morfram skeptically.

Hugo nodded firmly. "I can vouch for Albiorix, as well. Come, Miss Brewer. You're better off trusting us than those two."

Those two meant Tristan and Liam, and while neither uttered a word, Tristan's blistering expression practically screamed, *She's better off with me.*

On instinct, Natalie edged closer to Tristan, and the angry glow of his eyes dimmed.

When Hugo's eyes darted between them in an expression that said, *Well, well,* Natalie stepped away from Tristan. No, they were not an item. She barely knew the man. The fact that she'd fantasized about him didn't count. Tristan dated the likes of Jacqueline, not plain old her. Plus, he was a dragon, for goodness' sake!

But Hugo's eyes went right on studying, and a smile played over his lips.

"Enter," a grumpy voice boomed from the inner chamber. "I don't have all day."

Natalie cringed, but when Tristan touched her arm, she took a deep breath, ready to step forward. However, Jacqueline swept into the room first, giving a regal nod to the men at the door.

Natalie wasn't overly competitive, but Jacqueline rubbed her the wrong way, and she squared her shoulders and stepped in. If she'd learned anything over the past twenty-eight years, it was to accept who she was and be proud of the little things. So, in she went, directly past the wolf shifter, gargoyle, and vampire. God, was she nuts?

"Good gracious," Albiorix murmured as she went by. "She looks just like Amelie."

Who was Amelie? And was that a good or bad thing? Natalie swallowed hard as she stepped into the chamber — an oversized study, where a man sat in a chair. It was just a leather desk chair, but he managed to make it look like a throne. Jacqueline breezed forward, but he dismissed her with a curt gesture, commanding her to step aside for Natalie.

Jacqueline's eyes shot daggers, and Natalie hid an inner cringe. She didn't need another supernatural enemy. What was Jacqueline anyway? *Snake shifter* would have been her first guess, though it was probably something sleeker and more graceful.

Meanwhile, the king — er, the Guardian — watched her approach with laser-sharp eyes, and it took everything she had not to skitter away.

"Natalie, this is Alaric," Tristan murmured.

She made a mental note to have a word with Tristan about any further surprises. He'd mentioned *someone* who could help her, but not the size and intensity of the man.

Alaric's dark, weary eyes suggested he'd witnessed the follies of humans for centuries. His long, unkempt beard was streaked with gray. Even sitting, he had an edgy energy, like that of an evil wizard crossed with a... a....

Dragon, a voice in the back of Natalie's mind said.

She blanched.

Marcel took up position at Alaric's side the way an heir might, mimicking the older man's expression.

"Let me look at you, child," Alaric barked.

She raised her chin, determined not to be cowed. But the man was downright terrifying. And he was one of the good guys?

Tristan shuffled closer, and part of her exhaled at the subtle show of support. When Alaric scowled, Tristan didn't back down, and Alaric's expression darkened. An entire argument seemed to rage between them, though neither said a word. All their communication took place in a series of angry, flashing eyes and facial tics. Clearly, Alaric resented the challenge to his authority, but Tristan refused to step away.

In a way, the men were similar, separated more by age than character. They both had the same sense of coiled energy. The same intensity, the same brooding presence, and the same powerful stature.

Tristan, she wanted to say. *Be careful. I think he could be a dragon.*

But, crap. So was Tristan, and getting caught in the middle of a firefight did not seem like a good idea. The air filled with crackling energy, and even the others exchanged worried looks.

Natalie paled, ready to run. Her legs refused to budge, though, and it dawned on her that she wasn't caught in the middle of someone else's altercation. She was the cause of it. Tristan was standing up to a superior for her sake.

Summoning all her nerves, she slid between Tristan and Alaric.

"So nice to meet you, sir," she blurted in her best French. "Tristan said you might be able to help me."

Everyone in the room froze, and Alaric's chin jutted with an expression that said, *How dare you interrupt my stare-down?*

From the corner of her eye, Hugo gave her a subtle nod.

"Why would I want to help you, *mademoiselle?*" Alaric's voice cut into the frigid silence.

Natalie bit her lip, telling herself it was a test and not outright rejection.

"Because you don't like prowling vampires any more than I do. Because you don't want the city overrun by forces out of your control," she said, hazarding a guess from what Tristan had mentioned.

Alaric raised his bushy eyebrows at her then at Tristan, who stood perfectly still. Then he turned back to Natalie. "One vampire attacking a mere human hardly constitutes a force outside my control."

Natalie ignored the sting in his words. "But that's how trouble always begins, isn't it? With small, creeping problems. Little threats that come back to bite you if you wait too long." She winced and added, "No pun intended."

Thank goodness Hugo stepped forward. Was he hiding a grin?

"She's right, and you know it, Alaric. Paris is gradually slipping out of our control—"

Alaric jumped to his feet, roaring, "Paris is not slipping out of my control."

Everyone backed away — except Hugo, who leveled his steady eyes straight at the man. Everything about him screamed *loyal lieutenant* — the kind of man who could point out stark truths no one else dared utter.

Tense seconds ticked by, then a full minute. Natalie pictured a fuse racing toward a bomb, really to explode.

Finally, Alaric spun away with an angry *hmpf.*

Hugo shot Natalie a bolstering look, then stepped toward Alaric and spoke softly.

"You've dedicated yourself to the city for decades, my friend. Paris is in your debt for the stability it enjoys. Not that any humans realize it. But even you cannot keep the dark forces at bay."

Another quiet minute passed, and Natalie stuck close to Tristan's side.

"Increasing numbers of vampires... Rogue shifters... The return of the Lombardi clan..." Hugo shook his head sadly. "We've done our best, but you know as well as I do that it's been a struggle. And when our world destabilizes, the human world does too."

Natalie didn't know about the supernatural problems Hugo mentioned, but she knew about the issues Paris had faced in recent years — terrorist attacks, riots, the rise of right-wing groups. Were they related to the problems of the shifter world?

The less stable the shifter world, the more human conflicts escalate, Tristan had said.

"Look," Hugo finished, touching Alaric's shoulder. "She's here now." Then his voice dropped to the lowest possible whisper. "And I believe she may be The One."

Natalie frowned. The one what? Her knees trembled, because Alaric was staring at her. She edged toward Tristan, doing her best to conjure up her tough, business side. How many times had she appeared before the board of directors to propose a new community service project or to extend the level of staff insurance coverage? Those guys were blustery too, but she'd always held her ground.

She took a deep breath and ordered her hands not to tremble.

"We've searched for a Fire Maiden for so long," Alaric whispered.

Natalie didn't know what was more frightening — his haggard expression or the flicker of hope in his voice. Did he mean her?

"Fire Maiden..." Marcel echoed.

And, damn. Even Tristan gave her a funny look. Her and the crystal that dangled from her necklace. Natalie looked down. It was glowing a golden yellow, but so what? Crystals reflected any light they caught.

But Hugo nodded as solemnly as if she'd marched in with the Holy Grail.

"Fire Maiden," Morfram whispered. "Finally, our efforts have been rewarded."

"Her? You must be joking," Jacqueline muttered.

Albiorix wrinkled his nose. "But she's a foreigner. How can that be?"

Natalie looked around, bewildered. What was going on?

Hugo shook himself a little and shot her a thin smile. "Apologies. This is all new to you, no?" Then he called out. "Clara?"

Light footsteps tapped into the room, and Natalie turned to see a gray-haired woman — the type who defied nature and grew more beautiful with age. A warm smile played over the woman's lips, and her eyes sparkled.

Hugo's face warmed. No, it beamed. Clara had to be his wife, confidante, and lifelong lover. Nothing else would make a man glow at a woman in quite that way.

Natalie found herself glancing at Tristan and, whoa. He was looking at her — plain old Natalie, whom he'd only recently met — the same way. Her heart skipped, and a sequence of images flashed through her mind. Scenes she'd dreamed of her entire life, featuring her and a man, both impossibly happy, sharing joyous days and steamy, satisfying nights. Working side by side, growing old, not regretting a thing. But her dreams had always kept the man's face blurry.

Until now. She held her breath and nearly breathed, *Tristan...*

Everything but Tristan's glowing eyes grew dim and distant, and her heart thumped.

The older woman touched her shoulder, and Natalie blinked.

"I think Clara will do a better job explaining than any of us can," Hugo said. "Will you, my dear?"

Clara patted Natalie on the arm. "Oh my. You look like a doe in headlights." She pinned each of the men in the room with a stern look — even Alaric, who didn't seem to faze her one bit. "How many times have I reminded you not to treat everyone like a foot soldier in Napoleon's army?" Clara sighed and turned away, pulling Natalie with her. "Never mind them. Come with me, sweetheart. I'll explain."

Natalie looked back. As kind as Clara seemed, the only one who really put her at ease was Tristan. Then again, he confused her, too.

Clara followed her gaze and chuckled. "Ah, I know that feeling." Her eyes bounced over to Hugo and sparkled.

Then Jacqueline cut in, claiming center stage again. "I'll help explain."

Her words held a menacing edge, and Natalie got the impression *explaining* might mean *scaring away*.

"Jacqueline," Tristan growled.

Jacqueline turned toward him, giving her skirt a flirty spin. "Yes?"

But Alaric waved them away, and Natalie had no choice but to go.

Clara patted her hand and whispered, "Believe me, they're all bark and no bite."

Natalie studied the older woman's face. "I hope that's a figure of speech."

Clara laughed, and nervous as Natalie was, the sound put her a little more at ease. "I promise, I'll explain."

Chapter Ten

Half an hour later, Natalie stood stiffly, staring at Clara. Shifters? Dragons? Fire Maidens?

"Fire Maidens," Clara repeated from the couch in the sumptuously appointed parlor they'd moved over to for their talk. "Women descended from Liviana, the mightiest dragon queen of all."

Natalie's mind spun. She'd tried protesting that she was from Philadelphia and an unremarkable family line — a little Irish, a little German, a smattering of French...

But Clara had just shrugged. "Fire Maiden blood can slumber through generations before it flowers."

Jacqueline muttered something Natalie didn't quite catch, but she got the gist. *Flower? This woman? Don't make me laugh.*

Clara went on stirring her second cup of tea. Natalie's was still on the ornate ebony table, as cold as her fingers felt.

"Liviana..." she whispered. "That was my great-grandmother's name."

Clara nodded. "Families tend to carry on traditions without even realizing it."

"Coincidence," Jacqueline muttered from beside a huge Oriental vase in a corner of the room.

Natalie was inclined to agree, but somehow, her gut told her otherwise.

"The name goes back to Roman times," Clara explained. "The root word is *jealous*. Not that Liviana was jealous. Rather, other women were jealous of her power." Clara slid a sidelong glance at Jacqueline. "The Liviana of legends lived in medieval times. Back then, the greatest dragons were females, with male consorts to do their bidding." Clara's eyes twinkled. "Those were the days."

If circumstances had been different, Natalie would have laughed. But she'd just been informed dragons were real and that royal blood ran in her veins. Not enough to make her a shifter, but enough to be detected by a vampire's sensitive nose.

It would explain why the vampires wanted you, Clara had said.

But Jacqueline had just huffed. *Maybe they just wanted a quick meal.*

Natalie shook her head, reeling. "Vampires...shifters... Where did they come from?"

"Some, like my mate, Hugo, are born shifters," Clara explained with a warm glow in her eyes.

Mate. The word kept jumping out at Natalie. What exactly did it mean?

"Others are humans turned shifter, like me..."

Natalie was too frightened to ask what that entailed.

"Other than wolf shifters, there are bears, lions, and eagles. Gargoyles too, like Albiorix. And dragons—"

"Like me," Jacqueline said, tossing her chin.

Clara waved a hand, unimpressed. "All kinds. Like humans, shifters were embroiled in feudal wars throughout the Dark Ages. But occasionally, a leader emerged who used his or her power to unite all shifters in a common cause. They repelled evil forces, established law and order, and raised the quality of life for all — including humans. Liviana was the mightiest of those shifters, and she placed her daughters in each of the major cities of Europe to continue her work."

Natalie nodded dumbly, still shell-shocked. But it did make sense. The royal families of Europe had done a similar thing, preserving their power by intermarrying with other royal families. Marie Antoinette had been a Hapsburg, and Catherine the Great was born a Prussian princess. The Windsors of England stemmed from German royalty. Of course, those efforts were mostly to preserve power and royal bloodlines.

Natalie gulped. Did *power* and *royal bloodline* apply to her, too?

"Those were the days of powerful witches and warlocks..." Clara continued.

The blood drained from Natalie's face, but Jacqueline laughed. "Don't worry, they're all gone now. None but a few with very weak powers. Not like dragons."

Clara heaved a theatrical sigh. "If only dragons still had the power — and wisdom — they did in Liviana's day."

Jacqueline seemed to miss the dig, and Clara went on.

"Liviana hired the best witches of the era to cast a spell of protection for her daughters — and her daughters' daughters, and all female descendants of her family line. As long as one of Liviana's descendants resided in the city, shifter power remained strong, and a single good leader, like Alaric, could keep things running smoothly. But without one of Liviana's descendants..." Clara trailed off, frowning.

"Wouldn't the descendant have to be a dragon for the spell to work?" Natalie asked.

Clara tilted her head from side to side. "Yes and no. The spell is at its strongest with a female dragon shifter descended from the royal family. Alas, female dragons are few and far between. Dragon shifters have a notoriously difficult time breeding, and when they do, their offspring are usually males."

"There are, of course, some fortunate exceptions." Jacqueline fluttered her eyelashes. "Like me."

"True," Clara conceded. "But you are not of royal blood."

Jacqueline's eyes grew stormy, but Clara chuckled.

"It's not an insult, my dear. Just the truth. Alas, you are no more noble than me."

A deep scowl made it clear Jacqueline didn't entirely agree.

"In any case," Clara went on, "the bloodline thinned over time. Some of Liviana's descendants mixed with humans or other shifter species."

Jacqueline made a scoffing sound.

"Yes, plain old humans, as I once was. Imagine that." Clara winked. "Others left the cities, and consequently, their power waned. For a few generations, the residual power continued to protect the city from strife."

"When was the last time Paris had a Fire Maiden?" Natalie asked.

"After the Second World War," Clara said. "Amelie. She helped Europe rise from the ashes and rebuild partnerships. But she didn't have any children, and Paris has been without a Fire Maiden since then."

Clara's eyes drifted to Natalie then moved away again.

Natalie gulped. Her middle name was Amelie. Another coincidence?

"For a time, Alaric managed without a Fire Maiden, thanks to Hugo's support and alliances with Morfram and Albiorix," Clara said. "Lord knows we've done our best."

Her weary face said more than her words, and Natalie remembered the heavy bags under Alaric's eyes. Maybe he wasn't so much a tyrant as an overworked man doing his best to shoulder overwhelming responsibilities.

"But we're getting older." Clara sighed. "And, frankly, we thought we'd have someone to pass the torch to by now. You know, so we could enjoy a quiet retirement..."

Clara flashed a sentimental smile, and Natalie pictured her and Hugo on a sunny farm in the south of France. Alaric, she could imagine in a remote castle at the edge of the Alps, and gargoyles would probably find themselves a medieval church somewhere far from the tourist crowds of Notre Dame. How vampires retired, she had no idea. Hopefully, they went somewhere far, far away.

But fitting herself into that equation, she just couldn't do. Tristan, on the other hand, struck her as the perfect successor to Alaric, especially if the older dragon mentored him for a few years. Tristan had all the makings of a great leader, even if he was too modest to suggest as much.

But as for her... She was a foreigner. A human. A nobody.

"I am the least royal person I know, and my family is beyond ordinary. I wish I could help, but you must have the wrong person. I'm just me."

She looked out the window. In some ways, she wanted nothing to do with the supernatural world. But Tristan was part of that world, and her heart ached at the prospect of parting. How exactly would that go? Would he see her off at the airport if she decided to return to North America?

Well, thanks for saving me from vampires, she would whisper.

My pleasure, he'd rumble.

Their eyes would meet, and time would slow down, as it always did when they got close. Her breath would hitch, as would his. And then—

She frowned, imagining the *Last Call* announcement being made for her flight.

Bye, she'd whisper. *Take care.*

Three little words. A world of heartache.

You too, Tristan would say, slowly releasing her hands. The warmth of his touch would fade away, as would the hope in her soul. Somehow, she would have to force herself to board a plane and to say goodbye forever — not just to the man, but to Paris, too. Goodbye to her dream of living in the City of Lights.

Clara stirred her tea, and the quiet tap of her spoon against the china pulled Natalie back to the present.

"The wrong person? I think not." Clara pointed to the crystal around Natalie's neck. "May I?"

Slowly, Natalie pulled off the necklace, confused.

"You see?" Clara lifted the crystal, turning it this way and that in the shaft of light streaming through the window.

Of course, I see, Natalie nearly said. But the crystal that had been so bright a moment earlier dimmed in Clara's hands. Surely, that was just the way she held it, though.

Regardless of the angle, however, the glow was gone. But the moment Clara pushed the crystal into Natalie's hands, it glowed brightly again.

"It only shines for you, my dear." Clara stopped the housekeeper who had come in to check on the tea. "Marie, can you take this for a moment?" Clara rolled the crystal into the woman's hand, then pointed. "Again, nothing. It doesn't shine for anyone but you." She held the crystal out to the only other person in the room. "Care to demonstrate, Jacqueline?"

Jacqueline folded her dainty features into a deep scowl.

"Take it." Clara's voice was firm. An order, not a request.

The moment Jacqueline did, the crystal dulled, turning into an ordinary trinket instead of the shiny jewel it had been in Natalie's hands.

"See?"

Jacqueline thrust the crystal back, muttering, "Stupid thing."

"Wait. I think it lit up," Natalie tried.

Clara raised an eyebrow.

"Well, a little, at least," Natalie said, determined not to anger Jacqueline. But her words seemed to have the opposite effect, as did Clara's explanation.

"Jacqueline is a dragon, so yes, it might glimmer slightly. But for you..." She beckoned Natalie closer and placed the stone in her hand. "You see?"

The crystal went from a dull yellow-brown to a brilliant, golden jewel.

"But... But..."

"Do you truly know nothing of dragons?"

Natalie shook her head.

"No old legends in the family?"

She laughed. "The only legend in my family is the dog my mom had when she was eight. Harry. We have a million stories about him, but not a single dragon."

"Dreams, then. Any dreams you can't explain?"

Tons, Natalie nearly said. She dreamed of flying. She dreamed of vampires. But with Clara watching her so closely, she shut those thoughts away.

"I dreamed of Paris." That much, she was ready to admit. "But so do a lot of other people."

Clara shook her head gravely. "The city has been calling to you. Your blood has been calling. Your destiny."

Natalie wanted to laugh and point out that it had all started with Dean, the world's most boring date.

But when she thought about it, her dreams went way back. At twelve, she'd won a prize at the town fair and chosen a poster of the Eiffel Tower. She'd decorated her college dorm with Monet prints and minored in French for reasons she could never explain.

Then she shook her head. That hardly gave her the power to claim a vacant throne.

"See?" Clara murmured, touching her hand.

Natalie had been too deep in thought to pay attention, but when Clara spoke, she looked up. The older woman was holding her hand over the candle that flickered between them. Natalie pulled away, startled.

"You don't burn," Clara noted.

Natalie looked at her finger. "Not easily, no. But surely... Wait!" she protested as Clara thrust her hand into the heart of the candle.

"Does it hurt?"

Natalie closed her eyes, fishing for an explanation. "Um, I think it's starting to." Which was a lie, but heck. She couldn't exactly admit to only feeling a tickle. "It doesn't work with bigger fires." She'd learned that the hard way one summer at camp.

Clara nodded, unsurprised. "Your dragon blood protects you — as the crystal does."

Natalie looked down. "How can this little rock protect me?"

Clara glanced at Jacqueline, who scowled and huffed. "Don't ask me."

"The great dragons kept many treasures in their hoards — some so ancient, we do not recognize or understand their powers," Clara explained. "Over the past months, Alaric has distributed a few treasures throughout the city in hopes of identifying a Fire Maiden."

Natalie recalled the day she'd bought the crystal. "I just happened to find it. Anyone could have picked it up in that flea market."

"You didn't find it. It found you," Clara insisted. "If I had walked by, all I would have seen was a dull, everyday trinket. But a Fire Maiden would have seen it for what it truly was."

Fire Maiden. Natalie frowned. "Wait. First, I found the crystal. Then the vampires found me." She held her necklace at arm's length, feeling sick. Had she unwittingly drawn vampires to herself?

Clara shook her head. "Vampires have no interest in jewels, only blood. They sniffed out your royal ancestry."

Natalie froze, remembering what Olivier had said in the alley. *You think blood like that comes along every day? Royal blood?*

"So she might have a little dragon blood," Jacqueline griped. "That hardly makes her a Fire Maiden."

For the first time that afternoon, Natalie agreed with Jacqueline.

Clara's chest rose and fell in a sigh. "Perhaps hope makes me too eager to believe. But the spell Liviana commissioned survives to this day. Now, we need that power more than ever. We need a Fire Maiden."

"Need her to what?" Natalie asked nervously.

"To keep the spell active. Having a Fire Maiden in residence is part of that, but not all. She has to reside in the city. Love the city. Truly embrace it and its inhabitants."

Natalie considered. That didn't sound too bad.

"The city experiences its greatest periods of peace and stability when the resident Fire Maiden has children, because her instinct to protect them evokes the spell's power to protect the entire city."

Natalie frowned. She'd always figured she'd have kids someday, but whoa. There wasn't even a man in her life.

There's Tristan, a little voice whispered.

Her cheeks heated. It was one thing to entertain wild fantasies about a man. To actually act on them was entirely different. She barely knew Tristan, and as for his view on the matter...

Jacqueline paced through Natalie's line of vision, smirking at some inner thought — like how good the man was in bed, perhaps.

Natalie sank to the couch. "Okay. Maybe I have a drop of dragon blood. But it's hard to believe I could be your Fire Maiden."

"Of course you aren't," Jacqueline snipped. "Even if you were, you're hardly suited for the job."

Natalie looked up, her blood boiling.

Jacqueline shrugged. "It's not easy. A Fire Maiden is always a target. Especially when she's a mere human."

"Jacqueline," Clara warned.

But Jacqueline leaned in from behind Natalie's shoulder, breathing down her neck. "All those vampires..."

Natalie's skin crawled.

"And gargoyles..." Jacqueline's nails scratched over the backrest.

"Jacqueline," Clara barked.

The she-dragon went back to pacing. "Then again, there are... How do you say it? Ah, yes. Perks."

Natalie shook her head wearily. "If perks are all you're interested in, you're interviewing for the wrong job."

"It's not a job. It's a calling," Clara said, giving Jacqueline a stern look. Then she turned to Natalie and softened. "I don't deny that a Fire Maiden would be exposed to danger, especially early on. The spell will take time to fully awaken, and you're only a human, with no means of protecting yourself."

Natalie slumped. Was Clara trying to convince her or make her run?

"Also, we don't know precisely what your jewel is capable of. Clearly, it's been spelled."

Spelled? Natalie looked down at the crystal in her hand.

"There are stones that heal," Clara went on. "Stones that lend you strength, wisdom, or courage. Regardless, there is no denying who you are. A Fire Maiden." She held up her hands before Natalie could protest. "You'll have protection. I promise you that. This house is impenetrable..."

Natalie looked up, alarmed. *This house is dark and depressing.* She couldn't imagine a worse fate than becoming a houseguest to blustery old Alaric. Especially if Jacqueline lived under the same roof.

"I mean, just until you've settled into the city and learned more about our world," Clara added quickly.

Natalie forced herself to laugh, but it came out a nervous rattle. "I like my little apartment. That shows I'm not royal, right?"

Jacqueline cackled. "Let me guess. You're renting one of those tiny *chambres de bonne* in some obscure corner of the city."

Natalie furrowed her brow. Well, yes, she was renting what used to be a servant's room under the eaves of an old building. "How did you know?"

Jacqueline stuck up her nose. "Every deluded foreigner rents one when they come to Paris to find themselves."

I did not come to find myself, Natalie wanted to say. But maybe Jacqueline was right.

She shook her head quickly. Either way, it didn't matter. "My place is fine."

"It's not," Clara insisted. "The vampires who attacked you haven't been apprehended yet."

Natalie had been edging toward the door, but those words stopped her cold.

Clara mulled it over. "All right. I have an idea. Whether you accept you're our Fire Maiden or not, you need protection. Do you agree?"

Natalie ran her hands over her arms, trying to erase the goose bumps.

"Well... yes. I guess so."

Jacqueline made a disgusted sound that said, *Useless little human. If only you could defend yourself the way I can.*

Yeah, well. It would be nice to be able to turn into a dragon and fly away from vampires. Better yet, to incinerate them with a long plume of fire.

Natalie frowned. What a predicament. She had enough dragon blood to attract vampires, but not enough to defend herself.

Clara's eyes clouded, wandering over the tapestries on the walls. But when her gaze slid over toward the room where

Tristan and the other men waited, her face lit up with hope — and a hint of mischief.

"Don't worry, my dear. I know the perfect place for you to stay. And the perfect bodyguard for your protection."

Chapter Eleven

Every muscle in Tristan's body tensed. It had killed him to see Natalie led away, and he'd nearly followed like a lovesick puppy. A good thing Liam's cutting look reminded him of his situation.

Alaric is the boss, Tristan told his dragon. *He and Hugo and the others.*

All those old guys, his dragon grumbled.

Old guys who could kick his ass, at least collectively. Alaric and Hugo had been legendary warriors in their day, and while their hair might have turned gray, they were still forces to be reckoned with. Then there was creepy old Morfram, the vampire. Even if he was an ally, Tristan didn't trust the man. Morfram and his sidekick, Albiorix, were responsible for keeping their brethren under control, and yet a gang of vampires had attacked Natalie with the help of a gargoyle. So, no. Tristan didn't trust those old guys one bit.

Besides, what do they know about love? his dragon muttered.

Not much, he decided. Except for Hugo, perhaps. Even the grizzled wolf shifter couldn't hide a look of goofy rapture when Clara had appeared.

Tristan's dragon sighed. *That could be us and Natalie.*

Earth to Tristan, Liam called into his mind. *Ready to pay attention before you get your ass whipped? Or should I say, pay attention while your ass gets whipped, because Alaric is about to lay into you — and bad.*

Tristan steeled himself. Any moment now, the ranking dragon would explode with a barrage aimed squarely at him, the young gun who'd messed up yet again.

How could you fail so miserably? We hired you to watch for vampires, not to kill one. You're fired, hotshot.

Tristan clenched his fists. He'd never find a decent job again. He'd be forced to leave Paris. Worse, he'd be forced to part from Natalie.

But she's my mate, his dragon insisted.

He ground his teeth. Surely, he was mistaken — the way his mother had been mistaken about his father in the beginning. Natalie was amazing, but she deserved better than him.

Tristan... Liam called, pulling his attention back.

And not a moment too soon, because Alaric turned with a grave look. Beside him, Marcel folded his arms, trying to look menacing.

Brace yourself, buddy, Liam whispered, directing Tristan's attention to more immediate things. *And remember, I had nothing to do with your fuckup. Not this time anyway.*

Alaric stared Tristan down for a good long time.

Good luck, Liam added when Alaric finally began to speak. *You'll need it.*

"Monsieur Chevalier," Alaric started gravely. "You shall never defy me again, is that clear?"

Is that clear? Marcel's haughty expression echoed.

As if Tristan took orders from pampered brats like Marcel. He could barely swallow taking orders from Alaric, especially if those orders involved Natalie. But Hugo pinned him with a firm look that said, *Say yes, son.*

Tristan forced himself to nod — once.

"Good. Now on to the matter of the woman."

Tristan gnashed his teeth. Natalie was not just any woman. She was amazing. She was fascinating. She was—

"Well done, Monsieur Chevalier," Alaric murmured. "Well done."

He stared. Huh?

Liam looked just as puzzled, but he nodded. *Just run with it, man.*

"You have brought us the Fire Maiden we sought," Alaric said.

"Fire Maiden," Marcel echoed, his eyes glittering.

Tristan looked between Alaric and Hugo, utterly confused.

"Well, what do you have to say for yourself?" Alaric demanded.

Tristan waited for an *Aha* moment to strike and clarify what was going on, but none came. So he replied with a carefully even, "My task was to track vampires, sir."

Alaric nodded. "Olivier de Renoir. We know."

Tristan stared. Alaric knew about Natalie's attacker?

Wait a minute, his dragon muttered, growing angry.

"You know?" he grunted, incredulous.

Alaric nodded. "Of course."

The dragon's casual tone infuriated him, and slowly, he pieced things together. Alaric was desperate to find a Fire Maiden. Shifters had sensitive noses, but vampires were even better. Who better to sniff out royal blood?

"You used Olivier to lead you to her?" Tristan growled, his voice rising.

Take it easy, buddy, Liam tried.

No way was he taking it easy. Not with something as precious as Natalie's life.

"You used vampires?" he shouted.

Alaric's brow folded. "We sensed the presence of a Fire Maiden, but as her powers are still weak, we could not locate her."

"So you allowed vampires to do that?"

Alaric looked smug. "That was the idea, yes."

"Good idea," Marcel, ever the brown-noser, agreed.

It was a miracle Tristan didn't explode, given the way his blood pressure rose. "You didn't tell me. You put Natalie at risk."

"We told you what you had to know. Besides, we didn't expect the vampires to find her so quickly," Alaric said, clearly annoyed. "The idea was for you to report the vampires to us, and for Hugo to take over from there."

Tristan opened his mouth, then closed it, because he was about to roar and possibly spit fire. Sulfur was already stinging his throat as his fury increased.

"If I hadn't been there, Natalie would be dead."

"For which we are grateful, Monsieur Chevalier — if indeed she is the one we seek."

Tristan's mouth hung open. If Natalie didn't turn out to be a Fire Maiden, would Alaric simply abandon her to her fate, whatever it may be?

Liam quietly raised his hand. "Um... If I may intrude?"

Alaric turned to him with a sour look. "Intrude? Appropriate choice of words." Then he sighed and flapped a hand. "Yes, Mr. Bennett?"

"Why do you need her so badly?"

"Don't you see? We've been waiting — hoping — to find our Fire Maiden for so long," Morfram said. "We need her."

Tristan didn't like the sound of that. "Need her to what, exactly?"

Morfram looked down his nose at Tristan. "To revive the ancient spell set to protect the city. Simply by taking up residence, a Fire Maiden can accomplish that."

"A Fire Maiden can accomplish much more," Hugo added in a low, reverent voice.

Alaric nodded gravely. "Indeed, the greatest of the line have accomplished many important public works. But we can hardly expect someone of such watered-down blood to match the legends of her ancestral line."

Tristan wanted to snort. Obviously, these men didn't know Natalie.

But Alaric spoke first, shaking a finger at Tristan. "I warn you not to test the limits of my gratitude. You will not question my authority, is that clear?"

No, it isn't, Tristan nearly shouted. Not with his vision going red and steam about to come out of his ears.

Hugo pursed his lips, and his voice tapped at the edge of Tristan's mind. *Keep your cool, son. Force isn't always the way. Try finesse.*

Keep his cool? How the hell was he supposed to keep his cool when his mate's life was at stake?

Hugo's eyebrows jumped up, and Tristan winced. Shit. Had Hugo picked up on that thought? The wolf shifter studied Tristan closely, then looked in the direction Natalie had gone.

Tristan forced himself to look straight ahead, pretending he was as detached as a good soldier ought to be. But all the while, his inner dragon raged.

For the next few minutes, he endured Alaric's tempestuous speech about protocols employees were expected to follow and how long a man could expect to remain employed if he failed to comply. And on and on...

So blustery. Worse than a lion, even, Liam sighed.

Then there was Marcel, who'd always rubbed Tristan the wrong way. The man stood at Alaric's side the whole time, mimicking his uncle's facial expressions.

As if he'll ever rule anything, Liam scoffed.

Tristan tuned out, eying Hugo. The wolf shifter was Alaric's most trusted adviser. Was he going to rat Tristan out? Alaric had never found a mate, so he wouldn't understand how deep that bond ran. And, damn. Alaric would never stand for a commoner like Tristan mating with a Fire Maiden, if Natalie truly was one. That was like a pauper pining for the princess's hand. She was way, way out of his class.

Totally out of your class, Marcel's haughty expression agreed. *Not like me, Alaric's own nephew.*

Tristan stood sweating bullets, watching Hugo from the corner of his eye. Wishing he could beg the wolf shifter for mercy, because he desperately needed time to figure out how to win over his mate.

Finally, Alaric finished his tirade with another blustery, "Do you understand?"

Tristan forced out the obligatory, "Yes, sir," sick as it made him feel.

Hugo clapped once, drawing everyone's attention.

"Fine. Now that that's sorted, let's move on."

Everyone looked relieved, including Morfram and Albiorix, who had probably witnessed enough of Alaric's tirades for a lifetime.

"Move on?" Alaric furrowed his brow.

"Move on," Hugo said firmly. "First, we have to trace the young lady's lineage to be completely sure."

Alaric stroked his beard, and everyone nodded sagely.

"Good idea," Marcel said. Then he leaned closer to Alaric. "Allow me to investigate."

Tristan barely swallowed a snarl. Marcel's favorite form of investigation took place in the bedroom. That was about the only thing Alaric's nephew showed any prowess in. No way would Tristan let that happen.

Luckily, Hugo stuck up a hand, halting Marcel. "More important is the question of protecting her while she settles in. If she accepts her role as a Fire Maiden."

Alaric's frown deepened. "She'd better accept her role."

Tristan bristled, and his mind spun with crazy schemes to help Natalie escape if she didn't choose to stay. He and she could catch the first train to Calais, then head to London. Liam could find someplace for them to stay—

Hey, man. This is your mess, not mine, Liam muttered.

But Tristan was on a roll. After covering their tracks to London, he and Natalie could acquire forged passports and fly to America, where he would find a place to hide her from dragons or vampires. Then he and she would... They would...

He stalled out there, because it hit him how crazy it all was. Maybe Natalie wanted to stay in Paris. Hell, he sure did, but he would leave if it meant remaining at her side. But what if Natalie wasn't drawn to him the way he was drawn to her? What then?

Suddenly, he realized that Hugo had said something and that everyone was waiting for him to answer. He looked at Liam for help.

Oh, for God's sake, Hugo grumbled into his mind. Then he spoke aloud. "I said, congratulations, Monsieur Chevalier. You've been promoted."

Tristan frowned. Was that some kind of trick?

"Promoted to...?"

"Bodyguard."

"Bodyguard." Alaric heaved a heavy sigh. "We used to call them knights." His face took on a *Those were the days* expression.

Tristan and Liam exchanged glances. Exactly how old was Alaric?

"In any case," Hugo went on, "the young lady will need protection. And as my dear mate points out..."

Clara wasn't in the room, but Tristan figured she had to have used the private, mind-to-mind connection all mated shifters shared.

"...the young lady will need space and time to grasp the enormity of her new role. Since it might overwhelm her to stay here, the apartment on Boulevard Saint-Michel is a suitable place for her to stay. Temporarily, of course."

Tristan gulped. Had he just been granted his deepest desire or sentenced to a living hell? Protecting Natalie meant protecting her from vampires, gargoyles — and from himself. He was a hired gun. She was a goddamn princess, descended from royal blood.

"Is the apartment really suitable?" Marcel interjected with a deep frown aimed at Tristan.

"It's perfectly suitable," Alaric retorted. Then he pinned Tristan with his fiercest look. "Temporarily. Your job is to protect her until..."

Alarms clanged in Tristan's mind. "Until what?"

Alaric waved. "Until we find her a suitable mate, of course."

Tristan clenched his fists as his inner dragon roared. *No!*

Marcel stood a little straighter, and his eyes gleamed.

"Our Fire Maiden must remain in Paris, and she must be protected," Alaric declared. "Then she must produce an heir. A daughter, ideally. Several, in fact."

Marcel nodded eagerly, but Tristan couldn't believe his ears. "What if she doesn't approve of the mate you select?"

Marcel scoffed. Alaric tilted his head like he'd never considered such a thing.

"What she wants is not important, Monsieur Chevalier. What you think does not matter. What matters is the future of the city and the safety of its citizens."

Says the guy who dangled a woman in front of vampires as bait, Tristan nearly yelled.

But Hugo pinned him with a look of warning, and Liam spoke into his mind.

Shut up while you're ahead. We'll figure something out.

We. At least he'd have Liam's help. But did he have Hugo's?

He glanced at Hugo, beseeching him. *Please tell me you're not on board with this barbaric plan.*

But Hugo's gaze was distant, his thoughts firmly shut off from Tristan's mind.

"I'll send my nephew over to check on the woman soon," Alaric added.

Marcel flashed a lecherous grin.

Morfram nodded solemnly. "Meanwhile, we will track down the individuals who attacked her."

"I will find the gargoyle involved. One of the young ones, no doubt." Albiorix sighed.

Tristan made a face. *Young* for gargoyles meant less than a century or two.

"They will be punished," Albiorix finished gravely.

That was fine with Tristan. But what about Natalie? He stood mutely, horrified at what he'd led Natalie into. She'd trusted him to find help, but he'd never imagined this... this...

Mess? Liam finished, chipper as can be.

Tristan swung his jaw until it popped. *Mess* was right.

But the door swung open just then, and the women entered. Clara's eyes met Hugo's and glowed. Jacqueline licked her lips in open invitation, though Tristan hardly noticed, because Natalie entered next, and his vision narrowed, turning everything else into a blur.

Mate, his dragon rumbled so loudly, Liam coughed.

"Miss Brewer," Marcel said, stepped quickly to Natalie's side. "Allow me to see you out."

"No," Tristan growled, beating Marcel to Natalie's side. "Allow me."

Her expression was grateful, and her hand went straight to his arm. Best of all, she didn't so much as glance at Marcel. She just leaned against Tristan and headed for the door.

Then she squeaked, turned back to the others, and managed a polite *Au revoir* and even *Merci.* For what, Tristan wasn't sure.

"Tristan?" she whispered, turning quickly toward the door.

"Yeah?"
"Get me out of this place."
"With pleasure," he breathed.

Chapter Twelve

Natalie speed-walked back to the Metro, barely noticing the over-the-top displays of the red-light district. Her mind was spinning with everything she'd learned. Dragons... vampires... Fire Maidens. Her?

She felt numb, and she didn't notice how close she stuck to Tristan until they bumped for the second or third time. He didn't seem to mind. Thank goodness, because she desperately needed someone to lean against.

Which she did — literally — once they entered the subway car and took a seat. She sank against his shoulder, wrapped her arms around Tristan's in a sideways hug, and tried not to think as Paris's hidden depths rushed by. Bright stations alternated with dark tunnels, an apt reflection of her thoughts. For fleeting moments, she convinced herself that everything would be all right. But seconds later, she fought tears of despair.

We've searched for a Fire Maiden for so long...

Natalie squeezed her eyes shut. Maybe Alaric and the others were all crazy. Maybe there was no such thing as shifters or vampires. Even Tristan — who knew? He and Liam could be suffering from some rare form of PTSD that made them believe they could change into animals.

But then she remembered Olivier in the alley. The teeth. The fangs. Tristan's burst of fire.

So, no. They weren't crazy. But that was even worse. And as for the Fire Maiden part... What would happen when Alaric and the others found out they'd made a mistake? That she was plain old her, and no one special at all?

But then the crystal warmed against her chest, and echoes of past dreams darted through her mind. All those times she'd imagined flying. Her uncanny resistance to fire. The way Paris had called to her over the years...

Could it really be?

Her only solace was the soft brush of Tristan's hand on her shoulder and the steady murmur of his deep voice, telling her everything would be okay.

Liam, bless him, stood before them with his back turned, glaring at anyone who came close. He was the moat to the walls of Tristan's keep — another line of defense keeping her safe. But how safe was she, really?

You'll always be a target. All those vampires... Gargoyles...

She burrowed closer to Tristan. If she was a Fire Maiden, she would spend a lifetime looking over her shoulder, wondering when the next vampire might attack. Or would that lifetime be cut painfully short?

She glanced up at the subway map, tempted to transfer lines and rush to the airport. The subway car rattled around a turn, and the lights flickered, making her tense. The problem was, vampires could track her to Philadelphia. She slumped, burying her face in her hands as the metro car rattled along.

At some point, Tristan helped her up, and they transferred to a different Metro line.

"Not long now," he murmured.

She nearly laughed. Every second felt like a lifetime. But eventually, a garbled voice came over the intercom, announcing Luxembourg station, and soon after, she was back in the sun, striding briskly to Tristan's apartment.

"Monsieur Chevalier," the doorman greeted Tristan in precisely the same tone he'd used the previous night. Then he nodded to Natalie and Liam in turn. *"Mademoiselle. Monsieur."*

"Bonjour," Natalie mumbled, forcing a smile.

Tristan murmured a curt greeting before leading her to the tiny elevator. Then finally — finally! — they were home.

Home? Natalie stopped short. This wasn't home. It was a near-stranger's apartment, and a bare one at that.

Still, when Tristan closed the door with a decisive thump, she felt better. Still hollow and overwhelmed, but not quite as lost.

"Make yourself at home," Tristan murmured. "I'll be right back."

She headed for the red couch and sat there, staring out the floor-to-ceiling windows without registering the view. Bijou threaded between her ankles, meowing something she took to mean, *You look sad, but I'm sure petting me will cheer you up.*

Natalie scooped up the cat and cuddled him tightly, tuning in to his comforting purr. Out in the hallway, Tristan and Liam spoke in low tones. And out in the city...

She puffed out a long breath. It was a new day. Possibly the start of a new life. But, hell. Where would she begin?

A cup of hot chocolate and a good book, her mother used to say.

Natalie looked around. No hot chocolate, but Bijou was warm and cuddly, and Clara had given her a book as she'd left Alaric's mansion. She stared at the leather cover with its fancy gold embossing for a while. It looked like something out of medieval times.

A History of Dragons, the swirling script declared.

Slowly, haltingly, she opened to the first page and began to read.

∞∞∞∞

Two days passed — two long days and nights, during which time Tristan came and went. When he was in, he remained close, as restless and edgy as she felt. When he was out...

She shut the thought out of her mind. Mostly, he went to check in with Alaric or to hunt vampires. What if he was injured again? Worse, what if he died? He'd claimed shifters were "mostly immune" to vampire poison, which wasn't exactly comforting. And as for reporting to Alaric — he seemed to savor that duty even less.

Liam stopped by often, her only other link to the outside world, bringing treats, news, and good cheer. He'd picked up more clothes from her apartment, and those, together with some improvements Tristan made, helped her feel even more at home.

"*Voilà,*" he'd said when he set up a little nook for her with an end table and a lamp, plus thick cotton sheets and a blanket that looked brand-new.

"Still a terrible host," Madame Colette had muttered when she discovered Natalie was still sleeping on the couch.

"She insisted," Tristan said.

"I did," Natalie added quickly. "It's cozy."

"Cozy? *Impossible*," Madame announced in her thick Provençal accent.

"It is," Natalie insisted. "The apartment is big and empty, but the couch is like its own little room. A place where I don't feel so alone." The minute the words were out of her mouth, she winced. Oops.

Madame huffed, shooting Tristan a withering look. "A miserable failure of a host."

Tristan glowered and grabbed his phone. "I'll show you miserable..."

Within hours, a delivery crew was there, maneuvering in an antique writing desk with a fold-down top, plus a green, library-style reading lamp, some fluffy pillows, and—

Natalie laughed. "A beanbag?"

Tristan frowned. "You don't like it?"

"I love it. It's just a funny combination. A nice combination," she hurried to add. "Thank you. Truly. I mean it."

Madame Colette came in at exactly that moment, and Tristan folded his thick arms, daring her to comment. The housekeeper looked around with her flashing, eagle eyes, and a long, tense minute ticked by.

"I love it," Natalie announced. "I really do."

Tristan glowed. Bijou pawed the fluffy pillows, claiming them for himself. And as for Madame Colette...

She hmpfed and changed the subject. "I brought you a book. A good one," she emphasized, frowning at the stack Alaric had sent over. "Here."

She'd marked a chapter, so Natalie started there. The slanted, loopy script was hard to read, but the tome was filled with beautiful, hand-painted images. The pages were dry and ancient, and Natalie was terrified of damaging them. As far as she could tell, *Une Petite Histoire des Temps Anciens* was the epic saga of an eagle shifter clan. It read more like *Wuthering Heights* or *Pride and Prejudice* than history, which made a welcome change from the dry tone of Alaric's books. The only dragon in it was a side character named Claudine who made a brief appearance in Chapter Three before running off with a poor knight in Chapter Four and eventually returning in Chapter Eleven to run off a pack of marauding wolves.

"Claudine? Wait a second..."

Natalie flipped through Alaric's books, searching for the section that had stuck in her mind — one summarizing feats of great Fire Maidens over the centuries.

"Claudine," Natalie whispered when she located the page. Tucking her legs under herself on the couch, she began to read.

Claudine d'Islay, as it turned out, was one of the mightiest Fire Maidens Paris had ever known. After repelling multiple attacks and bringing vampires under control with the help of her consort, a knight named Breselan, she went on to develop public works in Paris. Under her leadership, the sewer system was expanded and running water brought to the poorest sections of the city. Claudine also established orphanages and schools for the poorest of the poor.

While the eagle shifter book only mentioned her in passing, Alaric's book detailed everything Claudine had done for the city and how she had lived to a ripe old age with Breselan.

Natalie sat back, comparing both books. Same Claudine, same knight. Then she sat back and sighed. The more she read, the more she decided she could never measure up. Liviana, Amelie, and other Fire Maidens had been able to breathe fire. They struck fear into the hearts of their enemies and fostered compassion in the city they loved. What could she do?

The doorbell buzzed, and she whirled. Tristan stalked over to the door and growled, "Hello?"

"Pizza delivery," came a voice.

That was Liam, joking as always. He didn't have a pizza, but he did have a shopping bag that smelled of fresh bread and cheese. He waved to Madame Colette, kissed Natalie on both cheeks, and thrust the bags into Tristan's hand.

"No pizza, but I did bring a very nice wine." Then he grinned and picked up Bijou, cuddling him under his chin. "Nice kitty. Sweet kitty."

Bijou's eyelids went to half-mast, and his purr echoed through the apartment.

Tristan rolled his eyes. "There's nothing sweet about that spitfire."

"Of course there is. Just look." Liam held out Bijou, who hissed at Tristan, then cuddled back up with Liam. "If you knew anything about cats—"

Tristan made a face. "I know lots about cats. Especially some overly talkative ones."

Natalie furrowed her brow. There it was again — that reminder that all was not as it seemed. She changed the subject quickly. "Were you able to find that sweater?"

Liam had brought over all her essentials, and he'd promised to stop by her apartment for the few items he'd missed.

"Your wish is my command." He took a deep bow and presented her with a shopping bag.

She half expected Liam to make a sophomoric comment about the bra she'd left hanging from her dresser, but he didn't, thank goodness. He did, however, deliver some chilling news, even if he related it in his usual cheery way.

"I stumbled across your landlady. Charming woman." *Not*, his expression said. "She didn't want to let me in at first, even though I showed her your key."

Natalie smiled. Her landlady was a lot like Madame Colette — a little brusque but good at heart.

"She said, 'I didn't let the others in, and I don't want you here either.'"

Natalie froze, and Tristan growled. "What others? Vampires?"

Liam pinched his lips briefly, but Natalie nodded him on.

"You know how it is — those bastards don't leave a scent. But I couldn't sniff out anyone else..."

Natalie wondered how good lion noses were. But then her mind caught up on the rest of his message. Vampires were still prowling the city. Worse, they had found her apartment. She brought together the sides of her button-down sweater and looked around. Would they find her here?

They wouldn't dare, Tristan's eyes assured her.

"You know what else the landlady said?" Liam went on, clearly ramping up to his next joke.

"What else did the landlady say?" Tristan replied in a bored monotone.

"She said 'That Natalie is a nice girl. Not your type. You leave her alone.'" Liam faked a hurt look, but his eyes sparkled. "Not my type? Who says nice girls aren't my type?"

"She's not," Tristan barked.

Liam grinned. "I don't know. What you think, Nat? Fancy a date with me?"

She laughed. "Maybe some other time." Then she grew somber again. She wasn't interested in a date with Liam, but heck. She was getting some serious cabin fever. Would she ever have the freedom to roam the city again? Or would she be locked up in a gilded cage for the rest of her life, gazing out the windows like Bijou did?

She'd already had to call in to work and beg for time off. She had only asked for a week, feeling terrible about the vague excuses she'd provided. Worse, she'd had to call in to *Solidarité du Coeur* to do the same.

But, Natalie! What will we do without you? the supervisor had pleaded.

It gutted her not to meet her responsibilities and to give up the routine she'd come to enjoy. Work, long walks through the city, and fascinating talks with people she met at the soup kitchen. Everything that had given her a sense of connection to the city she loved.

She must have been frowning, because Tristan nudged her. "You okay?"

She forced a smile, though she didn't know what to say. Yes? No?

"Oh, Clara sent you another book. One that looks even more boring than the last." Liam gestured back to the shopping bag. "I swear, Alaric has an entire library devoted to dragons, dragons, and more dragons. I think the latest one is something like, *The Dark Ages: Before We Dragons Came to Bless the Earth with Our Holy Presence.*"

Natalie opened the book the minute the others moved away. It turned out to be *The Great Shifter Wars and Their Aftermath: 1320-1597*. And yes, it did feature a lot of dragons. But it had an entire chapter on Liviana, and she pored over every word.

The mightiest dragon queen of all, she forged alliances, banished enemies, established charities... She also amassed a treasure greater than that of any other dragon...

Natalie mulled over the words, absently holding the crystal in one hand while petting Bijou with the other. As always, her thoughts drifted to the one dragon she couldn't get off her mind. Tristan. And as always, she told herself to think about something else.

But it was hard, especially now that she was spending so much time with him. Even when he was out of sight, she would catch a whiff of his rich, natural cologne, or hear his firm footsteps as he paced across the hardwood floors. She could sense him nearby. And at night...

Nights were the worst, because darkness had a way of shrinking the space between them and intensifying every sound. Every rustle of his sheets, every quiet breath set off fantasies she couldn't stop.

She took a deep breath, trying to halt those thoughts, and went back to reading. Hours passed, and the sun slowly set, layering the sky with bands of red, orange, and yellow. One by one, city lights came on. At first, too few to form a pattern. Then more lights came on, and the dots lined up to form a familiar network of boulevards and parks.

"Good book?" Tristan murmured, making her glance up.

She smiled, blushed, and promptly cursed herself. Why did he do that to her every time?

Maybe because he was leaning against the arched double doorway to the next room, arms folded over his chest like a warrior considering his next campaign. One ankle was crossed over the other, making him appear relaxed. Of course, *relaxed* was a relative term with Tristan, and he only ever seemed to hover in the red to yellow zone, always on alert. Were all dragons that way?

"Interesting, for sure," she replied a little lamely.

Then she tilted her head, studying Tristan more closely. Was his face a little flushed? Was his chest rising and falling in ever deeper breaths?

His mouth opened and closed, and she leaned forward, certain he was about to say something important, like, *Natalie, I keep thinking about you. Do you dream about me the way I dream about you?*

Another full minute passed with them gazing at each other, desperate to speak but unable to form words. The lights of Paris sparkled in the windows, as mute as they were. Even the Eiffel Tower, standing elegantly above the rest, seemed to hold its breath.

Finally, Tristan cleared his throat. He looked about to leave, but Natalie couldn't stand to see him go.

"So..." she started, not quite sure what to follow up with.

But Tristan leaned toward her, appearing as eager as she for an excuse to linger.

"Um... Shifters," she finally said, waving outside. "Do you only change under a full moon?"

His cheeks stretched into a smile. "No. We can shift anytime we want."

She gulped. In truth, she was dying to see him shift. To see a dragon — and not just the little glimpse he'd given her the other day. But something told her shifting was a private act. A little like sex, she supposed.

And, damn. That random thought made her body tingle all over.

She rushed to change the subject. "I guess your parents taught you how?"

Tristan mulled that one over. "Sort of. You don't shift until you hit your teenage years." He smiled. "I took off as soon as I could. My poor mother..." He laughed at first, but then his expression soured. "Mostly, I taught myself. My father wasn't around to help, and even if he were, I doubt he would have been much use." He cleared his throat. "But it's instinctive, I suppose."

She pursed her lips, trying not to wonder about his childhood. "I guess you have to be careful, though."

He snorted. "You learn that long before you can shift. Humans fear what they don't understand, and even if they're not as strong as most shifters, they have the advantage of numbers. In the Dark Ages, they burned any witch they could find and hunted some shifter species to extinction."

She frowned. "Like what?"

He shrugged. "Griffins. Harpies. Unicorns..."

Her eyes went wide. "Unicorns?"

He chuckled. "Where do you think the tapestries drew their inspiration from? Humans aren't that creative — unless it comes to instruments of destruction. They're champions at that." He gazed out the windows with a grim expression. "That's where we come in, doing our best to steer human ingenuity and energy in the right direction. But sometimes..."

A dozen tragic newspaper headlines ran through Natalie's mind, filling in where Tristan trailed off.

Natalie took a deep breath. Could she really make a difference? Dare she find out?

"Would a Fire Maiden really help?" she whispered.

The smile Tristan flashed was bright and genuine, but a moment later, he sobered as if he'd just remembered something.

"*Oui.* She would." His eyes lingered on hers, full of yearning and regret she wished she understood. "I know she would." Then he forced a smile and backed away. "Sorry. I'm keeping you up."

She was about to protest — *Please, I'd rather talk* — but Tristan appeared to have made up his mind.

"*Bonne nuit*," he whispered, sounding far away, as if he'd made the mental switch back to soldier mode.

"*Bonne nuit*," Natalie echoed, watching him slip silently away.

Chapter Thirteen

Bonne nuit.

Natalie sighed quietly. Tristan said that every night, though never as sadly as just then. And like every night, he didn't go to bed. Instead, he headed for the spiral staircase that led to the rooftop. She could tell by the tap of his steps on the metal stairs. A minute or two later, a breath of fresh air wafted through the apartment, and she pictured Tristan gazing over the city. Then there was nothing but silence.

She turned off her light and lay under her blanket, her eyes on the ceiling. Waiting. That silence, she'd learned, was the precursor to something else.

A car horn tooted on the street. Trees swayed in the park. Otherwise, nothing. But then...

Three heavy steps pounded across the roof, followed by a mighty *whoosh* of air. Natalie clutched her blanket while her heart thumped. Was that a dragon, soaring off into the night?

It had happened the first night, and the second, too. Each time, she lay still, waiting... wondering. What would shifting be like?

She closed her eyes, picturing herself soaring over Paris. She could almost feel the cool tickle of wind and see lights streak by below. She would soar toward the moon, then roll and dive toward the star-shaped intersection at the Arc de Triomphe. She imagined winging all the way out to Giverny, where Monet had painted water lilies. Would the ponds be dark patches, or would they shimmer in the moonlight like the effect of an impressionist's brush?

She heaved a deep breath. It was so easy to imagine, but flying was impossible, like so much else.

You're only a human, with no means of protecting yourself.

She'd been practicing the defensive move Tristan taught her, but it seemed like too little, too late. If a vampire got that close, she'd be a goner, for sure. She flexed her fingers, imagining claws in their place. If only she had enough dragon blood to shift! Then she could protect herself — and the city too. She could eradicate trouble with a single, fiery breath. She could conquer enemies. Head off trouble before it bubbled over into the human realm. She could...

An echo of Jacqueline's mocking voice sounded in her mind. *Just a human, not a dragon like me.*

Natalie drooped, looking at her hands. Those were plain old fingers, not claws. Even if she could change into a dragon, she doubted she could singlehandedly make the world a better place.

She sat up, switched on the reading light, and opened one of Alaric's books. If she couldn't sleep, she might as well learn more about dragons. But the views of Paris, as ever, caught her eye, and she sat there, fingering her crystal while taking it all in.

"Beautiful," she whispered.

But then Bijou arched and hissed. A shadow fell over the top right portion of the windows, and something fluttered outside. Natalie's heart revved, and goose bumps prickled her arm. At first, all she could see was her own reflection superimposed over the city view. But then another face appeared, twisting the features of her reflection into something sinister and distorted.

She saw a hooked, beaky nose. High, emaciated cheeks, curved ears, and a devil's horn. The creature's mouth opened, showing off pointy, widely spaced teeth. Then the grimace became a grotesque smile, and the eyes glowed.

There you are, my little pretty, its voice sounded in her mind.

Gargoyle. A real gargoyle, hovering outside her window. Spying on her for Olivier and his vampires?

Her blood ran cold, and she nearly screamed. But instinct took over, and she reacted without thinking.

She threw her blanket back and ran to the window, holding the crystal high. And while no sound came out, she was yelling inside. Practically roaring, in fact — as ferociously as a... a...

She gulped. As ferociously as a dragon?

The gargoyle's eyes went wide, and heck, she was just as surprised. Rays of blinding light shot out from the crystal, and the gargoyle lurched back.

Out of here. Out, lowly creature, she yelled in a voice not quite her own.

The light of the crystal obscured everything beyond the glass, but Natalie could just make out the gargoyle wheeling away in fear. The crystal's light intensified, forming a laser that followed the beast, and another voice registered in her mind. Deep and powerful, yet feminine, like a weary queen.

Go, and warn your masters we are not to be trifled with. You understand?

We? Natalie glanced at the crystal then pressed her face against the glass. The gargoyle was scrambling away in panic, and the voice she'd heard was... laughing in triumph?

As the intruder fled, the crystal's light faded, as did the sense of an outside presence. Natalie pushed away from the window, her chest heaving. Holy crap. What had just happened?

She stared at the crystal in her hand. If that was a dragon's, and if she really was descended from Liviana...

Her gaze shifted to her reflection in the windows, and she gulped. Was Clara right about her?

Then she jumped, because fire flared in the distance, and a second shadow chased the fleeing gargoyle. Natalie threw the French doors open and gripped the guardrail of the narrow balcony. Cool night air chilled her body, and the breeze toyed with her hair. But even the threat of gargoyles didn't frighten her, because that was a dragon out there.

Tristan, her heart cried.

Fire flashed a second time, and deep in her soul, she could hear his furious roar.

Long after both shadows disappeared, she stood there, sweating and panting as if she'd fought a physical battle. Then

Bijou meowed, and she backed away, closing the doors. Then she slumped on the couch. Had that really happened?

By the windows, Bijou sat, casually lifted one paw, and licked his belly as if to say, *Happens every day.*

∞∞∞

Natalie turned off her light and lay under her blanket, watching the windows. That gargoyle had been a spy for the vampires, she was sure of it. She huddled in a ball, wishing for Tristan. She stared at the ceiling, waiting for the thump-thump-thump that would signal his return. Minutes ticked by, then hours, and she began to fret. Was Tristan all right?

Then she frowned. This was an echo of the nights she'd spent waiting for Dean. Hadn't she vowed to change that? Paris was supposed to be her *me* time, not a time for another ill-fated romance.

For one long, wavering minute, she lay still. Then, in one sharp motion, she thrust the blanket aside and jumped to her feet.

Dammit, she was not going to be a passive bystander to her own fate. She was going to... to...

Her train of thought stalled out. Frankly, she had no idea what she'd do once she got outside. But she was through waiting — and wondering. So she yanked on a robe and stomped toward the spiraling staircase toward the roof. Bijou followed, jumping and playing with the long end of her belt.

"Hey, kitty." She stooped to pet the cat. "You think Tristan is okay?"

Bijou purred, dancing under Natalie's feet.

Obviously, the cat couldn't care less. But Natalie couldn't relax. She ascended the last few stairs and pushed open the door to the rooftop. It creaked, making her wince.

"Hello?" She peered around cautiously.

Bijou slid past her feet, sauntering ahead without even checking for gargoyles.

"Bijou!" Natalie hissed, hurrying after him with one eye on the sky.

And that was only one danger, because surely, the cat wasn't supposed to jump to the very edge of the roof and walk the inch-wide molding on the brink of the nine-story drop. And, whoa — what the heck was she doing, squeezing around the guard rail to follow him?

She glanced down, then blanched. It wasn't the first time in her life she'd stepped to the edge of a drop-off without thinking. But that was always followed by a terrifying moment of realization — like now — when fear set in. Not a fear of heights, but fear of her own boldness. Normal people didn't venture out on ledges. It simply wasn't done. Could it be the dragon blood in her, erasing what ought to have been instinctive fear?

Slowly, she tiptoed back. Dragon blood or not, she couldn't fly, and she certainly couldn't land on her feet like a cat, not after falling from that height.

"Bijou," she hissed, paralleling his path from the safe side of the guard rail. "Come back!"

But Bijou continued his tightrope walk until he settled atop a ventilation pipe. Then he sat, picked up a paw, and began to clean himself. A lick to the paw, a rub behind the ear, another lick, another rub-rub-rub, as casual as could be.

"Bijou..."

Natalie kneeled and reached toward the cat, smacking her lips. That position lined Bijou up with the Eiffel Tower and the nearly full moon. For a moment, she sat on her heels and admired the view in one of those *Wow, I'm really in Paris* moments that struck her from time to time.

Then she spotted a blur in the distance — a shadow among shadows, and slowly, shakily, she stood.

"Bijou..." she warned. That shadow was moving, and it was coming straight for her.

Her pulse skyrocketed. God, no.

Bijou took a break from cleaning himself to hiss at the intruder.

Natalie did a double take and stared into the darkness. Wait a second...

Bijou sprang to the terrace and disappeared down the stairs, but Natalie couldn't tear her gaze away from the creature rushing toward her. Its size might have been exaggerated by the backdrop of that huge, silver moon, but wow. It looked big. Dragon-big. The wingbeats were powerful and steady, the body streamlined in the air.

"Tristan?" Natalie gripped the railing.

Then she ducked, because the dragon was coming right at her. When it rushed overhead, her hair tossed. Natalie spun around, watching it execute a tight turn.

Over the past days, she'd thought constantly of dragons and studied them in books. But nothing had prepared her for this. This dragon was huge and powerful. Graceful, too, and leathery. His body was the same brownish-black color as Tristan's hair and so smooth, the moonlight reflected off his hide.

How did she know it was Tristan? The same way she could identify his footsteps without looking. The way her heart leaped an instant before he knocked on the door after running errands. She just knew.

He stuck his talons forward like an eagle ready to snatch a fish out of a river. The massive wings curled, backwinding his momentum, and he landed in three smooth steps.

Thump. Thump, thump.

Natalie's mouth hung open. The timing was exactly the same, every time. But imagining the maneuver and actually seeing it were two different things. Which meant she finally got to see what accounted for the long pause that always followed those three steps. Would Tristan reach his long neck back and comb his wings like a bird? Would he take a few deep breaths then rest?

She held her breath.

The dragon stepped forward to the very edge of the terrace, stuck out his chest, and opened his wings. He held his head high and tipped it back like a wolf preparing to howl. But the sound he made was low, rough, and growly, and it was followed by a tiny sliver of fire spat into the night.

Natalie gulped. Tristan might as well have beat his chest and announced, *I am mighty* or *This is my territory* or *Chal-*

lenge me if you dare. It was that commanding. That intimidating. That...

Princely, she thought.

But then he whipped his head around and bared a set of startlingly sharp teeth.

"Wait!" Natalie squeaked, falling flat on her rear. "It's me."

Panic filled her, and she screamed at herself. Oh God. She'd surprised a full-grown dragon on his home turf. If Tristan didn't recognize her, she'd be toast.

"It's me," she yelped, scuttling backward.

The dragon tilted his head, staring. It was terrifying, but slowly, the red of his eyes warmed to a friendlier orange hue.

Natalie, those hundred-carat eyes said.

She nearly crumpled in relief. "Sorry."

Slowly, carefully, the dragon folded his wings, taking care not to spook her. Just as slowly, and just as carefully, Natalie wobbled to her feet.

"Tristan." She gazed into eyes that appeared centuries deep. "Is it really you?"

The dragon's eyes shone, and the massive head bobbed.

She took a deep breath, steeled her nerves, and extended one hand. "Can I... Can I..."

Somehow, her lips couldn't get out all of *Can I touch you?* But Tristan's eyes swirled as if to say, *Be my guest.*

She inched forward, waiting for the illusion to break. Any second now, lights would flash on, someone would laugh, and Tristan would remove his mask, explaining how he'd pulled off that trick.

But it wasn't a trick. That was Tristan, totally different, yet somehow the same. She could tell from the eyes, the wary set of his jaw. His bearing — strong and proud, yet humble, like a man who'd learned life lessons the hard way.

Her fingers trembled in the tiny gap that remained between them. Finally, she stepped closer, placing her fingertip on the underside of his jaw, exactly the place she would scratch Bijou. His skin was warm, leathery, and just as tough as it looked.

So tough, she doubted he could feel her touch. But his head dipped slightly, coaxing her on.

She set the rest of her fingers down, sucked in another deep breath, and scratched.

His nostrils flared, and for a moment, her chest tightened. Forcing herself to relax, she scratched harder.

Nice, those bright eyes said.

It *was* nice, the way scratching a cat imparted a heartwarming, *he likes it* feeling. Growing bolder, she reached along the sharp line of Tristan's jaw. A wide, blocky jaw, as big as a bull's, with teeth the size of daggers.

Moments later, she let out a nervous little laugh. She was petting a dragon — and it wasn't all that different from petting Bijou. Especially not when the dragon stretched, guiding her to another spot.

She chuckled. "Bijou does that too."

Tristan rolled his oversize dragon eyes.

Natalie laughed outright. Meeting Tristan in dragon form was a little like seeing her company's CEO wearing shorts and a T-shirt at the community outreach events she'd organized. The same person with a different look.

Tristan nudged her lightly, and she hurried back to rubbing his long, pointy ear. Something moved in the shadows behind him — his tail, lashing the air the way Bijou did when she scratched his favorite spot. Natalie shook her head, awed.

Tristan must have spotted the motion, because he cocked his head.

"Sometimes, I can't believe it. Other times, it's like I always knew," she whispered.

He nodded solemnly, and she cupped his muzzle, stroking his nose with her thumbs. It looked as tough as the rest of him, but the front was as soft and velvety as a horse's nose.

"Wow," she whispered, dumbstruck all over again.

The dragon's eyes glowed brighter.

She peeked around the side of his body. "Can I see your wings?"

Slowly, he unfolded one glider-sized wing — a wing that could shelter a compact Renault. Hell, it was big enough to cover her entire apartment if the wind ever blew the roof off.

"You really can fly..."

He snorted. *Of course I can fly.*

Funny, how that made something inside her ache. In her dreams, she could fly, but she would never be able to soar through the air the way Tristan did.

His eyes darkened, and he tilted his head.

She forced a smile. "I might be slightly jealous. Of the wings, I mean."

He grinned. At least, she was pretty sure that was a grin among all those teeth.

"I might be jealous of that tail too," she joked.

He lashed it proudly, then gently rubbed her shoulder with his chin.

She broke into a smile, getting the gist of his message. Not everyone had a tail, but that was okay. Laughing, she wrapped her arms around his snout and leaned in.

She only meant to hug him for a moment, but somehow, she couldn't let go. Her eyes slid closed, and her breath bounced off his cheek. Her pulse slowed, and she found her mind drifting. Boy, was it nice. Warm. Cozy, somehow.

Then she caught herself. Whoa. She was hugging Tristan. Closely. Intimately. She'd fondled his ears, for goodness' sake!

Of course, she'd cuddled lots of dogs and cats in the past — even a few horses. But this was different. *Totally* different, because within that dragon was a man. And not just any man, but the one she'd spent the past days fantasizing about. Living beside. Seeing almost every hour of every day, and loving it.

She stepped back, sure Tristan would be as embarrassed as she was. But his eyes were at half-mast, and that edgy aura had eased.

Eventually, his eyes fluttered, and he blinked back to focus. Yet something about him remained a little forlorn.

Natalie cleared her throat. "Thanks. It's... You're..." She motioned to him, searching for the word. "Amazing."

She blushed, because you didn't just tell a guy he was amazing.

Then again, he was a dragon.

His nostrils flared, and she could have sworn she heard, *You're the amazing one* whisper through her mind.

Then he jutted his blocky chin, and she backed up. When the air around him shimmered, she peered around, thinking it was something in the sky. But then it hit her. Tristan was shifting.

He crossed his wings in front of his body and bowed his head. Everything happened gradually, yet still too fast for her to grasp. His back straightened, and his ears shrank. His tail curled until it was lost from view. His leathery hide paled to his normal skin color, and his wings made a smooth transition to arms.

Natalie had expected a painful, grotesque process punctuated by moans, but it was perfectly smooth and natural. And when his eyes opened...

Her breath caught. They were glowing softly — at her.

Her chest heated, and her rushing pulse echoed in her ears the way a shell echoed the ocean's hum. The lights of Paris grew blurry, and her lips moved.

She was dying to kiss him. To touch him. Absolutely aching to press her body against his and never, ever let him go. When she took a step closer, he did the same. But the door to the stairs creaked in the breeze, and they both spun at the sound. Then Natalie turned back, suddenly self-conscious. Had she really been leaning in that close? She inched back a little, giving Tristan space.

"That was amazing."

He flapped a hand. "Every shifter can do that."

She snorted. "Sure. Changing bodies? Flying? I can only do that in my dreams."

His eyes went wide. "You fly in your dreams?"

She winced. That sounded ridiculous, didn't it? She tried to cover up with a shrug. "Just sometimes. It's silly, really."

He took her hands. "It's not silly. It's... it's..."

He seemed truly taken aback, as if that were somehow significant. So significant, she was dying to hear what he would say. But then she glanced down, and—

Oops. Big oops.

Really big, a dirty corner of her mind said.

Blood rushed to her face, because Tristan was naked. Totally naked, from his broad chest to his checkerboard abs and a couple of fascinating scars. Or, they would be, if it hadn't been for his equally powerful lower body, and the cock that stood out like... like...

Like it did in her dreams right before she kneeled in front of him and—

She whirled away, turning pink. Make that crimson, judging by the fire in her cheeks.

"Oh. Sorry. I mean..."

Oh God. Please, please don't let him read my mind now.

"Sorry," Tristan murmured from behind her. "That's how shifting goes."

"Sure. Of course. Makes sense. Well, I'll just... uh... go to bed, I guess." She hurried for the stairs.

"Natalie..." Tristan called softly, almost imploring her.

She turned, still crimson. Thank goodness he held up his clothes, covering his groin.

"Yes?"

His chest rose and fell in a tiny sigh. Then he whispered, and his voice floated across the space between them. *"Bonne nuit."*

She warmed all over again then rushed downstairs after a slightly too sultry, *"Bonne nuit."*

Chapter Fourteen

The minute Natalie disappeared down the stairs, Tristan slumped. Dammit. She'd been so close, and a tingling, magical feeling had come over him as it had so often over the past days. A feeling of peace, as if the world weren't as messed up as he'd assumed it to be, and that life had a happier, richer side than he'd ever known. Natalie had felt it too. He was sure of it. But now...

He kicked at the safety railing, then cursed. Lashing out in frustration worked better with boots on.

When he'd first flown in and spotted Natalie, he'd been sure she would scream and run.

His dragon huffed. *Of course our mate didn't run. She recognized us.*

She had, and it had blown him away. And when she'd come over and touched him...

Warmth flooded his body as he relived her first trembling touch. Her awestruck expression. The soft, careful strokes along his ears.

Felt so good, his dragon hummed. *So nice.*

He took a deep breath, trying not to admit how much he'd needed it. The downside of being a dragon was not getting petted... well, ever. Dragons might be big and tough on the outside, but every creature needed affection from time to time. Cats got petted, while dogs got scratched around the ears and told, *Good boy!* Some lucky horses earned hugs.

But dragons... It was lonely going at times.

Doesn't have to be lonely. His dragon looked in the direction of the stairs. *She likes me.*

Tristan snorted. *She likes me.*

All right. She likes both of us, his dragon said.

He gazed up at the stars. It was true. That feeling of connection had remained even after he'd shifted. He'd tried controlling his eyes, but the hot, prickly feeling meant they'd been glowing. Not the ferocious gleam of battle, but the warm, gentle pulse of love. Best of all, Natalie's eyes had glowed back.

She'd known. For that brief moment, she'd known how he felt, and she hadn't shied away. In fact, she'd leaned closer, lips twitching in the prelude to a kiss. But then...

You ruined everything, his dragon grumbled.

He sighed. It wasn't his fault shifting left him naked. But he hadn't thought ahead, and when Natalie spotted him — worse, sporting a boner he hadn't even been aware of until that awful moment of realization — well, yeah. He'd ruined everything.

He ran a hand through his hair. A great night of flying and a spellbinding moment had all come to a crashing end.

My mate, his dragon sighed. *She can even fly in her dreams.*

He mulled that over. That must be a relic of her dragon blood. If so, was that fate's reminder that she was way, way out of his league? A few minutes earlier, he'd nearly come out and said how he felt about her. But if she was a Fire Maiden, that wouldn't matter. He couldn't have her, no matter how he — or she — felt.

What she wants is not important, Alaric had said. *What you think does not matter. What matters is the future of the city and the safety of its citizens.*

Tristan glared at the sky. He'd been out hunting vampires and ended up pursuing a gargoyle instead. The bastards were getting cheeky, that was for sure. He'd nearly incinerated it in full view of every human in Paris — and nearly roared his love for Natalie for everyone in the city to hear. But now, reality came crushing back in.

He gripped the railing, cursing his fate.

Everything all right up there? a voice drifted into his mind.

Tristan grimaced and peered down. Dammit, he'd forgotten about Liam. The lion shifter had been keeping watch over the building while he'd been out flying. Tristan searched the shadows of the sprawling park across the street. Was Liam crouched under the elm trees, or was he standing perfectly still by the statue of Queen Geneviève? Once a lion blended in with his surroundings, there was no spotting him — especially not Liam.

I'm fine, Tristan grumbled.

His dragon huffed. *Fine?*

Fine, he grunted. *Aerial patrols show no signs of vampires causing trouble tonight.*

Liam chuckled. *I didn't mean vampires. Is everything okay with you? Or should I say, with you and Natalie?*

Tristan jutted his chin from side to side. Great. Liam had probably witnessed the whole encounter.

She had to see me shift sooner or later, he said, trying not to sound too defensive.

See you shift? Yes. But getting up close and personal? I have the feeling Alaric wouldn't agree.

Tristan seriously considered shifting back to dragon form, launching off the terrace, and hunting down that damn lion. Instead, he gripped the railing tighter, trying to control himself.

Should I remind you she's off-limits? Liam asked.

No, you shouldn't. Tristan turned away.

That she's a Fire Maiden, and way, way out of your league?

Tristan frowned at the stars. *No.*

That Alaric will kill you if he catches wind of you messing around with Natalie?

We were not messing around, Tristan insisted.

You were thinking about it.

Tristan gritted his teeth. Yes, he thought about touching...kissing...even making love to Natalie — just about every hour of every day. How could he not? She was perfect in every way.

His dragon grinned. *Me and my mate...*

Tristan found himself drifting away all over again, replaying her soft touch. Her awestruck eyes. Her—

Not even tempted? Liam teased, ripping him out of his fantasies.

Shut up, Liam, Tristan roared back.

For a moment, he had his thoughts to himself, but Liam sighed and butted back in.

Listen, lust is one thing, but if you're thinking love, watch out. It's never as simple as you think.

Tristan frowned. What the hell did Liam know about love?

You think it's all about you and her, but there's a whole world out there, waiting to judge you. Waiting to tear you apart. To ruin everything — forever. For you. For her. For your kids.

Whoa. Kids? Who'd said anything about kids? Tristan glanced down at the park. He'd always thought Liam was another happy-go-lucky lion who didn't believe in long-term relationships. But the sadness in Liam's voice came from bitter experience. What had happened? When?

It's never worth it, Liam finished. *Believe me.*

Tristan frowned into the darkness. The words were an echo of the teary breakdowns his mother suffered every time his father came and left.

Every time he comes home, promising it will be different, I believe him. But then he disappears again, and I wonder what I was thinking. Love isn't worth it, my son. Nothing is worth this agony.

A lump formed in his throat. But Natalie was different, right?

Then again, that wasn't the point. His mother hadn't been warning him about getting his heart broken. She'd been warning him not to do the breaking. All those times she'd sighed and said, *You're just like your father...*

Sometimes, her words had a sentimental ring. But others...not so much.

Tristan circled his shoulders wearily. Up to that moment, he hadn't felt the least bit worn out by his patrol. But suddenly, every muscle ached, and his chin dipped. Boy, was he tired.

Anyway, it's all been determined now, Liam continued.

Tristan's chin snapped up. *What has?*

Alaric's people searched Natalie's family records. She goes right back to Amelie on her maternal grandmother's side. That's only four generations. Close enough to—

Tristan couldn't hold back the choking sound that escaped his throat. He'd been hoping Natalie wasn't the Fire Maiden Alaric sought. But if she was that closely related to Amelie, Alaric would force her to stay in Paris. She'd be a near prisoner. And as for him — if he remained in the city, he would forever be confronted with the woman he couldn't have.

Tristan? Liam called.

Tristan shook his head and moved out of Liam's line of sight. *Thanks for keeping an eye out. Good night.*

Tris—

Tristan shut his mind off from his friend and bent over the handrail, feeling sick.

Your job is to protect our Fire Maiden until we find her a suitable mate, Alaric had said.

Tristan tightened his hands so hard, the iron railing groaned. A multitude of stars winked down from the sky. Were they mocking or cheering for him?

Mocking, he decided. Then he took a deep breath and forced himself to look over the rooftops. He had come to Paris with one goal — to finally settle down in a nice place. To find a good job and do it well. And that's what he would do. The mission was straightforward enough — to protect Natalie and the city. That would have to be enough. And if he was ever tempted to give in...

He scowled, picturing his mother with her face buried in her hands.

He wouldn't allow himself to be tempted, and that was that. He would do his duty and stick to what he did best. Fighting, not feeling. Flying. Defending the woman he loved.

Natalie, his dragon whispered sadly. *Natalie...*

Chapter Fifteen

Another few days passed, and for Tristan, every one was torture. Well, each individual moment was great because he got to watch Natalie — out of the corner of his eye, at least — as she read, did yoga, or just gazed out the windows, thinking. She had a way of biting her lip and twirling a lock of her hair when deep in thought, and he ached to be the one doing that for her. Even more so, he longed to throw open the windows, grab her hand, and take her flying. Still, he got to talk to her, share meals, and fly home to her after patrolling Paris.

But then he'd remember he couldn't have her, and that was when the torture set in. She'd smile, and he would smile back, feeling all lit up inside. Then he'd frown because a smile was all he could ever give her, and a smile was all he would ever get in return.

So, treasure every one like a jewel, he tried convincing himself.

That was the thing with dragons — the urge to hoard treasures. He'd never been one to collect gold, silver, or diamonds, what with all the moving around he'd done. So other than the small change he accumulated in a jar and the snack food he impulsively stocked up on — a holdover from his time in the military — he collected memories. Like the one time his dad had taken him fishing, many years ago. That *Holy shit, you just saved my life* look fellow soldiers had thrown him from time to time. Other treasures in his collection were memories of kids in ragged war zones laughing at the funny faces Liam made, reminding them joy existed, if only for a short time.

But a single smile from Natalie...

He found himself grinning like a fool, then frowned.

Off-limits... Off-limits...

"Everything okay?" Natalie asked in one of those miserable moments after reality crushed his dreams.

Not really. You're a Fire Maiden. I'm a nobody you will never be able to count on, like my mom couldn't count on my dad. Also, you're as off-limits as a masterpiece in the goddamn Louvre. You're the Mona Lisa, the Venus de Milo, the Winged Victory. I can look, but I can't touch.

But he didn't say any of that. Instead, he bluffed. "Everything is great."

Then he walked off, making things worse, because she probably assumed he didn't like her.

Like? I love her, his dragon declared.

Meanwhile, Alaric had ordered him to check in daily, and the news was grim.

"We haven't been able to locate Olivier," Morfram reported. "Nor his accomplices."

Which meant the rogue vampires were still on the loose. Apparently, they'd given up on Natalie's apartment, but they'd been spotted around Paddy's bar, where Natalie worked as a waitress.

Where she used to work, Tristan thought glumly.

She'd been sacked after the end of her first week off. He could see the devastation in her eyes when she'd hung up the phone. *How will I pay my bills? How will I manage to stay in Paris?*

The fact that she wouldn't have to worry about those things as a Fire Maiden didn't seem to help. And the more he'd tried to explain, the madder she grew.

"I don't want a free ride. I want to earn my own living."

"It's not a free ride. Far from. Fire Maidens dedicate their lives to others."

Couldn't she see she was perfect for the job? But at that moment, the frustrations she'd kept bottled up over the past days came bubbling out, and he figured he'd better let her rant.

"I want to do something useful in life, not live off someone else's account. Not like... like... "

Jacqueline? he'd nearly filled in.

He didn't know who Natalie was thinking of, but Jacqueline certainly fit. A niece of one of Alaric's distant allies, she'd been living off his wealth for years without doing much in return besides flouncing around Paris in the latest, greatest fashions. She never flew patrols and rarely attended meetings. If she spent an hour a month working toward law and order in the shifter world, Tristan would be surprised. What did Jacqueline actually accomplish besides seducing warriors who passed through Paris?

Tristan scowled, having come close to falling for her charms. How he could have been so blind to Jacqueline's selfish, petty side, he had no idea. But that was further proof that he couldn't trust his feelings when it came to Natalie. He could be just as misguided about her as he'd been about Jacqueline.

His dragon huffed, making his nostrils burn. *She's nothing like Jacqueline.*

No, she wasn't, but still. He had to stick to what he did best — defending Paris.

Defending Natalie, his dragon insisted.

And that was getting harder and harder as her cabin fever increased.

"I came to Paris to live," she ranted one evening in one of her rare outbursts. "Not to live like a bird in a cage. Is this how a Fire Maiden would live?"

He opened his mouth, then closed it, not wishing to say, *It is for a vulnerable Fire Maiden who can't shift.*

Instead, he looked at her, mourning. He'd always felt a little sorry for humans, but most of them didn't miss what they were ignorant of. Natalie, on the other hand, had enough dragon in her to dream of flying. She could peek into a whole new world yet never enter it.

Then the doorbell rang, and Tristan frowned. Now what?

He strode to the door, sniffing the air, then scowling. Yves, the doorman, was a jackal shifter who would never permit an enemy through. Unfortunately, Yves had no orders to stop assholes.

"Marcel," Tristan muttered, opening the door.

"*Bonsoir,*" Marcel announced with a flourish.

Tristan made a face at the dragon shifter's tailored suit and skinny tie. Was he stopping by with a message from Alaric before rushing off to a hot date?

When Natalie stepped up behind Tristan, Marcel turned on a thousand-watt smile and patted his heart as if to say, *You beautiful creature, you.*

"*Bonsoir, mademoiselle.*"

Natalie murmured unenthusiastic greetings, but Marcel's self-important smile grew.

Tristan narrowed his eyes at the man's stylishly messy hair, carefully cultivated five-o'clock shadow, and arrogant bearing. Who was he trying to impress?

Natalie, his dragon huffed. *Hot date, remember?*

Tristan's blood boiled. *Non.* No way. Absolutely not.

Marcel started to move forward, but Tristan sidestepped, blocking his way. Which made the bastard step left, then right, only to be countered by Tristan each time. Finally, he spoke over Tristan's shoulder.

"Natalie, I've been thinking of you. How terrible it must feel to be — how do you say? — cooped up here." A sidelong look added something like, *Cooped up with this heathen. You poor thing.*

Tristan bristled. He might not share Marcel's noble blood, but he had been doing his best to keep Natalie in good spirits.

"The apartment is great," Natalie said quickly. *And so is the company,* her quick smile added, or so Tristan hoped. "It's just..."

She motioned toward the windows, and Marcel nodded sadly. "I know exactly what you mean. Free spirits like us are born to fly free."

Tristan coughed into his hand. Free spirit? Marcel? Everything the man did was calculated — including this visit to Natalie.

"That is why I petitioned Alaric on your behalf," Marcel announced. "Hugo and the others were adamant that you remain safely indoors. But I said, 'No!'" He raised a stern finger like a goddamn revolutionary. "I said, 'I will keep her safe.'"

Tristan rolled his eyes. Then something about Marcel's scent reached his nose, and he nearly bared his teeth.

Jacqueline, his inner dragon snarled.

Apparently, Marcel and Jacqueline had been sleeping together — again. They'd had an on-again, off-again relationship for months, although *off* didn't always correspond to the times each had pursued liaisons with someone else. Both had insatiable appetites for sex, but neither showed the kind of loyalty most shifters did.

So much for noble dragon blood.

But Natalie clapped with delight. "You mean I can go out?"

Marcel grinned indulgently and patted his chest. "I convinced them I would protect you. *Mademoiselle*, I am at your disposal for the evening."

And for the night, his glittering dragon eyes added.

Tristan stepped closer, ready to kick Marcel's sorry ass back down the hallway. But Natalie bounced with excitement.

"Great. Fantastic. I'll be ready in a second."

"Take all the time you need, *ma belle*," Marcel called.

She's not your goddamn belle, Tristan's growl said.

Oh, but she will be, Marcel's slick smile assured him.

Tristan pushed Marcel into the hallway, slammed the door in his face, and grabbed his phone. But Alaric, damn the man, confirmed that he'd granted Natalie an evening out under Marcel's protection, so there was nothing Tristan could do.

She put a hand on his arm. "Tristan, I love this place, but I swear I'll go crazy if I spend one more minute locked up here."

The contact made him warm all over, and the plea in her eyes gutted him. How could he deny her a taste of freedom?

Guilt washed over him. Her future as a Fire Maiden wouldn't offer much of that either. What had he gotten her into?

"Please," she whispered. "I need this."

Which was how Tristan found himself in the elevator not long later, counting to ten next to a smug Marcel and an excited Natalie.

Will not breathe fire at the shithead... Will not breathe fire...

"I can keep her perfectly safe on my own," Marcel insisted when they reached the lobby.

Natalie shook her head before Tristan could. "He is my bodyguard."

Yeah, asshole, he shot into Marcel's mind. *Her bodyguard.*

"Bodyguards keep a respectful distance," Marcel muttered, taking Natalie's arm and wrapping it around his.

Tristan's blood pressure spiked, but Natalie shot him a look that said, *Don't ruin this for me.* And she was right. He could never have her, so he ought to resign himself to playing bodyguard and not boyfriend.

But seriously — Marcel?

He wanted to forbid her from going out with the man. Better yet, from even thinking of the man. But if he did that, he was no better than Alaric. Only Natalie could map her own future, and only she could choose.

I want her to choose me, his dragon cried.

Marcel made a sweeping gesture when they stepped out into the street. "Ah, Paris."

Tristan scowled, trailing after them. The sky was the purplish blue of early evening, the air crisp. Paris was as beautiful as ever. But the city wasn't his problem. Marcel was.

"I know just where to take you," Marcel announced, steering Natalie away from the park she'd gazed at longingly for days.

"But..."

Marcel tugged her onward. "I know you'll love it."

Tristan balled his hands into fists. Every sentence Marcel formed started with himself. Did he think that would impress Natalie?

Marcel strode on, pulling Natalie past the bookstalls and shop windows her eyes lingered upon. "I will show you all of Paris, *ma belle.*"

She knows Paris, and she's not your anything, Tristan wanted to growl.

"I studied at the Sorbonne." Marcel gestured in one direction then another. "And I spent my childhood right over there."

"Nice," Natalie murmured, though she didn't look too interested. Instead, her eyes lit up as they roved over the city she loved. She turned her head to admire every intricate streetlamp, every carved facade. And when they reached the promenade on the banks of the Seine...

"Wow," she murmured, looking up.

"Yes, that is my family's villa." Marcel pointed to a building.

She meant the stars, asshole, Tristan growled, following her gaze upward.

It was one of those perfectly clear nights filled with stars in all their majesty, from Orion and Ursa Major to the long streak of the Milky Way.

"It's gorgeous," Natalie said, looking at Tristan, not Marcel.

His lungs tightened, his blood warmed, and for one breathless moment, the universe shrank down to just the two of them. Her chest rose the way it did when she gazed longingly over the park, and he swore his heart beat in time with hers.

Mate, his dragon whispered. *You are my mate.*

He'd never felt more certain about anything in his life. He nearly blurted it out, too.

I love you, Natalie. I need you.

But those were *me, me, me* thoughts like Marcel's. Couldn't he do better than that?

The evening breeze stirred her coppery hair, and Tristan bit his lip, wishing he could speak his mind. *You fascinate me. You amaze me. And you deserve better than Marcel.*

Her eyes took on a beautiful bluish tint, glowing like a shifter's.

You'd make a great dragon, he wanted to say. *You're already as tough, and you could learn the rest along the way.*

I could teach you. His dragon nodded eagerly.

He pictured coaching her through her first flight — a real flight, not a dream. Cheering for her once she became airborne and witnessing her delight. Then he pictured the two of them soaring in long, lazy circles over Paris, taking in the sights. Afterward, they would land on his rooftop and—

"It's true," Marcel said, breaking Tristan out of his reverie.

Natalie jolted too. Had she been just as swept away as he?

Marcel gestured to the mansion he'd grown up in. "The building was commissioned by Richelieu himself. *C'est magnifique, n'est-ce pas?*"

Natalie rolled her eyes, and Tristan hid a smile. Then he jutted his chin to the stars and did his best to shoot his thoughts into her mind. *Magnifique.*

"*Magnifique,*" Natalie whispered with a secret smile.

"I will take you there someday," Marcel went on, still talking about the mansion.

I will take you to the stars, Tristan countered. *Well, into the sky, at least.*

But Marcel was already towing Natalie along, pointing out every sight related to him. "My favorite brasserie... The apartment I lived in as a student... Oh, look, the new Mercedes model. Not as nice a color as mine, of course."

Natalie looked left when Marcel gestured right, tuning out. Tristan did too, focusing on their surroundings. They were out in the open, and he couldn't let his guard down.

Something fluttered overhead, and he cast an eye in the direction of Notre Dame. The cathedral was out of sight, but you never knew what its resident gargoyles might get up to. Some were just statues, but others were shifters who had survived the man-made fire at the cathedral. And although they were allied with Alaric, there was no telling when one might turn rogue.

And that was just the danger overhead. Tristan eyed every passerby, every shadow. There was no telling where or when a vampire might rush out at Natalie. If one did, Marcel wouldn't be much help. He was too busy babbling about himself and Paris.

"The Louvre... Oh, *regardez.*" He motioned as a classic motorboat zipped by on the river. "A classic Riva Aquarama, just like the one I keep in Saint-Tropez."

Tristan rolled his eyes.

It was a long, winding walk, but in spite of Marcel's endless monologue, Natalie bounced along. That is, until she stopped short, choked out something Tristan didn't catch, and rushed ahead.

Chapter Sixteen

No woman in her right mind would run toward a straggly group of homeless men in the shadow of the bridge, but that's what Natalie did. Tristan ran after her on high alert.

"Natalie!" one of the men called in delight.

Before Tristan could intervene, the two had clasped arms and air-kissed each other's cheeks while chatting excitedly in French.

"Natalie, it's been too long. You haven't been avoiding us, have you?"

By then, Marcel was rushing up as well, but Tristan stuck out an arm when he realized what was going on.

"*Solidarité du Coeur,*" he whispered.

"*Solidarité du* what?" Marcel demanded.

Tristan grinned as more men came out from the shadows. Many were regulars at the soup kitchen where Natalie volunteered, and clearly, her presence had been missed. They fussed over her like so many old friends and chattered away a mile a minute. And as for Natalie...

She smiled warmly and spoke in rapid French, looking happier than he'd ever seen her.

"You know these people?" Marcel interjected, aghast.

Natalie nodded and made introductions. "Philippe, Yan, Abdel..."

Tristan gave each a respectful nod, earning the same in return. Marcel, on the other hand, got looks of disdain. And no wonder, given the way he stuck up his nose.

"Really, Natalie. Let's move on."

But Natalie ignored him, stepping over to view the tents and makeshift shelters the men were eager to show her.

"Natalie," Marcel protested.

Tristan was about to shove him back, but Natalie turned and barked, "Give me a minute, all right?"

Marcel looked absolutely shocked, but Tristan nearly gave her a fist pump. Natalie might be kind, sweet, and polite, but clearly, she had her limits. What was it she'd said?

My father calls it my premature midlife crisis. But you know what? I love it. I love doing things on my own terms.

He grinned. Inside that sweet exterior was a woman learning to spread her wings.

Just like a dragon. His inner beast grinned.

But as Natalie followed Philippe on a tour of the little colony, his heart sank again, because she could never be his.

Perfect Fire Maiden, too, his dragon murmured a little mournfully.

It was true. She was a goddamn Princess Diana in the way she connected to this community in need. She asked questions and looked everyone in the eye, managing to look sorrowful and delighted at the same time.

"The *gendarmes* make us move every few days, but tonight, it's home," Philippe said, gesturing over the cardboard shelters set into niches under the bridge.

Tristan studied the little colony. How cold did it get under that bridge at night? How wet? How alone did the men feel? But it wasn't just somber thoughts that occupied his mind. There was admiration too. The men came from all walks of life and races, yet they'd found a way to get along. They scraped by on almost nothing, yet they maintained their pride. And they were all on their best behavior around Natalie.

"Bunch of tramps," Marcel sniffed, looking at his Rolex.

Tristan nearly punched him. Did Marcel have any idea how close to the edge some people lived?

No, he didn't, as was clear when Marcel trampled one man's sleeping bag on his way to extract Natalie.

"My dear, we really must be going."

Philippe and the others shot him dirty looks, and it was clear Natalie wasn't in any rush. On the other hand, she must have realized it would be better to leave before Marcel offended anyone, so she said her goodbyes.

"Will we see you soon?" Philippe asked, and a dozen pairs of eyes shone in hope.

"As soon as I can," Natalie assured them. Then she looked at Tristan, and uncertainty flashed in her eyes. How soon might that be?

Never, if Marcel had any say in the matter, Tristan figured. As for Alaric and the others, he had no idea. But he vowed to give Natalie the most freedom he possibly could — if she stayed in Paris. If he remained her bodyguard.

If, if, if...

The vow must have shown in his eyes, because Natalie smiled in gratitude.

"Now, then. Back to the beauty of Paris," Marcel murmured, hurrying her onward.

"The real Paris," Natalie murmured, glancing back.

"Yes, the real Paris," Marcel agreed, missing her point. "Now, coming up, you'll see the Musée d'Orsay..."

Natalie trooped on gamely. The color of the sky deepened, providing an increasingly dramatic backdrop to the monuments of Paris.

"The National Assembly... Le Grand Palais... Napoleon's Tomb..."

Natalie looked at the stars while Tristan kept an eye out for danger. The sky was clear, but clouds were gathering on the horizon.

"And here we are. The Eiffel Tower," Marcel announced, as if Natalie wouldn't have figured that out for herself. "I wanted you to see it at night, when it's most beautiful."

It was beautiful. All that steel shaped into graceful, curving lines that reached for the stars. Even the high fence and legions of souvenir hawkers couldn't ruin that view. Slowly, they skirted the security perimeter and wound along a leafy path. A flower-lined field opened on their left, with tidy footpaths that drew the eye in long, straight lines.

Again, Marcel stated the obvious. "The Champ de Mars. Beautiful, is it not?"

"Beautiful," Natalie agreed.

Even Tristan had to admit the place was especially atmospheric that evening. Floodlights lit the Eiffel Tower, making it glow gold against the indigo sky. Couples wandered by, and a jazz quartet played a swinging tune that seemed to climb the tower's latticework. Still, Tristan didn't let down his guard. He sniffed the air sharply, sensing another shifter. A moment later, he relaxed. It was just Liam, following them on a parallel path.

Good Lord, Liam muttered into Tristan's mind. *How can Natalie stand him?*

Barely, Tristan replied dryly.

Obviously, she'd tuned out of Marcel's ongoing monologue. She was studying the beams of the Eiffel Tower, not Marcel, who was still chattering away.

"A special place for a special lady..."

Tristan glared at Marcel, then at a souvenir hawker who approached them. The man's shoes hastily scuffed over the gravel footpath as he skittered back. If only Marcel would do the same. Tristan sighed and turned in a slow circle, checking the area.

Uh, Tristan... Liam warned.

Tristan spun to see Marcel take both Natalie's hands and drop to one knee. "Natalie, we are destined for each other. I know it. I want to give you the privilege of becoming my mate."

Tristan just about choked. The privilege?

"I will honor and worship you," Marcel went on.

Natalie stared. "What?"

"Yes, I mean it." Marcel grinned.

Natalie backed away, twisting her hand. But Marcel hung on, refusing to let her go.

"You will bear my children, and I shall raise our sons to be the mightiest dragons in all Europe. We shall—"

"You — what?" Natalie screeched, trying to yank away.

An angry gleam came over Marcel's eyes as he hung on to her wrists. Tristan saw red. He was on his way to punching

Marcel, but Natalie acted first, shoving Marcel hard enough to make him topple back.

Liam's chuckle sounded in Tristan's mind, but all he really registered was rage.

"But, darling," Marcel tried.

Tristan stepped between them, torn between kicking Marcel's ass and checking if Natalie was all right. He turned, then froze. Whoa. Wait. Natalie wasn't just glaring at Marcel. She was glaring at him, too.

"Mating?" Her cheeks turned crimson. "Giving you heirs?" She stuck her hands on her hips. "Is that how the dragon world works?"

Tristan's lips moved in protest, but Marcel beat him to it.

"Yes. We shall be mated, and you will be mine."

"Yours? What, like a carpet? A used book? A new car?"

Marcel stared, uncomprehending. "I already have a car."

Natalie threw up her hands. "I heard. The new Mercedes."

Marcel tilted his head. "You want one, too? I can get you one. I can get you anything."

"I don't want anything."

"Everyone wants something."

"Oh, really?" Tristan could practically see the steam coming out of her ears. "Then tell me exactly what you want, Marcel."

Tristan would have needed a couple of days — maybe even a lifetime — to answer a question like that. But Marcel replied without the slightest hesitation. "I want you. I want a Fire Maiden as my mate."

"Why? Because you love me?"

Marcel shrugged. "I'll learn to love you."

"Learn?" she shrieked.

Tristan couldn't believe his ears. He didn't need to learn how to love Natalie. It had happened all by itself. He loved the way she curled up with books on the velvet couch. He loved the softness of her voice and the passion in her eyes. He loved how strong she was, even when the going got tough.

"You will learn to love me too," Marcel assured her. "And that will give me power. A leading position in the city."

Natalie's eyebrows flew up. "Ambitious, aren't you?"

Marcel flashed a cocky smile, taking that as a compliment. "Isn't that what all men want?"

Natalie looked at Tristan, and he froze. Would she see him for who he really was, or did she think he was power hungry like Marcel?

She pursed her lips before he could read her expression. "I see. And what do women want, in your opinion?"

Marcel's smile stretched. "Women want men with power. They want nice homes and nice things. They want to live a good life and be well taken care of — them and their children."

The ultimate charm machine, isn't he? Liam's dry voice sounded in Tristan's mind.

"Are you done?" Natalie demanded.

Marcel nodded as if his list included everything a woman could possibly desire.

"Fine. Now, you listen to me." Natalie thrust a finger at Marcel. "If that kind of woman exists, I am not her. You got that? Furthermore, I belong to nobody. I am not yours. I am not his." She stabbed her finger toward Tristan. "I am my own person."

Tristan knew that but, ouch. He wanted her so badly.

"I didn't mean it that way," Marcel insisted.

Natalie's eyes narrowed. "This is about you getting a Fire Maiden. It's not about who I am. Who I *really* am."

"It's not," Tristan agreed.

But Marcel uttered the same words at the same time, erasing any earnestness Tristan might have conveyed. Worse, he stepped beside Tristan like they were a team or something.

"You're only interested in your own gain." Natalie shook a finger at Marcel. Then she shook it at Tristan. "And you...you've only been pretending. You were in on this all along."

Tristan's jaw dropped. "No! Natalie, I swear..."

"Darling, I swear," Marcel echoed. "I only want the best for you."

Tristan reached for her hand, begging with his eyes. But Natalie's face went hard, and her eyes took on an angry yellow sheen. "Get away from me, both of you."

"Be reasonable," Marcel said, throwing fuel on her fire.

"Get away!" she hollered, backing up.

"Natalie," Marcel insisted. "I will always protect you."

She moved from the footpath to the grass, ready to flee. "The only protection I need is from you." Then she spun and ran across the field.

Tristan's muscles twitched, insisting he take off after her. But he knew better than that. Marcel, on the other hand, didn't, and when he moved to chase down Natalie, Tristan grabbed his sleeve.

"Get out of my way," Marcel snarled.

"You will not touch her. You will not have her."

Marcel sneered. "Why? Because you said so?"

"No, because *she* said so."

Tristan shoved Marcel so hard, he stumbled into the bushes. When the dragon shifter recovered his balance, he squared his shoulders and glared. "You work for me, fool."

Tristan shook his head. "I work for Alaric."

"You're a hired hand. A mercenary. One about to lose his job, once my uncle hears about this. I, on the other hand, am of noble blood. A suitable mate for the Fire Maiden this city needs. She will be mine. Alaric promised her to me."

Tristan bared his teeth. "Listen to yourself. We're not living in medieval times."

Marcel snorted. "We live according to noble dragon traditions, not that you would understand."

Tristan's gums burned with the pressure of his teeth trying to extend, though he knew he couldn't shift. Not here, not now. But Marcel motioned him deeper into the shadows.

"You dare challenge me?"

I challenge you. I'd be happy to kill you, Tristan's dragon snapped.

His human side, however, made him stand his ground. "Not here, you idiot." Even with the jazz quartet drawing passersby to a distant corner of the park, the area was too public to risk shifting in.

"Coward." Marcel threw his jacket aside and loosened his tie.

Rage flowed through Tristan, and he barely held it in check. He couldn't let Marcel goad him into a fight. The shithead would find a way to twist the facts to make *him* look like the aggressor, and Alaric would kick his sorry ass out of town.

But Marcel wouldn't relent. Within seconds, his shirt was off, and his arms were morphing into wings.

"You want her, too. Do you think I'm blind?" Marcel's voice dropped an octave as he shifted. "We'll settle this as tradition dictates."

Tristan was pretty sure whatever tradition Marcel referred to had gone by the wayside when pistol duels had.

"Marcel..." he warned.

Isn't our mate worth fighting for? his dragon cried.

Of course she was. But fighting meant risking everything. His job. His future. Even his life. Was it worth it?

Hell, yes, he nearly barked.

Still, fighting wouldn't guarantee him Natalie's love. He had to be honest with himself. Was it worth it?

The answer was a mournful *yes.* He would fight for Natalie's right to choose a suitor, even if it didn't turn out to be him. No matter how dire the outcome was for him, the issue wasn't what he stood to gain. It was about what Natalie stood to lose.

Tristan took a deep breath, giving himself one more chance to rethink things. Well, he tried. But a nanosecond later, he yanked off his shirt. Marcel wanted a fight? He'd get one.

Yes, Tristan's dragon hissed. *Let's get the bastard.*

Chapter Seventeen

Natalie race-walked across the grass — a big no-no in any Paris park, but heck. She'd had it with men. Correction — she'd had it with dragons.

We shall be mated, and you will be mine.

Like hell, she would.

You will bear my children...

She couldn't believe her ears. And worse, Tristan had shouldered right up to Marcel, fully expecting her to go along.

Her face was twisted into so deep a frown, it hurt. All evening, Marcel had gotten on her nerves. And all evening, she couldn't help wishing he could be more like... like... Well, more like Tristan. But apparently, Tristan had been harboring an ulterior motive all along. Did he expect her to bear his children and lend him the prestige of a Fire Maiden, too?

Wisps of clouds drifted overhead, the precursors to a storm she should have seen building on the horizon. She stomped onward, furious with herself. Maybe she had some kind of hero complex when it came to Tristan. Maybe dragons had a heady scent that drove her wild. And she'd fallen for it, growing comfortable around him. Too comfortable, really, and far too trusting. Thinking he really cared about her, the plain Jane from Philadelphia, rather than a coveted Fire Maiden.

It had been hard enough to swallow the whole Fire Maiden thing over the past days, but two aspects had appealed: getting to stay in Paris and helping the world be a safer place, if Alaric, Tristan, and the others could be believed. But now...

She went from a jog to a run, desperate to get away. Could they force her to stay in Paris? Could they force her to accept Marcel's barbaric proposal?

Just as she was about to glance over her shoulder, the air overhead stirred wildly, and she stumbled to the ground.

"What the—"

She gaped as two dragons soared out of a cluster of trees and spiraled upward. Their mighty wings beat so hard, her hair tossed. One of the dragons was greenish-brown — Marcel? — and the other, a smooth, brownish-black hue.

"Tristan," she whispered.

Yes, she'd seen him in dragon form once. And yes, she'd even touched his smooth, leathery skin. But the dragon she beheld at that moment had a whole different aura. It was like seeing a friendly dog wag its tail then witnessing the same animal snarling through teeth that dripped with saliva. That, times a hundred, because Tristan was racing, snapping, and roaring at Marcel. The roar didn't register as a sound — only the rush of air did — but she could hear it in her mind.

The dragons circled the Eiffel Tower, keeping far enough away to avoid the floodlights, but close enough to show the outline of their wings. They were soaring. Darting. Fighting?

Natalie stared. Wait a minute. Weren't they on the same side?

Then she yelped and spun as someone grabbed her arm.

"Whoa, there," a familiar voice cried. The man held up his hands. "It's me."

"Liam?" She'd nearly pulled her one-two-three move on him. Then she huffed and marched away.

Liam was Tristan's buddy, and he took orders from Alaric. Was he there to force her into a barbaric arrangement with Marcel, too?

"Leave me alone," she barked when he hurried to catch up.

"Can't. Vampires, remember?"

She scowled, gesturing upward. "I'm starting to think dragons are a bigger problem." Glaring at him, she added, "Or lions."

When Liam grinned shamelessly, his teeth showed. His canines extended before her eyes, and the stubble on his chin thickened. Natalie jumped, and he thrust his hands up.

"Sorry, sorry. Lions have feelings too, you know."

"Don't do that to me," she yelled. Then she gathered her nerve and shoved him. "Go away. Go back to Alaric and tell him I'm out of here. I don't want anything to do with your crazy shifter world."

But Liam, damn him, kept hurrying along at her side. "I hate to point this out, but you're already part of it. Fire Maiden, remember?"

"What if I don't want to be a Fire Maiden?"

"Tell that to the vampires."

Natalie slumped.

"Listen," Liam said in a softer voice. "I'm not here for Alaric or any of the other Guardians. I'm here for Tristan."

He gestured upward. The dragons were so high, she could barely tell them apart, but there was no mistaking the fighting. One stretched out its neck, reaching for the other's wing. The second dodged and clawed at him. Natalie winced, picturing Tristan plummeting to the ground with shredded wings.

Still, none of it made sense. They were supposed to be on the same side. Unless...

Unless you misjudged Tristan completely? said a little voice in the back of her mind.

She bit her lip. It sure didn't look like Tristan was cooperating with Marcel. On the contrary, he was fighting the arrogant dragon away. Wait. Were they fighting over her?

Disturbing as the idea was, it was flattering too. But not if Tristan was purely interested in her Fire Maiden blood. Then again, he had come to her aid in the alley, back before either of them knew about that.

"Over here," Liam urged, pulling her toward the shadow of a tree. "Don't draw attention to them."

Natalie looked around. It was dark, and most visitors had drifted toward the jazz quartet. But how could anyone fail to notice two warring dragons?

Liam shook his head. "There's a veil that conceals our animal shapes — a holdover from the magic of old. It's faded over the centuries, but enough has held up that humans overlook us most of the time. But if they look directly at us and concentrate..." He trailed off, glancing around.

Natalie did the same, suddenly worried. What would happen if Tristan were spotted?

"That's another reason they're so desperate for a Fire Maiden," Liam whispered. "Her presence would stoke the magic and make the city safer."

She hugged herself, wishing she could go back to being the plain old Natalie no one took notice of. "Safer for shifters, you mean."

Liam shook his head. "Safer for everyone. A strong core of honest shifters helps stabilize the entire city. But even they need help. If the spell fades entirely, the city could revert back to the kind of fighting it saw in the Dark Ages. All those wars, all those diseases... They weren't kidding about needing you, Natalie."

She took a deep breath. Could she really help?

Then she looked back up at the dragons. "And they're fighting over..."

Liam snorted. "Over you, woman. Don't you get it?"

She went very still. It was one thing to flatter herself with such ideas. But for them to be true...

Glancing up, Liam muttered, "Let's hope they have the sense not to breathe fire."

Natalie's eyes went wide as she followed the aerial dogfight. The dragons dove, bit, and raked each other with their claws. But no fire — yet. Within a few steps, she and Liam were in the shadows at the edge of the park where they could watch more openly.

"Come on, Tristan," Liam muttered. "Show the bastard."

Shielding her eyes from the Eiffel Tower's floodlights, Natalie watched, sick yet fascinated. How could creatures that big be so nimble? With a snap of its tail, one of the dragons spun to face the other, and for a moment, they hovered in place, defying gravity — and each other.

"No fire, lads," Liam whispered. "Remember, no fire." A moment later, he cursed. "Bugger."

"Tristan," Natalie yelped as Marcel released a thin line of fire.

But Tristan rolled to one side and hammered Marcel's snout with his tail. The air crackled, but no one seemed to notice, especially with that storm brewing. A happy couple strolled by hand in hand, and the woman giggled at something the man said. Three young men walked in the opposite direction, noting that they'd better get moving before it rained. But no one noticed the battle raging overhead.

Liam leaned closer. "You can see them, right? Do you hear them too?"

Natalie gulped. Yes, she could. All too well.

Liam grinned. "Attagirl. It's the dragon blood in you. You see things humans miss."

The thing was, she didn't want to see — or hear — the furious roars. Tristan feinted to one side then twisted in midair to slash at Marcel. When he spun, he curled his wings with a flourish, like a bullfighter taunting a charging bull.

"Come on, Tristan." Natalie found herself echoing Liam.

But Marcel whipped his tail, smacking Tristan across the chest and sending him reeling through the air. A moment later, Tristan roared and counterattacked. Both dragons sped through the light of the quarter moon, then wheeled around and raced back toward the Eiffel Tower.

Natalie motioned upward. "Do something. Help him."

Liam stuck up his hands. "I can't."

"Can't or won't?"

Liam grimaced. "Lion, remember? Besides, Tristan would kill me if I did. He'll want to win this fight fairly."

She wrung her hands. "He will win, right?"

Clouds drifted closer, inching over the moon.

Liam frowned. "He'd better. Though his ass is toast either way."

She whipped around. "Why?"

Liam wore one of those *You really don't get it, do you?* expressions that made Natalie's gut sink. Then he explained, motioning with his hands. "For going against orders — again. He's supposed to keep you safe, not fall in love with you." A split second later, Liam winced. "Oops. Forget I said that."

Natalie's jaw dropped. She stood there, gaping, her heart thumping wildly as she looked up. Deep inside, she knew the past days had been about more than taking refuge in his apartment, no matter how much she'd told herself otherwise. But to hear Liam say it...

"Anyway," Liam continued. "Tristan is supposed to guard you, not kick Marcel's ass."

Natalie scowled. "I'd kick Marcel's ass if I could."

Liam chuckled. "Who wouldn't? The thing is, Marcel's lineage makes him the perfect mate for a Fire Maiden. According to Alaric, that is."

"Mate." She'd stumbled across the word in Alaric's books, but the concept still wasn't clear in her mind. "Marcel was talking about mating. He wanted me as his."

Liam nodded as if that were obvious.

"It's barbaric," she half shouted.

"True," Liam admitted. "But then again, if the woman feels the same..." His eyes went distant, and for the briefest of seconds, his sunny expression dimmed with some sad memory.

Natalie studied him. What secrets hid behind that cheery facade?

"And if she doesn't?"

Liam let out a pained snort. "Then you're not as lucky as you thought you were."

An uncomfortable silence ticked by before Liam gave himself a little shake. "Anyway, Marcel is a selfish bastard. Tristan is different."

She hugged herself, looking up. "Is he?"

Liam frowned. "After a week with him, you still have to ask?"

Natalie hung her head, ashamed. No, she didn't.

"Marcel covets power," Liam said bitterly. "Oh, and wealth. All Tristan wants is... is..." His eyes roved for a moment before coming to rest on Natalie. *You*, his eyes said. *He wants you.* But when Liam spoke, it was to whisper, "Honor."

He uttered the word like it was holy, and his jaunty expression became grave. His eyes flickered, and for a moment,

Natalie glimpsed another side of Liam. The warrior who'd do anything to help others.

Like Tristan, Natalie realized, though Liam kept that side hidden away. Why?

Liam sighed and looked up. "He's more honorable than any man I know. And he likes you, Natalie. You know he does. But he's forcing himself to give you space, because he wants you to have a choice. He wants you to be safe." Liam paused, then whispered, "He would die for you."

Five quiet seconds ticked by — seconds in which Natalie's throat felt drier than ever before, and the word *Honor* echoed through her mind. Tristan had risked his life for her from the very start. He'd been nothing but gracious as a host, and now, he was defending her at great risk.

"Dammit," Liam muttered. "Cut the fire."

Natalie looked up as another burst of flames split the sky. Then sparks broke out everywhere, and she nearly yelped. But then she realized that it wasn't dragon fire or lightning — just the hourly sparkle show at the Eiffel Tower.

Liam exhaled. "Well, that should help."

But the dragons only fought more fiercely, spitting huge plumes of fire. Natalie watched, terrified yet fascinated. She found herself leaning right or left as Tristan banked and even curling her fingers, imagining wingtips sensitive to the slightest change in pressure.

"Um, Nat?" Liam murmured.

She blinked, wondering why he was staring. Then she realized she'd raised her arms high, mimicking flight.

Liam raised an eyebrow. "Maybe that dragon blood is thicker than you thought."

Natalie dropped her arms back to her sides. Who was she kidding? Imagining was one thing. Truly flying was another.

"Oh!" She pointed. One of the dragons — Tristan? — released the biggest stream of fire yet. For a moment, his enemy was completely engulfed, a living outline in fire, and Natalie clutched at her sleeves. "Oh God."

It was one thing to want to be rid of Marcel, but seeing him burned alive?

"Don't worry," Liam murmured. "Dragons are pretty fire-resistant. If Tristan wanted Marcel dead, he'd be dead."

Indeed, a moment later, Marcel shook like a wet dog, dispelling the flames. Then he turned tail and beat a hasty retreat across the sky.

"Yes!" Liam cheered as Tristan nipped at Marcel's heels, harrying him into ever thicker clouds. "That's my man."

First Marcel, then Tristan, crossed in front of the quarter moon — two torpedo-like shadows, one fleeing, the other in hot pursuit. Eventually, Tristan broke off and hung back, watching Marcel flee.

Take that, Natalie imagined him shouting. *And don't you dare cross me again.*

She fought away the urge to jump in glee, but Liam sighed.

"Much as I'd like for Tristan to kill that ass, it's better he didn't. Things will be bad enough as it is."

Natalie glanced between Liam and Tristan, who was soaring back toward the Eiffel Tower with long, steady wingbeats. "Bad? How?"

Liam motioned upward. "I'll let him explain. Or try to, at least."

Natalie backed away as Tristan approached. He circled the area once then came in for a landing. His wings curved, catching the air, and his claws extended. But rather than the precision landing he'd executed on the rooftop, this was a long, jogged-in affair, graceful but weary at the same time. With every step, his dragon shape morphed, returning to human form, and Natalie found herself dashing alongside Liam to meet him. Then they both slowed, and Liam stuck an arm out, holding her back.

"Give him a second."

Natalie halted in her tracks. Oops. If she got any nearer, she'd be treated to another full monty view of the most heavenly body she'd ever seen. But much as the thought appealed...

Her cheeks heated, and she stepped back, summoning what dignity she could. "I'll wait here."

"Roger," Liam said, military-style, before trotting out to Tristan.

Natalie counted to ten, then twenty, secretly wishing Tristan hadn't come to a stop in such a shadowy location. She could see him in silhouette, lifting one foot then the other as he pulled on his pants — but that was all. Damn.

She could see Liam's mouth moving too — no surprise — along with little wisps of condensation in the fresh night air. Then Liam tipped his head in her direction, and Tristan turned.

When their eyes locked, Natalie's breath caught. Her heart thumped, and a deep voice murmured in her mind.

Mate. That man is your mate.

Was that destiny, speaking to her? Was it a trick?

Whatever it was, she found herself rooted to the spot, forgetting Liam, the Eiffel Tower, even Paris. Peering past the shadows, she focused on Tristan, picking out the hard lines of his face. His eyes had been an angry red when he landed, but now, they glowed a soft amber hue.

Mate, a higher, female voice deep inside her murmured. *That is my mate.*

Natalie shivered, partly in fear, and partly in... elation?

Time stood still, and her mind felt blurry. Blissfully so, like nothing mattered as long as Tristan was all right.

Then he crumpled to the ground, and she rushed forward. "Tristan!"

Chapter Eighteen

Tristan struggled to his feet, which was hard, even with Liam's help. For one thing, Marcel had landed a deep, ripping bite to his leg — the only real damage that bastard had managed to pull off, but still. On top of that was the momentary imbalance that always set in after a flight with lots of twists and turns. But most of all, what threw him was Natalie, looking so scared. Not scared of him — scared *for* him. Worried he might not make it back alive.

His dragon snorted. *As if Marcel can best me.*

The confrontation had only taken as long as it had because Tristan had been holding back. He'd learned the hard way about injuring arrogant sons of the ruling dragon classes. In the end, he would be the one in trouble, not Marcel. As it was, Marcel was probably rushing to Alaric at that very moment, spinning a story about Tristan challenging him rather than admitting it was the other way around.

And that was the problem. Tristan's dragon rage had burned high, but he couldn't vent much of it without his primary weapons. The claw marks he'd left on Marcel's sides were purposely shallow, and the tiny hiccups of fire he'd limited himself to were barely enough to singe the bastard's hide. He could have broken Marcel's ribs with a single whip of his tail, but all he'd left were bruises. No wonder his dragon was still raging inside.

But when Natalie rushed up, pale and worried, that rage softened to love.

"Are you all right?" She touched his arm, sending little bolts of lightning through his veins.

Oh, he was fine, other than the fact that his whole body was on fire.

She's our mate. Deep inside, she knows it, his dragon insisted. *We must claim her before some other bastard does.*

He grimaced. Now was not the time to approach Natalie with more talk of mates and forever.

At the very least, mark her, the beast insisted.

He trembled, fighting back the urge to hold her. To kiss her. To rub his chin along her cheek and mark her there. Better yet, to take her to bed and mark her all over.

Liam cleared his throat sharply and reassured Natalie. "I think he's fine."

"Are you?" Her voice was trembling, like her hands.

Tristan savored the moment. As a soldier, it had been better not to have anyone fret over him. But boy, was it nice to know Natalie cared.

Nice, his dragon agreed.

Briefly, he realized that was what the homeless in the soup kitchen might experience. That feeling of pain and problems vanishing, giving way to a flood of hope. Natalie had a way of making you believe everything would be all right, even if the odds said otherwise.

He straightened, croaking, "I'm fine. *Merci.*"

The word felt totally inadequate, because Natalie could have run screaming at what she'd just witnessed or laid into him about the outdatedness of dragon ways. But she didn't. She just stroked his arm gently and helped him up. And when he looked into her eyes—

"Whoa, there," Liam murmured as Tristan swayed for the second time.

Her eyes were aglow with dragon fire. The kind that stemmed from love, not anger.

She loved him?

Of course she does, his dragon said. *We are mates, destined for each other.*

"What?" Natalie asked, caught off guard by his reaction.

I love you, and you love me, he wanted to say. *Oh, and you might have more dragon blood than you thought. Noble blood.*

His dragon shrugged. *I don't care. I just know she's mine.*

Tristan nodded. He was a fool to have denied destiny for so long — that, or he deserved a goddamn medal for resisting an urge rooted so deeply in his soul.

No more resisting, his dragon swore. *To hell with Alaric and the rest of them. She's our mate.*

But, crap. What about his vow not to follow in his father's footsteps?

Easy, his dragon swore. *We love her. Protect her. Cherish her to the end of our days.*

It sounded so simple, but could he be the man she deserved?

Her hand was on his arm, her eyes wide and imploring. "Marcel didn't hurt you?"

Liam thumped Tristan hard enough to rattle his teeth. "It will take more than one snotty prep school dragon to whip this guy, right?"

Then Liam chuckled into Tristan's mind. *But it only takes one pint-size human to melt your heart.*

She's not pint-size, Tristan growled.

But she does melt your heart?

Tristan ignored him, because somehow, he and Natalie had ended up face-to-face and holding hands.

"Nothing serious," he whispered. "I'm fine."

Was he, though? Natalie had a way of taking his breath away at the least expected times. Like now, with her soft touch doing all kinds of crazy things to his body. Then there were her eyes, full of sparkles as bright as those illuminating the Eiffel Tower. A whole fascinating universe he could have studied forever.

If it hadn't been for Liam muttering, *Man, you do have it bad,* who knew who long he and Natalie might have stood there?

"Let's get you two home, shall we?" Liam finally sighed.

Was the bastard hiding a smug smile? Tristan couldn't tell. He didn't care much either. Not with Natalie there, helping him along. Her scent was heavenly, and the whiff of worry in her fragrance slowly gave way to the sweet scent of arousal.

"Home sounds good," he said, struggling to keep his voice even.

Very good, his dragon murmured, replaying his wildest fantasies. Vividly.

He swore and counted to ten. Natalie didn't want a caveman bastard.

She wants me, his dragon promised.

The hand she'd kept on his side started wandering up his chest, making that hard to deny. Was she as tired of resisting the electric attraction between them as he was?

"Metro or cab?" Liam asked.

Tristan pinned him with a murderous look, and Liam chuckled.

"Right. A cab. Let me go find one. But don't dawdle. It will be raining soon."

Which left Tristan alone with Natalie for a few blissfully quiet minutes, though he didn't know what to say. *I love you. I need you. I want you?* He wasn't sure it would come out right. *You're my mate* was definitely out, as was *I told you Marcel was an ass.*

In the end, he held his tongue and looped his arm over her shoulders, keeping her nice and close. Every breath he took brought him a whiff of her tempting scent, and his inner dragon refused to settle down.

The approaching storm intensified that feeling, too. By the time they made it to the cab Liam had hailed at the end of the park, the clouds grew darker, and the distant sound of the jazz concert broke off. Natalie hurried ahead to open the door.

"Here, let me help you." She bent to help him maneuver his injured leg in. Then she hurried around the cab, got in, and slid all the way over to his side, fretting over him the whole time.

Going soft, Monsieur Chevalier? Liam chuckled as he took the front seat.

Tristan ignored him. Was it a crime to feel good? To enjoy a woman's touch in a way he never had before? Her hands were so gentle, her voice so soft. And the silky wisps of her hair on his shoulder so...so...

Tempting, his dragon growled.

"Natalie..." he whispered, reaching for her hand.

She laced her fingers through his and stroked his palm. At the same time, her chest rose and fell in a deep breath. One a lot like his — the kind you took to settle down.

"We have to stop meeting like this," she joked a moment later.

He laughed. "Maybe I like meeting like this."

It was too dark to see her blush, but the heat rising from her face gave it away.

"You like getting hurt?"

He shook his head. "Call it my cheap excuse to get close to you."

She nestled closer, whispering, "Maybe we can find an easier way."

He grinned like a fool, admiring their reflection in the window. Him and her, so close and comfortable. Like a real couple without a care in the world.

His dragon snarled away the little voice that wanted to point out they were anything but. *Tonight, we are a real couple without a care in the world.*

Her knees rested against his thigh, and her hand lay over his heart. He kept his arm over her shoulders, and when her hair brushed his hand, he inhaled sharply. How good would it feel to run his hands through her hair — all ten fingers through the full length of those long, silky locks? How good would it be to feel her hand against his bare chest instead of through his clothes?

You aren't forgetting the forbidden *part of what Alaric said, are you?* Liam murmured into his mind.

No, he was actively ignoring that order. All his life, something had been off-limits. Well, not his mate. Not tonight.

Liam sighed. *You know you smell like ash, right, champ?*

Tristan grimaced. Shoot. If Natalie got any closer, she'd back off, for sure.

Told you not to spit fire. Liam sighed.

Natalie nestled closer, not appearing to mind one bit.

Streetlights flashed as the cab cruised along, casting them into alternating strips of darkness and light. Tristan's reflection in the cab window was worn and haggard, and outside, rain started to splash the sidewalks. By the time the cab pulled up outside his building, it was pouring.

Tristan leaned forward, speaking to the driver in French. "My friend will pay when you take him home."

"I will?" Liam protested.

"Yes. Good night." Tristan pushed the door open decisively. Liam owed him dozens of favors. Hell, he owed Tristan his life. The same was true in reverse, but right now, Tristan had a chance too good to pass up.

Liam sighed and waved. "Have a good night, kids."

Oh, Tristan planned to, if he was reading Natalie right. A moment later, he and she were dashing through the rain.

"Mademoiselle. Monsieur Chevalier," the doorman murmured as they rushed through the lobby.

"*Bonsoir,*" Natalie said, polite as ever.

"*Bonsoir,*" Tristan growled, slamming the gate to the elevator closed. It took off with a lurch, climbing toward the top floor.

They looked at each other, and an entire conversation passed in silence. Their eyes danced, while their nostrils flared, and raw, pulsing energy crackled between them. Then, a moment later—

Tristan didn't know who initiated the crash of a kiss they fell into next. Was it him, with his step toward her, or Natalie, who'd reached up to touch his cheek? Either way, they went from quiet yearning to hot-blooded action in the span of a heartbeat. Their lips met, their arms tangled, and he pressed her body against the elevator wall.

"Please tell me you want this," he murmured, barely breaking away from that breathless kiss.

"Not obvious?" she panted, setting him off all over again.

If he consumed her lips, she smothered his, and the way she squeezed her hips against his groin left no room for doubt. He tilted his head, kissing deeper and harder. Little whimpers escaped her lips while her hands traced the muscles of his back.

"At first, I thought that was a dragon thing," she panted at their next gasp for air.

Tristan traced a line of kisses along her chin. "What was?"

She waved at nothing in particular. "This fire. This need. This hunger for you that's been driving me crazy."

Tristan retraced his kisses back to her lips. "Maybe it's a dragon thing."

She shook her head. "No way. Marcel proved that. Total dud."

Tristan snorted. "Surprised?"

She laughed, cupping his face in her hands. "Not really. I thought it was you, but I had to make sure."

He paused, still burning. "And now you're sure?"

Her eyes dropped to his lips. "It's not a dragon thing, because I felt nothing around Marcel — except bored. And it's not all shifters either. Take Liam..."

Tristan stiffened.

"—he's funny and all, but no. Not a spark there."

Tristan exhaled.

"So, it's you. Just you."

He shook his head. "It's us."

We're mates, his dragon added, though he was glad she couldn't hear.

"Us," she agreed.

Then they were kissing again — not to mention groping and touching so desperately, his vision blurred.

"Oh," she cried, breaking away. "Your leg."

He shook his head and dove back into a kiss. "Already better."

All too soon, the elevator chimed, and they broke apart as if caught by a witness. But there was no one, just the ragged sound of their own breath.

Still, Tristan hesitated, thinking of all the reasons he should try to resist. After all, Alaric had declared Natalie off-limits. But Natalie pushed the gate aside, erasing all doubt. She was his mate. And since there was no greater authority than destiny...

He fumbled for his key, but getting it into the narrow slot was tricky, what with Natalie kissing him at the same time. When he finally threw the door open, Bijou stepped forward with a meow.

Tristan groaned. Damn the cat, distracting Natalie.

But Natalie only gave Bijou a rushed pat before sliding right back into Tristan's arms. He held her, inhaling her scent, desperate for more but frightened of moving too fast. It was she who moved first, backing him from the corridor to the empty living room while nuzzling his chin.

"You know how long I've wanted this?" she whispered.

Rain streamed down the windows and tapped on the roof.

"I know how long I've wanted this."

"So, there's only really one question left." Her voice was pure temptation, her smile a tease.

"What's that?"

Bijou padded over, winding between their legs. But Tristan didn't feel any pity. The cat had been sleeping in Natalie's bed all week. It was his turn now.

Natalie glanced right then left.

"Your place or mine?"

He looked between the velvet couch and his king-size bed. He had dozens of fantasies that played out in both places, which ought to make it hard to pick. But his dragon was already barking a reply.

My woman. My bed.

Which definitely had its appeal. It would be so easy to sweep Natalie up, carry her to his bed, and release every animal desire that had accumulated over the past week. But he was painfully conscious of the domineering jerk his father had been, so he turned the question around.

"Lady's choice."

Just please, please make it fast, his dragon begged.

Her eyes sparkled, and he caught a brief glimpse of the fantasies playing through her mind. Like the two of them intertwined on the narrow red couch, or her splayed out on his bed while he explored every inch of her bare, beautiful body.

Or even the two of them humping wildly on the floor in no-man's-land.

His pulse hammered in his ears when she leaned forward and whispered in his ear.

"Your bed." Her voice was raw with desire, her body calling to his. "I want you to take me to your bed."

A hallelujah chorus might as well have broken out in his ears, he was so relieved.

"Just one thing," she added with a smile that managed to be both shy and sultry.

He cocked his head.

"I wasn't kidding about the *take me* part."

Chapter Nineteen

Natalie didn't know what had come over her. Had Tristan's raw, animal energy rubbed off? Or had that flood of irresistible desire welled up from a hidden part of her? Either way, she wanted him so badly, she ached.

"Watch what you wish for," Tristan murmured, stepping behind her so they both faced the huge windows.

"Watch? I could get into that," she replied, teasing shamelessly.

In truth, she was shocked at herself. Where was the tame, quiet girl who kept her eyes shut during sex? Where was that virtuous side that steered her clear of any hint of dirty or wild?

Gone, apparently, or superseded by a whole new side of her soul. Something deep inside that she'd only ever faced in her fantasies.

But watching? Being taken? He was a dragon shifter, for goodness' sake!

Hell yes, a voice sounded in her mind. It was low and rough, like a barmaid who'd smoked too many cigars.

Her eyes went wide. Maybe that was her dragon side. Maybe Paris — and Tristan — had awakened a part of her soul she never knew she had.

But Tristan started kissing her neck at the same time, and when he drew lazy circles on her belly, she stopped caring about anything else.

"Beautiful," he murmured, sliding his hand along her ribs.

She stuttered through her next breath, because he was gently circling her breast by then, and it felt so good. Her hips swayed, pushing against his. He pushed back, and the hard prod of his erection promised he enjoyed the sensation, too. Everywhere he touched tingled, and the nipping kisses he trailed along her neck throbbed.

"Oh," she cried out when lights sparkled through the rain.

The hourly show at the Eiffel Tower must be going off again. That, or her blissed-out mind was projecting its own show.

"Is this good?" he whispered, slipping his hand down the front of her jeans.

She practically purred her answer. "Yes."

Then she inhaled, making space for his hand. But even that was too tight, so he popped her fly and zipper, then went back to caressing her in slow, masterful movements. The hand that cupped her breast moved to the same rhythm, and soon, she was rocking against him.

"And how about this?" he whispered, slipping a finger between her folds.

She tipped her head back. Penthouse views were very nice, but there were only so many sensations a woman could process at one time. Like his thick finger, touching her where she needed it most. His huge hand, lifting her breast. His warm breath, ruffling the hair by her ear.

"*Ma belle,*" he whispered between kisses.

Her heart raced. Not only was she his, she was beautiful? Then she giggled out loud. Maybe she wasn't the only one operating in a sweet, sensual haze.

"What?"

She laughed. "I just feel good."

He snorted. "You'll feel even better soon. I promise."

Natalie glanced at her faint reflection in the window in one of those *Pinch me, I'm dreaming* moments. The man of her dreams was not only touching her, but promising her more?

Yes, please, that low, feminine voice purred in her mind.

Her eyelids drooped as he reached deeper, stroking her most sensitive spots. Her nipples peaked, and her breath came in pants. The lights of Paris became a blur, like they would if she were speeding past in a car.

Or flying really, really fast, that inner voice chuckled.

Part of her felt deliciously drowsy, as if her human side were nodding off while her dragon woke from a long, satisfying slumber. Opening her eyes, she focused on her reflection, superimposed on the lights of Paris. Her top and bra were gone, her hair drifting back over Tristan's shoulders. She looked — and felt — like a sensual model in the studio of a master painter. A little blurry, like one of Degas' dancers crossed with one of Picasso's *demoiselles*, thanks to the way she held her arms up and back.

When she wiggled her hips, Tristan caught the hint and worked her jeans and panties down to her ankles, then pushed them aside. He did the same with his pants, and when he took off his shirt, layers of muscles rippled along his abdomen and sides.

"No fair," she mumbled, turning slowly in his arms. "I get all the pleasure."

He chuckled, making her hair stir. "If you believe that..."

When their eyes met, he trailed off, and a moment later, they were locked in another kiss. Natalie wrapped her arms around him, drinking in her own sculpted masterpiece. His back was lined with its own ridgeline. His abs were a washboard, marked by a few battle scars. And below...

He stiffened as her fingers brushed his cock, and when he pulled back from the kiss, his eyes were glowing a pure, golden color.

Our mate likes our touch, her inner voice hummed.

Natalie gulped and looked down.

"What are you doing?" Tristan asked in a voice gritty with need.

That second self — that vixen inside her — made her chuckle. "I'm watching what I wished for."

A split second later, they both burst into laughter, though she didn't stop stroking him. Then Tristan released a low, growly sound, lifted her right off the floor, and rushed her toward his bed.

"We did say my place, correct?"

She barely had time to nod before they sprawled over the mattress, so desperate, they couldn't coordinate their kisses properly. But that was fine, because wherever Tristan's lips landed sizzled. He kissed her chin... her neck... her collarbone. There, he hesitated like a man choosing from a vast menu of options.

She trembled in sheer need. Up to that point, any sex she'd had was always a straightforward affair. A little kissing, a little groping, and eventually, a blink-and-you'll-miss-it climax. But Tristan drew it all out, speeding ahead then slowing down. And nothing — absolutely nothing — he did could be called *little*. His kisses made her dizzy. Wherever he touched her, bonfires seemed to erupt. Then his eyes flared, and he ducked, lips reaching for her nipple.

Whatever little groans Natalie had let out so far were whispers compared to the cries she could no longer hold back. And when he shifted lower...

Watch what you wish for, the vixen's voice whispered in her mind.

She dragged a pillow over, propped it under her head, and watched, fascinated. Was that sleek, bare body really hers? Was Tristan really bobbing between her legs and his tongue doing the most exquisite things to her core, or was it all a fantasy?

Then he glanced up and—

Mate, Tristan's voice whispered in her mind.

Mate, her inner dragon echoed.

His lips glistened, and his hair hung low, giving him a decadent, bad-boy look. His hands stayed firm on her thighs like that was his turf, and everything about him screamed alpha male.

He flashed a wicked grin, then ducked and licked her all the way over to her first orgasm.

First of many, his hands assured her as her body shuddered wildly.

The first *ever*, it felt like, because the sexual highs of her past seemed laughably amateur.

Lightning flashed behind her tightly shut eyes, and blurry visions rippled through her soul. She'd thrown her arms back at some point, but her imagination turned them into wings, and she swore she saw a pair of dragons coupling in midair. One of them was Tristan, and the other one was... her?

Afterward, she lay limp, panting at the ceiling as heat raged through her body and slowly, deliciously, subsided. She was unable to move, unable to think. Apparently, orgasms were neither overrated nor impossible. Just hard to attain without the right, er... stimulus.

She laughed. Tristan was stimulating, all right. But, whoa. What about that dragon part? Was it just a sex-induced fantasy, or was it more?

She snorted the thought away. Clearly, she'd spent too much time reading about dragons lately.

Tristan cozied up to her again, lying along the length of her body, stroking her sides. At her chuckle, he raised one eyebrow.

"What? *Ça ne va pas?*"

She shook her head, not quite able to speak. Of course, it was good. But the vines of the ceiling's delicate plasterwork were only gradually coming back into focus. An instant later, the embers of her desire flared again, and her eyes heated.

"Nothing." She chuckled. "Everything."

Then she tugged him up and wrapped her legs around his waist.

"Do you have a condom?" she breathed, trying not to yowl. Because holy hell, there really was something about dragons that set off smoldering passion.

Then it hit her. If she truly had dragon blood, then she and Tristan would really make sparks fly.

The sultry voice inside her snorted. *No wonder you've never felt such rapture.*

Tristan's lips moved, and she worried that he might say *No, I don't have a condom*. But after a moment of staring at her neck, he nodded and reached for the bedside table. Natalie closed her eyes. The dresser drawer rolled, and the sheets rustled. Foil ripped, and Tristan's weight shifted. Natalie reached out, covering his hand with hers as he unrolled the condom. Then he resettled over her, drawing her arms over her head.

She lay trembling, waiting for the painful push of his entry. But instead, his lips fluttered over hers. She opened her eyes, caught off guard. Power pulsed off every coiled muscle in Tristan's body, but his fingers were gentle as he smoothed a wisp of hair aside.

"Natalie," he whispered, lending it that rising rhythm she loved, full of hope and promise.

He might as well have lit her with a thousand bulbs, the way she beamed. Then she drew her leg along his in a hint.

For a moment, he looked lost, as if he would be perfectly content just to admire her for a while. But then the glow in his eyes intensified. He nudged her legs apart, tightened his fingers around hers, and—

Instead of plunging in, he eased in, rocking forward and back, giving her time to adjust. A bead of sweat formed on his brow, and she could sense him leashing his own power. He watched her face intently, making sure it was as good for her as it was for him. And then — only then — did he shift into another gear, going from slow slides to powerful thrusts.

"Oh," she cried out.

The motion burned in the best possible way, and she rocked against him, begging for more.

"Yes..."

When she pulled her legs higher along his sides, Tristan reached back, pinning her knee against his hip. Then he went back to deep, sharp thrusts, making her howl. Eventually, he switched over to the other side, lighting up an entirely new set of nerves.

By all rights, she should have come to a screaming orgasm right there, but something in Tristan's face told her to hang on. So she did — barely — flexing her inner muscles, making him groan.

Show him, that inner voice insisted. *Show him what his mate can do.*

Natalie bucked upward, suddenly determined to prove something — to herself, not to him. That she wasn't as plain as she'd told herself a thousand times. That she could rock a man's world — even a man who'd experienced so many things. She could be the center of his world, and he the center of hers.

Mates, her inner voice murmured. *Now you know what it means.*

She wasn't entirely sure about that, but she did know she belonged with him. So she pushed her shoulders back, pumped her hips, and flexed one more time.

Tristan groaned, and she watched as he came absolutely, utterly undone. His mouth opened in suppressed cries, and his biceps bulged. Then he made a garbled sound and reared back on his heels.

"No," she cried as they separated.

But Tristan was already on his knees and lifting her hips off the bed. A split second later, he thrust in, and she cried out.

Deep took on a whole new meaning at that angle, but damn, did it feel good. Blood rushed to her head, and a wave of emotion gathered within her, steamrolling everything away. Tristan bowed his head in total concentration. Then, when she thought she wouldn't last a moment longer, he pumped in one last time.

Her body shuddered, and her head spun with a thousand images, though none of them made sense. She was flying — no, soaring over the ground. Fire crackled around her lips, and the air around her heaved. A church bell tolled, and the green slopes of a vineyard blurred under her wings.

Whoa. Wait. Under her what?

Wings, that inner voice laughed.

A shadow moved over her, and she knew it was Tristan with her in bed. But her mind reassembled the image, making him a dragon flying directly over her, spreading his wings and roaring into the night, daring anyone to come between them.

Mate, she whispered. Or had Tristan said that?

She opened her eyes slowly, and there they were, naked, sweaty, and wrapped around each other in bed. At first, Tristan's eyes were vacant, as if he were living that scene too. But when he focused on her—

She arched, hit by an aftershock of pleasure. Tristan tightened his arms around her, holding her as she shuddered. Then, when she was panting and exhausted, he settled her on the mattress and brought his lips to hers in a searing kiss.

Her eyes flew open. That kiss was hot. Hot as... dragon fire?

Tristan's eyes remained closed, his lips sealed around hers. *Really* sealed, taking away her air, but giving her air at the same time. It filled her lungs, warming her from the inside. The heat spread through her chest, to her arms, and all the way to her toes. She found herself cupping his face, hoping he'd never let go. Because holy crap — what a kiss. One that was all the way over on the other side of the ecstasy meter from where she'd just been. One extreme was the sheer exhilaration of sex. The opposite was that kiss — peaceful and serene, yet every bit as intimate. If sex was an inferno, this was a warm, sensual bath, and she sighed, letting it sink in.

It might have been seconds later or an hour when she opened her eyes. Tristan had slumped over her, his cheek along hers. When she stirred, he did too, slowly rubbing up and down.

Natalie's mind spun. The best sex of her life. Visions of flying, even breathing fire. A kiss like none other...

"What was that?" she whispered, reliving it.

Tristan stopped nuzzling long enough to look her in the eyes. "Dragon kiss."

His mouth remained open as if he might say more, but after a pause, he went back to nuzzling.

"Dragon kiss, huh?" She wrapped her arms around his shoulders and let her fingers caress his back.

He rolled to his side, propping himself up on one elbow quietly — nervously? — awaiting her judgment.

She licked the last hint of heat off her lips and nodded. "I like it."

Tristan broke into laughter, and for the next minute, the huge, empty apartment echoed with the sound. Enough to make Bijou appear around a corner, then scowl and stalk away.

Slowly, Tristan settled down again, and his face grew pensive.

"What?" she asked.

He shook his head, then murmured in French. "Where were you?"

She blinked, caught off guard. "Where...?"

"Where were you my whole life?"

She bit her lip, and for the next happy thumps of her heart, they lay there, marveling at each other.

"Where have you been my whole life?" she whispered at last.

Tristan broke into a smile that was a lot like hers — part sorrow at what they had been missing all along, and part wonder at finally feeling...

Complete, her inner voice filled in.

Natalie bit her lip, studying Tristan. Yes, *complete*. But there was still so much she didn't know about him — or even herself. Then she shooed those thoughts away. She'd done enough thinking — and discovering — for one night.

Tristan shuffled around, spooning her from behind, and they lay together without uttering a sound. The few times Natalie opened and closed her eyes, she focused on his fingers, wrapped around hers, keeping her close. Keeping her safe.

Then, feeling more tired and satisfied than she'd ever thought possible, she slowly, peacefully, drifted off to sleep.

Chapter Twenty

Tristan woke with a groan, reluctant to budge from Natalie's side. He'd been sleeping so well — the sleep of the just, as a former sergeant of his would say — but now, a boulder was rolling at his bedside, or so it seemed. He cracked an eye open. He had been planning to sleep through till morning, but judging by the darkness, it was only three or four a.m. Paris was still sleeping, and dammit, so should he.

He turned, ready to turn one hand into a claw and lash out. It was a special night. An amazing night. The first ever with his mate. Who dared disturb that?

Two shining eyes regarded him in silence, and that awful rolling sound broke out again.

"Bijou," he groaned.

If Natalie hadn't been sharing his pillow, he would have thrown it at the cat.

Bijou blinked then batted at the watch on the bedside table. It rolled, bumping and rattling as it went.

"Bijou," Tristan hissed.

The cat purred as if to say, *Do I finally have your attention?*

If wrath counted as attention, then yes, Bijou had it. Tristan flopped back and stared at the ceiling, counting to ten. The last time Bijou had made a racket like that, he'd locked the little beast out on the roof. But the cat had started yowling, and Tristan had been forced to let the monster back in. And when he had...

He growled at the memory. Bijou had sauntered in then strutted right back out. The cat didn't care where he was. He just enjoyed torturing dragons. There was no winning with him.

"You'll wake Natalie," Tristan tried.

Bijou seemed to consider for a moment, then smacked the watch again — a little more softly, so it didn't make quite as much noise, but enough to get under Tristan's skin.

"What do you want?" he demanded.

Bijou looked up smugly as if to say, *Guess.*

Tristan swung his jaw from side to side. God, did he hate cats. Little ones, at least. Liam and the other feline shifters Tristan knew were mostly okay. Of course, they all had that prima donna streak in them, just like Bijou did.

Did the cat want food? Did he want to go out? Or was it all a ploy to lure Tristan out of bed so Bijou could sneak in next to Natalie?

The cat rattled the watch again, and Tristan finally gave in.

"Okay, okay, j'arrive." I'm coming.

Sliding out of bed shouldn't have taken much effort, but with Natalie there, Tristan almost gave up. It was only Bijou taking aim at the watch that made him force himself to his feet. Bijou scampered to the kitchen, but Tristan stood at the bedside for a moment, watching Natalie sleep.

Her hair was mussed, and her hands still clasped at her chest, leaving space for his fingers to curl around hers. She looked so peaceful, so content. So... part of his life, somehow. She fit right in. Or she could, if she wanted it as much as he did.

His heart just about tripled in size as his dragon murmured, *I want it. More than anything.*

The problem was, she was a Fire Maiden. The proof was in the visions that had swept through her when they'd bonded. Normally, he couldn't read her mind, but those images had come through loud and clear. In them, she was a gorgeous, copper-colored dragon. Most dragons were brown, black, tan, or green. The rare shades between copper and gold were the sign of a legend.

Fire Maiden, his dragon breathed.

He took a deep breath. That Natalie had dragon blood, he knew. That she was special, any fool ought to be able to see.

But part of him must have been hoping she wasn't descended from Liviana, Queen of the Dragons, just to make things easier for them. But now, reality sank in.

She was a princess. He was a nobody.

He pursed his lips. That didn't matter, did it? They would find a way. But, hell. Alaric and the others would put up a fuss, and—

Bijou popped his head around the doorway, glaring. *Must I summon you again?*

Tristan sighed. There were times he could have sworn the cat was a shifter, but no. Just a pint-sized monster who thought he could boss dragons around.

Tristan walked to the kitchen slowly, resolving not to ruin an amazing morning with thoughts of *forbidden*. Bijou, meanwhile, wound between his legs, nearly tripping him.

"Natalie fed you, you beast," he murmured, reaching into a cabinet for a packet of cat food.

Bijou looked on eagerly, then turned up his nose.

"*Et maintenant, qu'est-ce que tu veux?*" *Now, what do you want?* Tristan demanded. When Bijou looked back at the cabinet, Tristan shut the door with his foot. "You get what you get, mister. I don't eat salmon most nights."

Bijou looked on, miffed, as Tristan thumped the packet over the edge of the food dish.

The nice lady uses a spoon, Bijou's sour expression said.

Yeah, well. Food was food.

Wrinkling his nose at the smell, Tristan toed the dish closer to Bijou, then turned to the sink. Footsteps sounded behind him, and he whipped around. It was Natalie, padding to the bathroom, still half asleep and as gorgeously naked as she'd been in bed. He gulped and forced himself to go back to bed. Much as he would have liked to wait for her — and maybe even replay that sensual embrace by the windows — that probably wasn't best. Americans were shy about their bodies, though he didn't know why. Especially not a body as perfect as Natalie's. So he went back to bed and stared at the ceiling, waiting.

The sheets carried Natalie's heavenly fragrance along with the sticky-sweet scent of sex. He licked his lips, savoring the last traces of Natalie's kisses. A perfectly unique, perfectly *Natalie* taste that made him love her even more. Other women tasted like something else — cherry, strawberry, or whatever the heck was in the stuff they put on their lips. But Natalie tasted like Natalie. Pure, honest, unpretentious.

He reached out, touching the space beside him and gazed toward the windows. In a few hours, a new day would dawn. What kind of day would it be?

He would give anything for a nice, quiet day for the two of them. A stroll in the park, hand in hand. A stop for a crêpe or at the *confiserie*. Then they'd walk home with a nice bottle of wine and maybe spend a few hours in bed.

But a sinking feeling warned him of what really lay ahead. The confrontation with Marcel meant it was time to see Alaric and exercise damage control. But, *merde*. How? He'd nuzzled Natalie hard enough that no shower would erase her scent.

Not that he wanted to erase it. He wanted to flaunt it — not as a trophy, but as a sign of his intent. Natalie was his mate, and he had every right to celebrate that. He wanted to parade his love around like Hugo and Clara, who got to exchange all the *I'm so in love with you* looks they wanted. But Tristan couldn't, not when it came to a Fire Maiden.

He frowned. Finding one's mate ought to be a joyous occasion, not a dilemma. What if Alaric kicked him out of Paris? What then?

"Hey." A whisper pulled him out of his thoughts. It was Natalie, standing beside the bed, her arms held shyly over her chest. But the minute their eyes locked...

Natalie smiled, and her shoulders relaxed. Tristan's blood surged with that instant pull, that instinctive recognition.

Mate, his dragon hummed.

Mate, a faint voice echoed, making his heart swell.

He could feel the dragon stirring inside her. A powerful, confident presence that had been there all along, like a single jewel hiding under all the treasures of Natalie's personality.

Just wait till we make her our mate, his dragon murmured.

His heart skipped. Then she would be a dragon, too. A formidable one.

Fire Maiden, his dragon whispered.

Then Alaric's words echoed in his mind. *Forbidden.*

Wordlessly, he held up the sheet, and Natalie slid right in. Not just into bed, but into his arms — and into a nice, soft kiss.

"You're worried about something," she whispered.

He shrugged. "That stopped when I saw you."

She lit up and cupped his face, stroking his chin with her thumb. He leaned into her touch, practically purring like that goddamn cat.

"So soft," she murmured, tracing his stubble. Then she bit her lip. "Your eyes are glowing again."

So are yours, he wanted to say. Faintly, but definitely glowing with a mix of contentment and apprehension.

He gave a tiny nod. "Dragons do that when they're happy."

Happier than I've ever been, he wanted to add. *But a little scared of the future too.*

Her lips curled into a broad smile that faded all too quickly. "Your eyes were glowing red after you fought."

He held his breath. Did that scare her?

Maybe she read his mind, because she shook her head and whispered, "I think you've proven yourself trustworthy. You're my knight in shining armor."

He smiled, relieved. "Nowadays, we call them bodyguards."

"No, you're definitely knight quality," she assured him with a smile. Then she went somber again, and her eyes slid away from his. "So, last night, you conquered another dragon, and then you conquered some woman?"

He shook his head immediately. "You're not some woman. One particular one." He ran a finger along her cheek. "Besides, I'm pretty sure she conquered me."

Natalie's grin stretched, and he went on.

"A special woman."

She flashed a wistful smile. "Special, huh?"

He hesitated, because he'd seen her reaction to Marcel's proposal. But he had to say it.

"You're my mate, Natalie. My destiny. You're the one."

She went still but didn't bolt. Her hand remained on his chest, her legs still snuggled along his. "The one you recognized at first sight?"

His heart thumped wildly, and his dragon lashed its tail. *Yes! Yes!*

He nodded quietly, trying not to hope too hard.

She crooked an eyebrow. "The one you want to bear you lots of offspring?"

He grimaced at the echo of Marcel's words. "The woman I want to love. To honor. To protect. The one I've been burning to touch for so long."

He held his breath, hoping that extra glow in her eyes wasn't just a reflection of his.

She nodded slowly. "Something you felt the first time we touched, and every morning, noon, and night ever since we met?"

His pulse skipped. So it wasn't just him. She felt it too.

"All my life, I've been waiting for you. I just didn't know it until now."

Natalie's chest rose in a deep sigh, and then she stuck a finger at his chest. "You promise this has nothing to do with power?"

"If I wanted power, I wouldn't be working for Alaric. All I know is I want you. I need you."

She nodded as if she felt exactly the same. "Destiny..."

Her eyes met his, and he nodded. *I felt that lightning bolt too.*

Then she faked a frown. "Wait. Do I blame destiny for the fact that I heat up every time I see you?"

He grinned. "Must be."

Her hands slid farther down his rear, kneading as they went. "And it's all destiny's fault that I want you again right now?"

He nodded gravely.

"Hmm," she mumbled, sweeping her tongue over his lips. "I guess we shouldn't mess with that."

"Definitely don't want to mess with that." He rolled, coming over her.

For a few breathless minutes, they lay there, kissing, touching, exploring. Tristan kept reaching for a condom, then stopping, because he just couldn't let her go. Natalie made greedy little kitten sounds, driving him wild. When he finally broke away, lunging for the side table, she reared up with a wicked grin.

"What do dragons think about doggy style?" She rolled to all fours, glancing back at him.

His eyes already felt hot as coals, but the sight of her perfect rear made them burn harder.

"Let me show you," he rumbled, fumbling with the condom. In truth, he was dying to skip that step and enter her skin-on-skin.

Someday, his dragon promised as he rolled on the condom.

Someday, he agreed, kneeling behind her.

Slowing down long enough to kiss her shoulder, he snuggled up, running his hands over the perfect curve of her ass. Then he reached around, kneading a breast with one hand while tracing her folds with the other.

"Oh..." she breathed, swaying under him.

His cock ached in anticipation, but he held out, savoring the sweet scent of her arousal. Savoring everything about the moment, in fact. The trust. The raw need.

He dipped his fingers deeper, anticipating the rush of burying himself in that sweet heaven. The kisses he rained along her neck turned to nips, and it was hard not to imagine a mating bite.

"Tristan," Natalie murmured, bumping back against him.

He held her hips, ready to give her what she wanted. He only paused long enough to finger-comb her hair away from her back and off to one side. That view was better than anything in Paris, London, and Rome combined, and there was no way he was going to miss it.

"Tristan," Natalie groaned.

Her cry went right to his cock, and his dragon roared inside. Then he pushed in, making Natalie cry out. His mind exploded with a thousand floodlights, and thinking became impossible. Only doing. Moving. Satisfying the burning need to connect.

Again and again, he thrust forward. The faster he moved, the more Natalie pushed back against him. Her head was on the pillow, her rear high in the air, and the sounds of their lovemaking drove his dragon wild. A bead of sweat dropped from his forehead to her back. He gritted his teeth, giving her everything he had.

"Oh!" Natalie hit a high note and clamped down around him, making him explode.

Every muscle clenched. A flood of pleasure flowed through his body, and his cock pulsed. It was ecstasy — pure ecstasy, like nothing he'd ever felt.

Mate, his dragon said with sheer certainty.

This was no accident. It was not a mistake. It was destiny, telling him where he belonged.

Slowly, he slumped, delirious with pleasure. Moments later, he stumbled away, disposed of the condom, and hurried back. Then he stretched out, pulling Natalie against his chest. Panting and cooing, she clung to him.

"Destiny," she whispered into the dark.

Tristan closed his eyes. Fire Maiden or not, she was his. Let any fool try to get between him and true love.

His dragon huffed. *Let them try.*

Natalie's soothing touch brought him back to the dreamy cocoon of the bed, and he slowly settled down. Dawn was only a few hours away, and when it broke, he'd give anyone who protested a piece of his mind. But right now...

He caressed Natalie's shoulder and breathed softly into the night. "Destiny, my mate."

Chapter Twenty-One

Natalie woke slowly, having slept like a log — or as the French said, *comme une marmotte* — like a marmot. That fit, considering how she'd burrowed under the sheets and cuddled against Tristan, where she would have been happy to hibernate for the next few months. The man was all muscle, yet she fit perfectly into the curve of his chest. And the way he kept his arms looped around her...

She sighed. Heaven.

Opening her eyes reinforced the impression. Light streamed through the windows in bold streaks of gold, and outside, a chorus of birds sang.

She flexed her fingers around Tristan's, thinking about everything they'd done. She'd never had anything but plain, predictable, missionary-style sex. Now, in a single night... She puffed a breath of air over her face, trying to cool off. It was uncanny, how her body and Tristan's communicated. When one of them moved, the other always knew exactly what to do, like they'd been born for each other.

Destiny. Could it really be true? She'd heard of soul mates, but shifter mates seemed to go beyond that. When she'd first encountered the word in one of Alaric's books, it sounded crude and possessive. But now, snuggled in Tristan's arms...

"Mate," she whispered, trying it out for herself.

He was hers as much as she was his. She could feel it deep in her bones. She'd even sensed it before Tristan had entered the soup kitchen that first night. Her world had shaken in its own little earthquake, as if some force had taken her by the shoulders and said, *Brace yourself. This is it.*

Destiny?

Then she frowned. Could it just be hormones, making fantasies all too easy to believe?

Tristan rubbed his thumb over hers, and she broke into a huge smile. If it was hormones, then fine. The man could keep stirring them as far as she was concerned.

When she rolled in his arms and murmured, "Good morning," he lit up.

"*Bonjour*," he rumbled, keeping her nice and snug.

A minute passed before their lips met, but it was almost as if they'd been kissing the whole time. Kissing in the way their eyes lingered on each other or in each soft caress. And when their lips actually touched...

Natalie closed her eyes, savoring his oaky taste. Was it all real, or was it a dream?

Then Tristan's phone chimed, and they both groaned. Tristan stuck an arm over his eyes as the phone rang and rang.

She nudged him. "Are you going to answer that?"

"No," he declared. Then his face clouded, and his eyes drifted to the phone.

"I don't mind," Natalie fibbed.

She would rather have tossed the device out the window, but she knew how it was. That might be Alaric, and duty was duty.

Tristan rolled, grabbed it, and barked a very French, "*Allô?*"

When he stiffened and sat up, Natalie did, too. Who was on the line?

"When? Where?" Tristan barked. "Now?"

Natalie waited, wondering what was wrong.

"All right. Tell him I'm on my way." Tristan sighed then threw down the phone.

"Trouble?"

He snorted. "That was Jacqueline, so, yes. Trouble." He looked pained. "Alaric wants me to report, *tout de suite*."

She stroked his arm. She hated to let him go, but orders were orders in the shifter and human world.

Tristan eased his legs over the side of the bed, shaking his head. Then he turned and kissed her — a long, lingering kiss full of fire, longing, and regret.

"*Merde.* I hate to go," he murmured barely an inch from her lips.

She hugged him tightly. "For the last few days, I felt so cooped up. Now I'd give anything to be cooped up with you."

Her body heated at the thought, and Tristan's eyes sparkled. "Can I take a rain check?"

She grinned, nodding a mile a minute.

He kissed her one more time then sighed. "Somehow, we'll figure this out. But I'd better get over to Pigalle before I get chewed out." Then he made a face. "Well, I'll definitely get my ass chewed out."

"For what?"

"Breaking orders."

She furrowed her brow. "Orders?"

"Alaric made it perfectly clear I wasn't supposed to touch you."

A wave of anger swept through her. "How about I march over and tell him I wanted to be touched?"

Tristan smiled. "That, I'd love to see." Then he sobered. "But it doesn't work that way. Not with shifters. When the alpha gives an order, you follow."

"Maybe I'm not good at taking orders."

"Neither am I." His lips quirked into a brief smile. "But, like Hugo once said, I need to... to... " He motioned vaguely, then went on, mimicking the wolf shifter's deep voice. "'Force isn't always the way. Try finesse.'" Tristan frowned. "I think Clara taught him that. But I'm not sure I have finesse in me."

Natalie laughed. "You never know."

He cracked a tiny smile then stood.

She steeled herself to say goodbye, but then a cold draft reached her, and the hairs on the back of her neck stood.

Tristan turned immediately. "What is it?"

She tried shaking it off, but the chill persisted. "Nothing. Sorry." She forced herself to laugh. "Just the thought of you leaving makes me worry about vampires."

Tristan pulled her closer, armoring the space around her with his body. "They wouldn't dare. I won't let them. Besides, you know what to do."

She snorted. That move he'd taught her? "Sure. One, two, three." Her voice was surly, but her arms twitched with the sequence Tristan had taught her. Arms snapping up, elbow jab, then a blow to the nose. When she didn't overthink it, her body knew what to do. But when she consciously imagined herself fending off a vampire, it seemed hopeless.

Reluctantly, Tristan released her. "Anyway, Liam will be keeping an eye on the place, and the doorman, too."

She knew he was right, but still. She hated to see him go. "Maybe I should come with you."

Tristan sat beside her. "Think about it. Alaric will be furious, and Marcel is likely to be there. Marcel and whoever else Alaric has lined up for you to choose from."

His voice was bitter, so she hugged him. "I already know who I want."

He cupped her cheek. "I know who I want, too."

For a moment, they stayed close, speaking volumes without uttering a word. But eventually, Tristan pulled back.

"You'll have to talk to them at some point. But I know they're going to chew me out. They might even fire me or banish me from the city." His eyes roamed the room once. Then he shrugged, like none of that mattered, though sorrow filled his eyes.

I can lose this apartment, his expression said. *I can lose my job. I can lose living in Paris, but none of that would hurt as much as losing you.*

She took his hands and squeezed tightly. "If they want me as their Fire Maiden, they'll have to listen to me, won't they?"

He smiled weakly. "If only it were that easy."

The longer they held each other, the more a warm cloak filled the space around them. Natalie bowed her head, tuning in to the sensation. "Is that part of being mates?"

"Is what?"

She motioned around. "That energy. That heat. The way the world zooms out of focus when I'm around you."

He nodded. "I think so."

"So, if destiny wants us together, we'll be okay, right?"

The pause before his reply worried her. "Destiny has a way of throwing obstacles in a person's path. But, yes. We'll be okay."

Natalie forced her hands not to tremble. Tristan sounded more determined than convinced.

"Anyway," he said, changing the subject. "I'd rather you didn't witness me getting reprimanded. You know, to keep my dignity and all."

She laughed, running her hands over his steely shoulders. "Your dignity, my ass."

He grinned and dropped his hands to her rear. "You mean this?"

"No, this." She smacked his rear.

For a moment, they smiled, and it felt good, even if she knew there was trouble ahead. But eventually...

She forced herself not to follow Tristan around like a smitten puppy as he prepared to go. While he showered, she dressed. Then she brewed a couple of strong coffees and held Bijou, pensively stroking his fur.

"Little beast," Tristan muttered when he ducked to kiss Natalie goodbye.

Bijou jumped away, and Natalie looped her arms around her man. "His loss. My gain."

She kissed him, wondering if that was how damsels once felt when their knights departed for battle. Then she straightened her shoulders. She was no damsel, and when the time came to face Alaric, she'd give the old dragon a piece of her mind.

She hugged Tristan one more time, then all but pushed him to the door to get it over with. "See you soon."

Tristan nodded. "See you soon. Stay safe."

"You too," she whispered.

The door clicked shut, and she turned all three locks. Then she stood, staring at the door as silent minutes ticked by.

"Tristan," she whispered, aching all over.

The more time they spent together, the more he felt like part of her. A lot like Paris, in a way. She turned and looked out the windows, hugging herself. When Bijou wound around her ankles, she picked him up.

"Why can't you and Tristan get along?" she scolded.

Bijou put on a miserable look that said, *Because he's so mean.*

Natalie nuzzled him. "Tristan is not mean. He's sweet. Kind. Considerate."

The fact that Bijou kept nuzzling probably meant he wasn't paying attention, but Natalie continued anyway.

"Tristan cares. He's honorable. He does the right thing — or, he tries to." She smiled. Tristan might not always get things right, but he did try.

Bijou wiggled out of her arms and jumped to the floor, then meowed and led the way to the kitchen.

"You already ate."

Bijou sauntered on, and Natalie laughed, following him. "I wish I could get away with eating every time I thought of it."

She picked out a packet of beef flavor — Bijou's favorite — and scooped it carefully into the dish while the cat studied her every move. The moment Natalie stepped aside, Bijou rushed in as if some no-good dragon had left him to starve for days. But a moment later, he tensed and whirled, ready to flee at a noise at the door.

Natalie nearly laughed. Maybe Tristan was returning sooner than she'd hoped. That would be nice.

Then a cold finger of air sliced into the room, and she tensed. Bijou rushed for the rooftop. Outside, birds stopped singing, and Natalie stood still, her heart thumping away.

What? What was going on?

The feeling was so eerie, she backed away at the footsteps approaching the front door rather than rushing forward in anticipation of seeing Tristan again.

Not Tristan, the hairs on the back of her neck said.

Chapter Twenty-Two

A knock sounded.

Natalie slowly put the spoon in the sink, afraid to make a sound.

"*Il y a quelqu'un?*" a woman called through the door. *Anybody there?*

Natalie gripped the edge of the counter. Jacqueline?

Still, Natalie didn't move. Jacqueline was the last person she wanted to see. Plus, there was that icy sensation in the air. A warning that zipped through every on-edge nerve in her body.

She shivered. Vampire?

"Hello?" Jacqueline demanded in English.

Natalie held perfectly still. Maybe Jacqueline would go away if she thought no one was there.

The doorknob rattled, and Natalie nearly jumped. Jacqueline wasn't just checking if the door was open. She was testing its strength.

"We know you're in there, little human. Let us in," another voice called.

Natalie froze. Was that Olivier? But, wait. Why would Jacqueline be with a rogue vampire? And why had the doorman let them in? God, where was Liam?

Tristan, she wanted to scream.

But Tristan had been gone at least a quarter of an hour, and with a Metro station so close to the building, he could be halfway across Paris.

"Of course she's in there," Jacqueline snipped. "I can smell her." She raised her voice. "I can smell you. I can—" Her voice broke off, and an ominous silence set in. "I smell Tristan all over you. Good Lord, girl. How on earth did he fall for your charms when you have none?"

"She does have royal blood," Olivier murmured.

Natalie shivered, picturing the vampire licking his lips. At the same time, the heat of anger burned her cheeks. Tristan wasn't interested in royal anything. He loved her for her own sake.

"Well, I'm sure you enjoyed it. Tristan never disappoints," Jacqueline said with a knowing sigh. "On the other hand, he did leave rather quickly. Perhaps you disappointed him?" She laughed. "But of course. How could a man possibly be satisfied with you?"

Natalie balled her hands but kept her mouth shut.

"Let me in so I can tell you the truth about Tristan. What he's really after."

He isn't after anything, Natalie wanted to scream. But somehow, her insecurities welled up, making her stomach churn. What if it had all been an act? What if Tristan had an ulterior motive for sleeping with her?

"He's using you, sweetheart, just like he tried to use me."

Natalie covered her ears. Jacqueline had the tongue of a serpent. If there was any truth in her words, it was that she had used Tristan.

"*Ouvre la porte!*" Olivier called. *Open the door!*

Natalie glanced at the kitchen knives. One was wickedly long and sharp, and another was three inches wide. But neither would stop a vampire, would it?

She took the long one, trying to think rationally. Maybe it was all a mistake. Maybe Morfram had found Olivier and disciplined him, and Jacqueline was about to explain that Natalie's nightmare was over.

The chills running down her spine told a different story, though. She was anything but safe.

She glanced around, desperate for a way out. Following Bijou to the roof wouldn't help, not unless she could hop from ledge to ledge like a cat — or soar away like a dragon. Jacqueline and Olivier were at the door, so that was out. Which left…

Slowly, she turned to the rear corridor. There was the back stairwell — the dim, creepy one.

She faced the small door for a full minute without making a move. Then the front door shook with a blow powerful enough to make Tristan's jar of coins rattle, and she hurried forward.

"I want your blood. I need it. And I will have it," Olivier snarled.

Natalie rushed over and yanked open the back door. Then she paused, contemplating the dark, eerily silent shaft. Did she really want to spiral eight stories down through that?

Olivier banged on the front door, and she spun again. Did she have a choice?

"Bijou," she whispered, hoping for some company.

But the cat had fled, and it was time she did the same. So she took a deep breath and stepped onto the creaky staircase, closing the door behind her and fumbling for a lock. There didn't seem to be one, so after another minute of gathering her nerves, she started the descent.

Tap, tap, tap. She winced at the echo of her steps through that huge, empty space. Keeping her right hand on the banister, she spiraled around and around, counting floors as she went. Seventh floor... sixth floor... fifth—

Several stories above, the penthouse door flew open, and a beam of light shone in.

"Now, now. Do you really want to make this so hard on yourself?" Jacqueline called.

Natalie moved faster, trying to keep her steps quiet. But that was futile, and she quickly gave up on anything but racing down as fast as she could.

Fourth floor... third...

Arctic air whooshed down the stairs behind her, hounding her as she went.

First floor... ground floor...

She rushed for the lobby door, then froze. The small, one-way window showed three men in the lobby, all clad in black. Not Yves, nor another doorman she recognized. Not Liam either. Just those three... vampires?

She backed away as one whirled, sniffing. Oh God. Were Liam and Yves all right?

Move, a little voice insisted. *Now.*

She ran back to the stairs and hurried down.

"Run, little one. Run," Olivier taunted from above. "It makes your blood pump and fill the air."

Disgusted, Natalie raced on, trying to remember what came next. A corridor with two forks. She raced down the left one. Soon, she'd pop out the secret entrance to the alley. Then she could run to the Metro, hop on a train, and escape. Ideally, to Pigalle, where Tristan had gone.

But a second set of footsteps sounded ahead, making her halt in her tracks.

"Oh, that blood. I can already taste it," a man murmured in lusty French.

"So, get moving," a second man urged.

Natalie's heart pounded. Jacqueline and Olivier were coming down the stairs behind her. At the same time, two more vampires cut off the way to the Metro. That left her no choice but to hurry back to the fork on the right. There, she pulled up short, staring into the darkness.

The catacombs. The place of the dead.

Not the part open to tourists, Tristan had said in a tone so grim, it still echoed in her mind. But what choice did she have?

She hurried down that tunnel, only to come out at an iron gate. Grabbing the bars, she rattled it. The narrow space amplified the grating sound, and she winced.

"So close," one of the vampires called in glee.

Natalie yanked at the chain that kept the gate locked, then reached blindly along a rock ledge. Her skin crawled as she groped around, finding a damp cloth... spider webs... a small metal stick figure...

No, wait. That was a skeleton key. She nearly cheered. Did it fit the lock?

Her hands shook so hard, she could barely fit the key into the lock. The vampires' footsteps grew louder, and she cursed.

But finally, the lock creaked open. When she pulled the chain through the gate, it made a loud, scraping sound.

Come and get me, it might as well have advertised.

She rushed through the gate then turned and wrapped the chain around it again. That might help, right?

A pair of glowing red eyes appeared at the end of the tunnel. "Get her!"

She fumbled, nearly giving up. But at the last possible second, she got the lock on the chain and closed it with a sharp click.

"Got you!" A hand reached through the gate.

Natalie jumped back, heart thumping in terror.

"My pretty," Olivier murmured, grasping for her hand.

Natalie nearly screamed. When her legs finally registered her command to run, she stumbled backward. Then she caught herself and ran into the catacombs.

Into the realm of the dead.

Within a few steps, the tunnel split, and she took a blind guess on the right side. If she squinted, she could just make out her feet. When she tossed the skeleton key down a side tunnel, it pinged, making her wince. Worse was the ear-splitting rattles of the gate and the angry voices of those trying to break through.

"Dammit, get her!" someone yelled.

"I lead you right to your prey, and you still can't catch her," Jacqueline complained.

Natalie ran as fast as she dared, her mind spinning. Was Jacqueline in cahoots with the vampires? Why?

She slowed down, searching the darkness. Did she really dare run headlong into the maze of the catacombs? People perished there each year — and that was without vampires breathing down their necks.

In places, faint light illuminated the tunnels, though she couldn't trace the source. Other sections were so dark, she had to pull a hand along the wall and keep the other stuck blindly ahead so she wouldn't crash into anything. She could feel the tunnel bending right or left but had no sense of anything beyond. At one point, the rough tunnel walls grew bumpy, and her fingers traced a series of knobs.

She yelped, jerking her hand away. That wasn't a bumpy wall. It was a stack of arm bones, as the dim light revealed. Hundreds and hundreds of them, carefully stacked with the ends pointing out. Every yard or so, the pattern broke, leaving space for an artfully arranged collection of vertebrae encircling a skull. Natalie stared into the empty sockets, then gulped and hurried on.

The air was thick with the dust of death — centuries' worth, filling tunnel after tunnel. The whole place was one macabre celebration of death. There were entire niches devoted to femurs and others for ribs. Pelvises were placed side by side like ghostly butterflies, and skulls dotted the collection at intervals — grisly reminders of the spirits who had once inhabited those bones. Someone had spent a lot of time arranging those bones into flowers, arches, and even hearts. Leg bones danced, skulls gaped, and tiny foot bones clawed at the earth.

Natalie spun when a loud crack thundered through the air, followed by the crash of iron and cheers. The vampires had broken through the gate. How long would it take them to track her through the maze of tunnels?

She rushed toward a promising chamber that was slightly brighter than the rest. There, she stopped, peering up at the light filtering down through a long, deep shaft. How far was she beneath the surface of Paris?

Too far, she knew. Too far to have any hope of help.

As she turned, looking around, her foot hit something that rolled. The dim light sparkled, and a crunch registered under her foot. She leaned closer, discovering broken glass. There was a ring of stones, too, and a pile of charcoal.

She huffed. Seriously? Someone had come to this horrifying place to party?

She glanced around, then froze, covering her mouth. That chamber wasn't just any place. It was an altar of sorts, with three mummies suspended against one wall. Honest-to-God, full-size mummies dressed in medieval robes. The two on either side wore hooded monks' robes, with ropes as belts and rosaries in their wizened hands. The one in the center was taller and covered in armor, and his hands held a dagger carved from ivory.

Natalie turned away. She was already plenty spooked and didn't need more. But the vampires were still out there. Their voices carried from along different tunnels as they fanned out, searching for her.

She covered her face with her hands as her mind galloped in a dozen directions at once. Some of her thoughts were regrets — of all the mistakes she'd made, opportunities she'd passed up, or kind words left unspoken. Others were desperate, disjointed plans of escape. *Run! Hide! Climb the overhead shaft!*

Then there were thoughts of Tristan, and those were *really* mixed up. Some were mournful, others suspicious, and the rest warm and comforting despite how desperate she felt.

But none of that would help her, so she forced herself to look around and consider as calmly as she could. Whoever had partied in that chamber had left a mess. There were wine bottles and half-stripped wooden pallets. She stepped to a niche lined with burned-out candles. Was there a lighter there? She pictured herself sweeping a torch in a huge circle like Indiana Jones, then frowned. A torch would only draw the vampires' attention. And as for Indiana Jones... Well, she wished.

Then her eyes wandered to the mummies. Rosaries. Would they help against vampires? She stepped closer. No vials of holy water, no wooden stakes...

Then she stopped short. The dagger. She reached out, then jerked her hand back. She wasn't really going to steal from a monk, was she?

A dead monk, survival instinct pointed out.

She looked closer. The dagger was decorated with ivory, but beneath that was wood. Again, she reached out, and again, she snapped her hand back.

Tristan, she wanted to cry.

She nearly crumpled to her knees. Even if that dagger counted as a wooden stake, there were six vampires after her. Plus, there was that bitch of a dragon, Jacqueline. Natalie flexed her fingers, wishing for claws to scratch out Jacqueline's eyes.

"Where are you, my pretty?" Olivier's voice echoed through the tunnels.

Natalie gritted her teeth and gently pried the dagger from the mummy's hands, trembling the whole time.

"Sorry. I'm so sorry." Then she added a few *pardons*, because it was France after all. That and a prayer that the mummy's hands wouldn't come off with the dagger. They didn't, thank goodness, though she had to grasp one leathery hand to ease the weapon out.

"Sorry," she whispered one more time. Then she shrank back, dagger in hand.

The footsteps grew louder, closing in from both sides. Natalie hurried to a recessed niche at one side of the chamber. It smelled of urine — yuck — but that might cover her scent. Then she crouched in the shadows, closed her eyes, and rocked on her heels, wishing herself out of that place.

Thoughts of home didn't help, and neither did imagining her favorite spots in Paris. But when she pictured Tristan...

Her revving heart calmed slightly, and the chill around her shoulders eased a tiny bit.

She pictured Tristan at breakfast on the rooftop, patiently explaining things she couldn't grasp. Him valiantly fighting the vampires that fateful night. She remembered Tristan stepping forward to glare at Alaric when no one else dared and soaring off after Marcel. Finally, she pictured Tristan in bed, blinking at her in love and wonder.

"Tristan," she whispered, wishing he were there to whisper back.

A vampire ran by — a dark, flowing shape among all those bones and shadows. Natalie held her breath and listened as his footsteps faded down the next tunnel.

"Any trace of her?" someone yelled.

"Her scent leads here," another replied.

"And here," another added.

Natalie shivered. They were closing in.

Another vampire cursed, and Jacqueline huffed. "Fools. How hard can it be to track her?"

The nearest vampire backtracked, returning to the chamber of mummies. Natalie shrank back, not daring to breathe. He kicked the wine bottle, making it roll, then shatter. She winced at the explosion of sound but didn't budge.

"*Tu ne l'as pas vue, mon vieux?*" he muttered at one of the mummies. *Hey, buddy. You haven't seen her, have you?*

Natalie hunched her shoulders, wishing she could reply. *No, he didn't. Please go away.*

The vampire turned, sniffing, and Natalie gripped the dagger tightly. He stepped out of view, but the scrape of his shoes indicated he was checking another niche in the chamber.

Broken glass crunched as a second vampire ran in. "Anything?"

"She's close," the first murmured.

Natalie's heart beat so hard, she was sure they would be able to hear. But then she recalled what Olivier had said in the stairwell. *Run, little one. Run. It makes your blood pump and fill the air.*

She forced herself to exhale, trying to slow her racing heart.

Tristan...

His name became a mantra, and she silently repeated it as more vampires explored the chamber. They headed in one direction, turned around when her trail faded, and returned to the mummies, cursing. And all the while, Natalie kept up her inner chant.

Tristan...

She was so desperate for hope that she imagined him replying, *Hang on. I'm coming.*

She smiled at the little fantasy. Now, that would be nice. The deathly cold of the catacombs was seeping into her bones, and she could barely keep her teeth from chattering.

Jacqueline sashayed into the chamber, looking completely out of place in a stunning cream gown.

"So, where is she?" Olivier demanded.

Jacqueline scowled at someone outside Natalie's narrow field of vision. "You're the bloodhounds."

"The deal was for you to deliver her to us. Where is she?"

Natalie clutched the dagger harder, wishing she had the nerve to jump out and yell, *Right here.*

"Not far." Jacqueline sniffed, then crinkled her nose at the niche Natalie had concealed herself in. "Keep looking. And remember to save some of her blood for me."

Natalie stared at the veins on the backs of her hands. What was it about her blood, dammit? It was just plain old A positive.

Fire Maiden, Alaric's voice boomed through her mind.

Fire Maiden, her inner voice growled. *Watch what I can do.*

Slowly, carefully, she reached up to touch the crystal hanging from her neck. The fabric of her shirt kept it from shining — thank goodness — but it was warm against her chest.

We don't know precisely what your jewel is capable of, Clara had said. *There are stones that heal. Stones that lend you strength, wisdom, or courage...*

Natalie wished for all three — or for a single Tristan. He was faithful, while Jacqueline was the liar. The trickster. The one plotting for power.

The one I'll kill, her inner dragon said.

Natalie fingered the dagger. She couldn't shift into dragon form, but maybe she could harness that inner power.

And God, she needed it, because the nearest vampire muttered, "Save her blood? I swear I'll drink it all myself."

Then a roar exploded. The ground shook, and orange light burst into the chamber from a tunnel on the left. Jacqueline and the vampires flinched, and in the distance, someone screamed.

"*Merde.* What was that?" one of the vampires muttered, throwing up a hand.

The light flickered and faded before a second roar sounded and the light flared for a second time.

"Fire," the second vampire breathed. "Dragon fire."

Hope flooded Natalie's heart, and her lips parted. Tristan?

"Don't be ridiculous," Jacqueline snipped. "The only dragon around here is me."

Another burst of flame lit the tunnel system, and dust cascaded from the ceiling.

"Dragon!" another vampire yelled, fleeing through the chamber and out the other side.

"Shift!" one of the vampires bayed at Jacqueline. "Shift!"

"Impossible. There's no room in here for a dragon."

"Tell him that," another vampire muttered when the next roar sounded.

An instant later, a voice boomed through the tunnels.

"Jacqueline?"

Natalie recognized Tristan's voice, and boy, did he sound mad. But she must have squeaked, because one of the vampires spun and squinted into the niche.

"Wait a minute..."

Her stomach folded in on itself, and she scuttled back.

Too late. A moment later, the vampire dragged her out into the circle of his accomplices. She barely managed to slip the dagger up her sleeve before they wrestled her hands to her sides.

Jacqueline turned up her nose. "What a fitting hiding place you found."

A fitting place for you to die, Natalie wanted to say. But the same could apply to her, so she kept her mouth shut.

Another burst of fire ripped through the tunnel, and everyone jumped.

"Natalie!" Tristan boomed. "Run!"

Natalie spun, breaking free. Running sounded like a great plan.

But a few steps later, she pulled up short. Running from the vampires in the alley had saved her life, but it had nearly cost Tristan his. And that had been against fewer enemies than they faced now. How could she leave him?

"Not so fast." Olivier grabbed her in that moment of hesitation and yanked her to his side.

Close as she was to panic, Natalie forced herself to think. She had the dagger and the element of surprise. But she would have to use both if she had any hope of escaping the catacombs alive.

"*Arrêtez, ou je lui tords le cou,*" Olivier yelled to Tristan. *Stop, or I'll wring her neck.*

Natalie jabbed an elbow into his ribs.

"Don't, you fool," one of the others said. "We need her blood fresh from the vein."

Olivier hissed for him to be quiet, and Natalie parked that information away. The thought made her gag, but it did provide a glimmer of hope. The vampires couldn't kill her on the run — they had to keep her alive to feed off her.

Tristan sprinted into view, then halted in his tracks and breathed, "Natalie."

If Natalie had any nagging little doubts about Tristan, mates, or destiny, they all vanished at the sight of him. His face was a mask of determination, his jaw set hard. The furious red glow of his eyes softened at the sight of her, and he whispered her name again. "Natalie."

Warming all over, she smiled. That was all she managed to do, because words fled her, lost in the rush of emotion inside.

Love, she realized. That wasn't just relief, heating her up from the inside. It was love.

Tristan, I love you. She bundled up the thought and did her best to push it into his mind, as she'd read shifters could do. Then she looked around at her grim reality and managed a joke.

"We have to stop meeting like this."

Tristan's lips curled slightly, and he shook his head. "Any way I get to be with you is fine."

Natalie beamed. Olivier rolled his eyes. Jacqueline huffed.

"Aren't they adorable." Then she snapped her fingers, motioning the vampires toward Tristan. "Kill him."

Chapter Twenty-Three

Tristan took a deep breath, trying to settle his inner dragon. Thank goodness he'd made it in time. He'd been halfway to Alaric's mansion before a sinking feeling crept into his soul. When he'd reached his mind toward Natalie's, he'd sensed her panic and immediately rushed home. Her trail had led to the catacombs, and he'd feared the worst. But, no. She was alive and unharmed — so far.

But why isn't she listening? his dragon demanded. *Why didn't she run when she had the chance?*

He smiled faintly. *Because she's brave. Because she loves us. Because she truly is a Fire Maiden.*

He could have stood admiring her courage all day. But there were five vampires and a traitorous she-dragon to deal with first, so he turned his attention to Jacqueline. How he'd ever been tempted by her warped charms, he had no idea.

"Showing your true colors, Jacqueline?"

"Doing what needs to be done, you fool."

He squinted. "Which is?"

Jacqueline scoffed. "You wouldn't understand."

They both spoke in cutting, rapid-fire French, and he could see Natalie concentrating hard, trying to follow along.

Tristan prowled closer. Seeing Natalie had abated his fury, but it flooded back with a vengeance now. His whole body burned with malice, and the vampires shrank back.

"No, I do not understand. Alaric ordered us to protect her. Do you dare disobey his orders? The city needs her."

"The city needs me," Jacqueline hissed so forcefully, two of the vampires cringed. "A born leader."

"Pity you weren't born with the right blood," Tristan said, knowing that would cut deep.

But Jacqueline didn't glare. She smiled. Not a good sign.

"Ah, yes. Luckily, I have a way around that." She held out a vial. "Liviana's spell is stirred by the blood of a Fire Maiden? Well, fine. I'll get myself some. They can have the rest."

She gestured, and five pairs of vampire eyes glittered in the darkness.

Tristan's stomach turned as the extent of Jacqueline's betrayal became clear. She'd made some kind of deal with the vampires — something along the lines of handing Natalie over in exchange for support in her bid for power. Did she really think a vial of blood would be enough to reinvigorate the spell over Paris?

It was crazy. But times were such that anything was possible. Evil was everywhere, waiting for its chance. As Jacqueline had been, he realized.

"Listen to yourself, Jacqueline. You've gone mad."

"Have I?" she half screamed. "Alaric's power is slipping. You know that as well as I do. At first, I thought you might be the one to help me topple him."

Tristan's jaw dropped. Is that why she'd attempted to seduce him when he'd first arrived in Paris?

Jacqueline scowled. "But I quickly realized that you, with your misplaced sense of honor, were of no use."

It ought to have felt like a compliment, but all Tristan felt was anger. Had Jacqueline really thought him capable of turning on Alaric? The alpha had his faults, but his heart beat for justice and peace.

"So I was forced to bide my time," Jacqueline growled, then smiled. "And *voilà* — along came our dear, innocent *mademoiselle*, rewarding me for my patience. We need to reinvigorate the spell if we are to maintain power."

Tristan held up his hand. He didn't want anything to do with that *we*. But Jacqueline rushed on, gesturing wildly.

"The city needs a strong leader, and that is me. Besides, I deserve to rule. I'm the one who has devoted her life to this city, not this foreigner."

Tristan snorted. "You've devoted your life to parties and fashion shows." He pointed at Natalie. "She's been in soup kitchens and out in the streets."

Jacqueline huffed. "We don't need to concern ourselves with that rabble. Only with preserving our power."

He couldn't believe his ears. "Power comes from honoring the Guardian vow to protect the city — for the good of all, not just ourselves."

Jacqueline shrugged. "It's called trickle-down. The wealth and power we accumulate will eventually help the poor with their own sorry lives — if they're capable of such a thing. We create jobs and keep the economy running. The rest is up to them. But I don't suppose you'd know much about that." She sniffed. "You're a warrior, Tristan, not an economist."

"And you are?"

Jacqueline tossed her hair over her shoulder. "I've gone to the best schools. I have the best contacts. Whatever I don't know, I'll get the top advisers to help me."

"What advisers? Who will work for a traitor like you?"

Jacqueline grinned proudly. "As I said, I have contacts." She leaned closer, whispering as if he were in on her conspiracy. "The Lombardis. They shall be my lieutenants, and I shall be their queen."

Tristan's jaw dropped. He knew that power-hungry dragon clan was back in Europe after an unsuccessful bid to grab power in North America. They'd even sent Alaric a nasty message after the fire at Notre Dame, threatening to inflict similar damage on other monuments if Alaric didn't cede power. So far, Alaric had held the Lombardis at bay, but Jacqueline could open a back door to that unscrupulous clan.

"Just as you betray Alaric, the Lombardis will betray you," he warned.

Jacqueline laughed. "They wouldn't dare."

Tristan shook his head. It was madness, all of it.

But it got worse, because Jacqueline leaned closer and whispered, "Last chance."

He frowned. Last chance to what? Run? Save Natalie? Kill Jacqueline?

"Last chance to come out on the winning side." Jacqueline's eyes glowed with greed. "You could be the man at my side. My personal bodyguard."

Her eyes swept over his body with a look that revealed exactly how *personal* that could be.

"Forget it, Jacqueline. I'm no traitor."

He looked at Natalie. She was the woman he had sworn to protect. The one he would sacrifice his life for.

In the corner of his eye, something flashed, and Natalie screamed, "Watch out!"

Jacqueline spat a ball of fire that flew across the chamber, barely an inch over his head.

"I said, last chance," she screamed.

He looked up to see a monster — half human, half dragon, the features twisted in a horrific mismatch.

Usually, shifting was a quick, smooth process. But Jacqueline couldn't shift fully in the confines of the tunnel, and she hadn't mastered the fine art of a partial shift. Her body kept morphing back and forth. For a split second, she was a human with a grotesque, protruding snout. Then she was a dragon with painfully small eyes and minuscule ears. A moment later, those ears extended wildly, but her face was all wrong again, with massive dragon nostrils on her human face.

The vampires scattered, and pandemonium broke out. Tristan rolled, and Jacqueline chased him into one of the niches with a long blast of fire. He jumped to his feet, took a deep breath, and leaped back into the open, spraying the chamber with flames.

One of the vampires screamed as his jacket caught fire. Two others beat the flames out, while another ducked behind Jacqueline, who spat more fire. When Tristan's flames crashed against hers, both erupted outward, crackling and hissing as the heat sought an outlet.

Tristan roared as Olivier dragged Natalie backward into a tunnel.

"Natalie!"

But calling out stopped his stream of fire, and Jacqueline let loose with another fiery volley. Tristan spat a counter flame just in time, and again, they stood locked in a ferocious battle of fire against fire. Tristan huffed with all his might, driving Jacqueline back. But she countered when he gulped for breath, and the stalemate continued.

It was madness, and nothing like a proper dragon battle. Tristan kept raising his arms, intent on taking the fight to the sky in the time-honored dragon way. But when he bumped the sides of the tunnel, he remembered that wasn't possible.

"Dammit..."

Jacqueline cackled, and it occurred to him that she had been counting on that all along. Keeping him in tight quarters worked to her advantage, where the vampires' nails and fangs could slash at his human body.

One of the vampires rolled, screaming horribly as flames engulfed his clothes. He kicked and screamed, then went still and collapsed into a pile of ash. Two others leaped at Tristan from opposite directions. He punched one aside, but the other raked his arm with long, pointed fingernails, leaving a stinging trail of poison in his flesh. Not enough to bring him down, but hell. Another couple injuries like that would eventually take their toll.

Tristan squinted, trying to see past the flames. Where was Olivier taking Natalie? And, crap. How could he stop Jacqueline?

Punch through her fire, his dragon shouted. *Throttle her with your bare hands, and save our mate. Hurry!*

"Tristan!" Natalie cried, struggling against Olivier.

He lunged to help, but the vampires leaped at him, and it was all he could do to keep them at bay. They grinned fiendishly and eyed his neck, no doubt planning to overpower him and feast on his blood. Tristan let out his dragon claws and slashed back. But it was three against one — plus Jacqueline, ready to throw flames whenever the vampires faltered.

No matter how fiercely Tristan battled, he couldn't make any headway toward the woman he loved.

Everything was a blur, but he caught glimpses of Natalie amid the onslaught of nails and teeth. Olivier held her up against his chest, pinning her arms while he bared his fangs. At first, terror colored Natalie's face. Then hope crept in, followed by despair.

Natalie! he wanted to yell. *I'm trying!*

But then he caught another glimpse of Natalie, and by then, her face was twisted in anger. Anger that intensified until her eyes glowed as red as a dragon's. At the same time, another point of light glowed at her neck — the pendant, as bright as a bulb.

Yes, he wanted to cheer. *Use that inner power. Harness it.*

He didn't know what that crystal did, but it looked as ferocious as Natalie.

One of the vampires jumped at Tristan from behind, and he spun to fend it off. The next time he caught sight of Natalie, she looked frighteningly calm and determined. Her arms were pinned, but she'd managed to work one hand to her side. As she wiggled, something thin and pointy appeared. A dagger.

Her eyes met his, and a dozen conflicting emotions blazed away. Anger. Fear. Desperation. And above all, horror at what she was about to do. Natalie was a kind, gentle soul. Violence didn't come easily to her, not even in self-defense.

Do it, he yelled, willing the words into her mind. *One, two, three. Like we practiced.*

The remaining vampires used the distraction to tackle Tristan from behind, and he wrestled madly. He dug his claws into their arms, but they didn't give up, and he could feel one's breath on his neck.

"And so the mighty dragon falls," Olivier chuckled, glancing his way.

Tristan gritted his teeth. He had another few tricks up his sleeve, but Olivier seemed mesmerized by the idea of watching his friends sink their teeth into a dragon shifter's neck to drink. So Tristan stalled as long as he dared. The vampires inched closer to his neck, and one murmured in glee.

"We'll call this our appetizer."

Now, Natalie, Tristan urged. *Now or never.*

Her chest rose in a deep breath, and she tightened her fingers around the dagger. Olivier didn't notice, and neither did Jacqueline, who tut-tutted at Tristan.

"You should have joined me."

He would rather die. And hell, he was getting awfully close.

But at exactly that moment, Natalie sprang into action. *One.* She snapped her hands up, gaining a little space. *Two.* She jabbed her elbows into Olivier's ribs.

Hurry, his dragon yelled as the nearest vampire opened his jaws wide.

Three! Natalie whipped around, thrusting an elbow into Olivier's face. He staggered back in surprise.

Now, run, Tristan wanted to yell.

But Natalie didn't run. Her face hardened in determination, and she raised the dagger high.

Tristan gulped. *Do it. Finish him.*

Natalie's hand trembled, but she plunged down with a vengeance, burying the dagger in Olivier's chest.

Yes, Tristan nearly cheered.

At first, Olivier simply looked down, annoyed. Then his eyes widened in surprise at the black blood soaking his shirt, and he staggered.

"Tristan!" Natalie yelled.

He whirled, knocking away the vampire at his throat. Following up with a furious spurt of fire, he set his enemy ablaze. The vampire screamed and ran down one of the tunnels, trailing flames as he went.

The other two vampires jumped Tristan. In the whirlwind of action that followed, he caught sight of Olivier dropping to his knees. Jacqueline leaned over in surprise, then glared at Natalie. But Natalie was already leaping at the mummies suspended from the chamber wall, grabbing at...

The sword! The middle mummy was a knight, or he had been, centuries before. But that sword still glinted in the light. Tristan would have cheered, but he was too busy clawing away a vampire.

"You wouldn't," Jacqueline dared Natalie.

Natalie braced her feet and swung the sword back, then hesitated.

Jacqueline laughed. "Afraid to use it?"

A lick of lingering dragon fire glinted off the sword, and Natalie yelled, "Stand back."

Summoning his last reserves, Tristan pushed one vampire away and body-checked another against the tunnel wall. Then he extended his claws and moved in.

"Die," he roared.

There weren't many ways to kill a vampire, but slicing its head off was one. Gory, but effective. Moments after the vampire dropped, the body crumpled and turned to ash.

Tristan spun, blinking the sweat out of his eyes. There was one vampire left. Where?

A blur ran at him, screaming like a banshee. Acting on reflex, Tristan slashed at the vampire's neck. He missed on the first try, but not on the second, and a moment later—

"No!" Jacqueline screamed as her last accomplice went down.

Tristan caught himself a heartbeat away from stumbling. Panting wildly, he leaned against the tunnel wall, willing his vision to clear. How many enemies left?

One, he decided, now that Olivier had dropped to the ground, dead. The last survivor looked around, then turned tail and fled, the coward. Other than his receding footsteps, the catacombs fell into eerie silence.

The silence was brief, though, because Jacqueline cackled. "Bravo, Tristan. Bravo."

Tristan gritted his teeth, trying to straighten. The poison might not kill him, but it did cloud his mind. He swayed toward Natalie, who stood with the sword raised.

"Let me help you, darling," Jacqueline purred, stepping toward him. Her eyes shone, and not in a good way. "There's still time."

Time? Tristan frowned. Time for what?

Then it hit him. Jacqueline didn't need vampires to finish this off. She could still kill Natalie, collect some blood, and carry out her crazy plan to seize power.

Tristan growled, tempted to hurl her down one of the tunnels. But poison pooled in his midsection, and he doubled over in pain.

"My poor darling. Let me help you," Jacqueline murmured, making his blood go cold.

She wasn't going to help him. She was going to kill him, then Natalie.

"Stop right there," Natalie cried.

Jacqueline ignored her, reaching for Tristan. Her hands turned to claws, and excitement flashed in her eyes. The thrill of a kill, Tristan knew.

He threw up a hand in defense and croaked, "Natalie, run."

But Natalie didn't run, dammit. Her face turned crimson, and she stalked up behind Jacqueline.

"I said, stop!"

Jacqueline turned, laughing. "Seriously?"

"Seriously," Natalie whispered, raising the sword. "I mean it."

But Jacqueline turned her back, tossing a hand as if to say, *I knew she didn't have it in her.* Then her eyes narrowed on Tristan, and he figured he was about a minute away from dying at the hands of the woman who'd caused him so much grief.

Jacqueline's claws reached for him. Natalie swung the sword, uttering a final warning. A warning Jacqueline didn't heed, and a split second later—

Jacqueline's eyes went wide, and her shoulders jerked against the impact of the sword. The vial she clutched shattered against the flagstone floor. Natalie winced but hung on, and seconds later...

"You bitch..." Jacqueline whispered then collapsed to the ground.

Natalie watched in horror, stumbling backward. Then she edged around Jacqueline and rushed to Tristan's side.

Wait. Watch out, he wanted to yell. But he couldn't. Meanwhile, Jacqueline swayed to her feet, her eyes glowing in fury. She reached around her back, groping blindly for the sword. That blow would have killed a human, but Jacqueline's shifter powers gave her the strength to pull it out with a scream. Then she grimaced and raised the sword, looking at Natalie.

"Tristan..." Natalie touched his shoulder, ignorant of the danger behind her.

A roar split the air, and it took Tristan a moment to realize that was him. The arm that pushed Natalie aside was his, too, as was the next explosion of fire. Jacqueline screamed and ducked, but Tristan had no mercy left. He kept up the blaze, reminding himself his mate's life at stake, along with the future of Paris.

"Stop," Jacqueline screamed. "Stop!"

No, he would not. Not even when Jacqueline fell to the ground, engulfed in flames. She rolled, screaming, and the sword clattered out of her grasp. Even then, Tristan kept up that lethal burst of fire.

"Wait!" Natalie cried. "Stop!"

He shook his head. But Natalie begged him, and something in his heart gave way. So he cut off his fire and bellowed instead.

"Out. Get out of my sight and out of Paris. And don't even think of returning."

Jacqueline rolled to her knees, moaning. "How could you?"

He nearly hit her with another plume of fire, but Natalie touched his shoulder, and he couldn't ignore her silent plea.

"Go," he barked at Jacqueline. "Before I change my mind."

When Jacqueline rose to her feet, Tristan almost hoped she would attempt something sneaky, giving an excuse for him to finish her off for good. But she turned and stumbled into the shadows, croaking as she went.

"Fools. I will be back, and I will have my revenge."

He took a step forward, but Natalie held him back.

"Enough." Her voice was rough and weary as she gestured to the carnage all around. "Enough killing."

He wanted to protest, but Natalie was right. The sword was lying on the ground, and in its reflection, he saw one last swirl of fire. Then that, too, went out, taking the last of his energy with it.

He slumped, aching all over. His lips were chafed, his tongue burned, his legs too tired to support him.

Natalie bent over him, her eyes filled with tears. "Are you all right?"

"*Oui.* Are you?"

Natalie nodded, and a moment later, they swayed into a hug. Still, he pointed one shaky hand in the direction of Jacqueline's receding footsteps.

"She means it, you know. She will be back. Or she'll try to seize power somewhere else."

Natalie nodded wearily. "I know. But there has to be a better way."

He cocked his head. "What way?"

She smiled weakly. "If I'm going to be your Fire Maiden, we'll have to find a better solution than blasting every enemy with fire."

He grinned. "We?"

She nodded firmly. "We."

He would have loved to bask in the sound of that word for an hour or two, but footsteps sounded in the tunnel, and Natalie tensed.

"More vampires?"

The footsteps broke off, and a familiar voice called through the dark. "Did someone say vampires?"

Tristan exhaled. "Liam." Then he raised his voice and called, "You're late. As usual."

Natalie's pale face slowly filled with color when Liam strode into view. He toed a pile of ash, then whistled at the dagger within it and the carnage all around.

"Well, it looks like Natalie is all you need. I'm more like the cleanup crew."

Tristan held Natalie's hand, swelling with pride. Yes, she was amazing. Still, it would have been nice not to cut things so close.

Dammit, you were supposed to be guarding Natalie, he barked into Liam's mind.

Then it hit him. Liam was playing it cool, but his hair was a mess, and his sleeves were torn. His musky scent indicated a recent shift. Apparently, Liam had been fighting, too.

Liam's stiff bearing hinted at hurt pride. *A couple of gargoyles rushed the roof of your building, and I had my hands full with them. Make that, my claws.* He flexed and straightened his fingers a few times. *I had to leave my post to deal with them. If I'd known they were diverting me from the vampires...*

Tristan nodded wearily. Without Liam, things would have been twice as bad, but damn. Cleanups came with explanations, which meant he had to face Alaric. Plus, there was Jacqueline.

The moment he murmured her name and motioned, Liam nodded and ran off. "I'm on it."

The last of Tristan's energy drained away, and he sat down hard. Shifters had great regenerative power, and he could feel his body fighting away the vampire poison. That didn't change the level of pain, though. He closed his eyes and pulled Natalie against his side. He would deal with Alaric later. Right now, all that mattered was his mate.

"You're really all right?" she whispered.

He smiled. Even in this place of death, her hair smelled like flowers, and a ray of sunshine poured into his heart.

"Of course."

She snorted. "Of course?"

He nodded, quietly reveling in the healing touch of his mate. "With you, I'm always all right. It's the rest of the world I get fed up with."

She chuckled softly and cupped his cheek. "Funny, I was thinking the same thing."

Chapter Twenty-Four

As much as Tristan's body ached, he refused to let Natalie stray from his side until they got home, where they both collapsed on the couch. He drifted in and out of consciousness for hours, letting his weary body break down the rest of the poison. When he finally woke, sunlight was slanting through the windows, indicating afternoon. Natalie was at his side, gently stroking his cheek. He'd already rested for hours, and now he was basking like a cat under her loving touch. But, hell. Who could blame him?

Then he looked down at his ragged clothes and groaned. What a mess. Slowly, he sat up, relieved to find he wasn't half as sore as before. But his nose wrinkled a moment later.

"Ugh. Sorry. I need a shower."

Natalie shook her head. "You need to rest."

"I'm fine, but I'm a mess."

She motioned over her body. "Join the club. Even Bijou turned his nose up at me."

When Tristan caught sight of her cuts, bruises, and torn clothes, he pulled her into a hug.

"Hey, I'm okay," she protested.

"Yes, but it was close," he murmured into her hair. "Much too close."

They cuddled for a minute, but then her body hardened, and she slowly pulled away.

"There's one thing I have to know. Just one."

Tristan's nerves twitched at the tone in her voice. He forced himself to nod. "Anything."

Natalie ran her tongue over her teeth, then spoke haltingly. "Jacqueline." She motioned around. "Did you... I mean..." Her hands trembled in his. "Did you and she ever..."

Tristan cursed himself as Natalie's eyes wandered over to the bed. No, he hadn't slept with Jacqueline, but he had to admit, it had been close. When he spoke, his voice cracked.

"I never slept with her, Natalie. I swear. She came on hard, and I nearly fell for her...charms." He soured, because the word didn't fit. "But, no. We never went that far. Honestly, I have no idea why I let her get close. I figured out my mistake quickly, though. I promise you."

Natalie searched his eyes for a long time, and he could see the hurt in hers. Hurt that he'd even considered someone like Jacqueline. That was something he could never take away, short of traveling back in time — and not even shifters could do that. But Natalie was right to ask. They had to get that out in the open before they could move on.

To his relief, she nodded. "Well, it took me years to figure out my mistake. With Dean, I mean."

"That moron didn't deserve you," Tristan growled.

Natalie laughed. "You don't even know him."

Still, Tristan frowned. "I just know. I'm not sure I deserve you."

She touched his cheek. "I could say that about you." Then she wrinkled her nose and pushed him away gently. "But, yes, you could use a shower. Me too."

So they headed to the bathroom together and took the longest, most sensual, and least soldierly shower Tristan had ever indulged in. Natalie soaped his back, and he soaped hers, moving gingerly over her scrapes and bruises. Then she claimed the bar of soap and smoothed it over his front. First his chest, then his belly, and then...

He closed his eyes, because what Natalie did to him with her hands and — sweet Jesus, her mouth — did more to cleanse his mind, body, and soul than any soap could.

In the end, he carried her over to the bed in a rush, dripping as they went.

"The bed will get wet," she squeaked.

"The bed is already a mess, and we can change the sheets later."

He laid her down, and that was all the talking they did for the next hour, if he didn't count the little whimpers and soft moans of their lovemaking. The first round was hot and hard, marked by the same urgency and desperation they'd battled the vampires with. Not long after, they were at it again, taking it slow and sweet. Eventually, they sank back into the sheets, and Natalie chuckled.

"I need another shower."

Briefly, Tristan considered running over to Alaric while she did. He really had to check in with the Guardians. Jaqueline was on the loose — unfortunately, she had narrowly escaped, as Liam had reported shortly afterward. The lion shifter was still kicking himself over it, but Jacqueline knew the catacombs, and she'd had enough of a lead over Liam to get away. But someday...

Tristan's inner dragon growled, putting a firm halt to those thoughts.

Not leaving my mate. Not at a time like this. Are you crazy?

No, he wasn't. He followed Natalie back into the bathroom like a duck who'd imprinted for a lifetime, and that time was a little more business, a little less fun. Natalie traced the long scars on his chest and arms, shaking her head.

"What a world we live in."

For a moment, every human injustice Tristan had ever witnessed paraded through his mind. But when Natalie hugged him, he saw blue skies... gorgeous sunsets... and the smiles of both strangers and friends. Life had its dark moments and even periods of utter despair. But hope and sunshine could come out of nowhere and make a man want to live again.

"What a world we live in," he echoed. A world where twists of fate could lead to love, joy, and relief.

He stroked her long, wet hair as warm water sluiced from his body to hers. Yes, a man could definitely learn to live again, especially with his mate at his side.

Natalie looked up at him through the steam, then smiled and waved around. "I think you have the best water heater in Paris."

He laughed. Not too many buildings in the city had modernized their plumbing, but his building had recently upgraded.

"One of the few perks of the job."

It was a joke, but they both sobered, and Natalie took his hands. "Speaking of which..."

He nodded wearily. She was right. They really had to talk.

Slowly, they dried off and got dressed. Natalie wrapped herself in his robe, and Tristan pulled on some boxers. Then a soft knock sounded on the door, and Tristan froze. If that was Madame Colette, he was not letting her in.

Then the visitor's scent wafted in, and he relaxed. "Liam."

By the time he opened the door, Liam was silently disappearing around the corner, leaving a basket of food on the doorstep.

"*Merci, mon vieux,*" Tristan called.

Liam waved like it was nothing, but what struck Tristan was the wistful look on his friend's face as he whispered, "Enjoy your mate."

Did Liam pine for a special someone? Did that jovial exterior hide deeper feelings inside?

Tristan watched him go, promising himself to check on his friend.

Later, his dragon growled. *Right now...*

He turned back into the penthouse. Right now, he had a mate to take care of.

He and Natalie made quick work of the fresh bread, cheese, and wine, then moved from the kitchen to sit on the bed.

Tristan kissed her hand before speaking, remembering what a close call it had been. His eyes wandered over the bare apartment. During the past week, Natalie had filled that space with energy and life, but if he had lost her... He swallowed away the lump in his throat. Life would be as empty as the rooms stretching out in a long row, and the view, no matter how beautiful, would always be bleak.

Then he turned as Bijou jumped on the bed and pranced by, holding his tail high as a flag that said, *Life is good. Life is great.* Then he wound himself around Natalie, purring. *See? She loves me.*

Tristan smiled. Apparently, he and the little monster had one thing in common. They both loved Natalie, and she loved them back.

Then he hesitated. So much to explain, but where to start?

"So, about Fire Maidens..."

She made a face. "Let me guess. They attract vampires and power-hungry jerks."

He squeezed her hand. "I guess so. But the blood of the ancients runs through you, giving you power."

Natalie made a face. "Power? I wish."

"You stood up to Alaric and to Jacqueline. You resisted the thrall of the vampires. Most humans can't do that."

She looked at her hands, unconvinced.

"And as for the rest... Well, call it potential. I can feel it coursing through you."

She ran a hand up his thigh and shot him a sultry look. "Oh, we have potential, all right."

He smiled then motioned at her crystal. Much as he would have loved to make steamy love for the rest of the afternoon, he had to stay focused.

"Then there's that. May I?"

She dipped her chin, and he cupped the crystal in his hand. The moment he did, its glow dimmed. When he pressed it into her hand, it brightened again.

"See? It doesn't glow for just any dragon, Natalie."

"But I'm not a dragon."

He took a deep breath. This was it. His chance to finally say it.

"You could be if you mate with me."

Her eyes widened. "I could... what?"

He took a deep breath. "Well, technically, it wouldn't have to be with me, but I'd like that. A lot. I mean..." *Merde.* He ran a hand through his hair. As usual, the words weren't coming out right. "Mating with a shifter would make you a shifter too."

She sat perfectly still. "A dragon? Me? For real?"

Her tone was impossible to read, and he held his breath.

"You mean, I could fly? Breathe fire? All of those things?"

He exhaled slightly. That sounded promising.

Then she tapped her lips. "And I could accomplish that with any shifter? Say, Marcel? Liam?"

Tristan's blood heated, and he nearly roared. But Natalie chuckled and play-smacked his arm. "Hey, I was only kidding. Yes, I would love that. But mainly, I want you. You could be a human and I'd still want you. Heck, you could be a gargoyle. Even a vampire..."

He raised an eyebrow.

"Well, maybe not a vampire." She laughed, then took both his hands. "Honestly, I don't really care as long as it's you. You're the only one I want."

He kissed her hands, though he wasn't done. "I want you, and you want me. But there are others who won't agree. Fire Maidens aren't supposed to mix with guys like me."

Bijou butted between them at that moment, accentuating his point.

She gently moved the cat aside, then huffed. "Alaric, you mean."

He nodded. "Alaric and many others. They can make things...complicated for us."

Her face flushed, and she muttered, "I'll show them complicated."

Then her eyes sparkled, and her gaze wandered to the books stacked by the couch at the opposite end of the apartment. Abruptly, she stood and handed him a surprised Bijou. Then she hurried across the apartment and came back, leafing through a huge, leather-bound volume.

"I read something in here..."

Bijou gave Tristan the evil eye. *What are you doing, holding me?*

Tristan had no clue. But obviously, Natalie was onto something.

The moment she sat down, Bijou sprang back into her lap, but the book was in the way, so he wound around her body instead, meowing pitifully.

"One second, Bijou," she murmured. "Here." She stopped on one page and traced through the text. "Claudine d'Islay... Breselan..."

Tristan squinted at the page, but she dropped the book a moment later and caught him in a tight hug.

"Um... Natalie?"

She laughed, and he wondered if she was suffering from some form of shock. But when she pulled back, her face glowed with excitement. "Don't worry about Alaric. I've got that part covered."

He tilted his head, tempted to ask. But, heck. A man had to trust his mate, right?

Then Natalie sobered and searched his eyes. "Tell me about mates. Tell me everything."

Tristan glanced at the stack of books. How much had she read?

She nudged him, so he started with the basics. "Most shifters believe in destined mates. That there's only one person out there for them, and the moment they meet, they both know it."

His mind drifted back to the first day he'd laid eyes on Natalie, and how the earth had shaken under his feet.

He went on quickly. "Shifters don't get married. They mate for life."

Her eyes met his. "For life, huh?"

For life, his dragon murmured.

Then he looked at his feet. "At least, that's what most shifters believe."

Natalie touched his arm, and a little electric zing traveled through him. "What do you believe?"

He stalled, studying Bijou before answering. But he'd promised Natalie the truth — the whole truth — so finally, he plowed ahead.

"For a long time, I didn't believe in mates. My mother and father..." He trailed off, clearing the gruffness out of his throat. "They mated, but it didn't work out. Not the way true mates are supposed to. My dad came and went, and my mom was... full of regrets."

He balled his fists, thinking of all the times his mother had stared off into the distance, hoping for her mate to return, then hoping he'd leave.

"But now..." Natalie whispered.

He met her eyes, because she had to know how serious he was. "Now, I believe. The minute I met you, I knew. Not just that I wanted you. More like I wanted to do anything for you. Love you. Protect you. Lay down my life if I have to."

She squeezed his hand. "Hopefully we'll never come that close again."

He pursed his lips. He'd do it again — a thousand times over. But, yeah. He'd rather dwell on the good parts. "I love having you in my life. Just watching you read or look out the windows — or smile. I love watching you smile."

She lit up, giving him the confidence to go on.

"It's like my whole life up to the moment I met you was just a warm-up. I didn't know why I was living until I met you. And now I do."

She looked a little breathless at that point, which was good, because so was he.

"Why are you living, then?" she whispered, clutching his hands.

At any other point in this life, he would have struggled to answer. But now, he could reply without the slightest hesitation. "To love you. To make you happy. To let you make me happy too."

Her smile stretched and her eyes glowed. "Pretty good speech, mister."

He flashed a smile. Whew.

Then she grinned and threw her arms around him, murmuring in his ear. "I want that, too, Tristan. I want you. Forever. But dammit..." He pulled back, alarmed, but Natalie smiled. "Stop doing this to me."

"Doing what?"

"This." She sank into the mattress, pulling him with her. "Stop making me crave sex all the time."

Relief made him burst into loud laughter that he muffled in the sheets. "Not my fault. That's a side effect of destined mates. What was that word again?"

"A perk," she murmured, nibbling on his ear. "Fringe benefit."

He rubbed his jaw along hers, marking her with his scent. None of the emotions Natalie aroused in him were *fringe* anything. They caught him up and swept him away, whether she was sad, scared, or — like now — hungry for contact.

But there was one more thing he had to tell her, so he forced himself to hold back.

"Natalie."

"Hmm?" she mumbled, more interested in the way his abs led down to his groin.

"There's one more thing you have to know."

She groaned. "I think my brain is full. Now, it's my body's turn." Her hands snuck lower, stoking his desire.

"To mate, I have to bite you."

"Fine," she mumbled, working his boxers down.

He blinked. Fine?

His shock must have shown, because she laughed. "Honestly, I'd say yes to anything right now. But seriously — yes. I read about that. I trust you." Then her voice dropped to a purr, and she wrapped one leg around his side. "Right now, I want you. I want us. I want everything." Then she laughed. "Greedy, huh?"

"Not so greedy," he mumbled, barely holding back a growl. "But seriously—"

He broke off when she surged under his body and tucked her hand into the hem of his boxers. Then she palmed his cock, and he hissed in raw need.

"I don't want anything or anyone to ever come between us again," she whispered, grinding her hips against his while wrestling with the knot of her robe. "I need this. Please."

Her words were an order that went straight to his heart, and he couldn't say no. Without thinking, he snuck a hand between the folds of her robe and palmed the soft flesh of her breast. His mind blanked out everything — all the questions, all the answers, all the unknowns. Everything but the burning need for his mate.

Their next few kisses were rushed, fueled by pure lust. Then, guided by instinct, Tristan started to nip and sniff along her neck, homing in on the right spot to place the bite.

His mind spun with the sheer thrill of it all. A mating bite. *His* mating bite.

Her nipples pressed against his chest, and his hand itched to explore her core. So he touched her there too, and soon, she was wrapping her legs around him. Then there was no holding back. When he rose up over her and thrust in, they both cried out.

Within seconds, his mind was a blur of sensual impressions. Her warm, slick heat. The light scratch of her nails across his back. The sound of her eager cries, and the slap of their bodies meeting, again and again. He could sense her blood rush, beckoning him.

"Yes..." she cried, clutching him closer. "Yes..."

He inched his mouth along her neck. Slowly, his canines extended, adding to the haze of pleasure-pain in his mind. When he scraped his teeth along Natalie's neck, she arched.

Take me. Please, my mate, her inner dragon called.

He was so far gone that it didn't really register how amazing it was to hear her inner dragon so clearly in his mind. It just felt natural, the way the fire building inside him was natural.

Bite her. Take her. Seal your bond, a faraway voice whispered in his mind, low and sure. The voice of destiny.

He thrust one more time, deeper than ever, making Natalie howl. Then he sank his teeth into her neck so quickly, it scared him. But an instant later, a hot gush swept through his veins, and he inhaled.

Now. Do it, the voice urged.

Without thinking, he channeled his inner fire and puffed past his bite. Natalie cried out, and part of him worried he'd gotten it wrong. But a heartbeat later, her cry turned to sheer ecstasy, and she shuddered beneath him.

Every muscle in his body burned as the fire circled through her veins then whooshed back into his, making his inner dragon roar.

Mate! My mate!

It was thrilling. Exquisite. A rough, rugged high with a delicate edge that made him teeter in ecstasy for minutes on end. Natalie was right there with him, clutching his sides while her body trembled with need.

"So good..."

Tristan never wanted to let go, but at some point, the fire subsided into satisfied little embers — a signal to let go. Carefully, he sealed his lips around her skin and retracted his canines. Natalie shuddered as he did, coming for the second or third time. He kept his tongue over the bite, making sure the wound healed. Then he melted over her as his body shut down, utterly spent.

Panting, he mumbled her name and combed his fingers through her hair, though he was probably tangling it. Nothing registered but the heat inside him and the voice in his head — Natalie's voice, singing in joy.

Love. Mate. Never have to be lonely again.

For a moment, sorrow washed over him. They'd each locked away how alone they'd felt — until now, when it all tumbled out like a wave. Tristan pressed his face against Natalie's hair, letting her sweet scent remind him there was nothing to be sad about now.

"Tristan," she sighed, going limp. "I love you so much."

Light flooded his soul, and he bobbed his head up and down. "I love you."

She patted him on the back and chuckled. "Wow. Who knew?"

He smoothed a strand of hair away from her eyes. "What?"

"That being bitten could feel so good."

He laughed and scrubbed his cheek against hers.

"And wow — what was that? That fire part," she asked.

"That's a dragon thing," he said, trying to sound casual about something he'd never really believed in, then had been blown away by.

Natalie thought for a moment, holding him close. Then she whispered, "Do we get to do that again?"

He laughed. "We can do that as often as you want." Then he groaned. "Of course, I really should go report to Alaric..."

She shook her head. "I need more time getting to know my mate. Thoroughly." Her voice dropped to a sensual whisper, and when she put a finger to her neck, she groaned. "Wow. I could give myself an orgasm just thinking about it. Even touching it feels good."

Tristan nosed her finger out of the way and started kissing the tiny scars of the mating bite. And, hell. He nearly moaned at the sensation, too.

Natalie started moving her leg over his, heating up all over again.

"You're a dangerous man, Tristan."

He laughed. "You're a dangerous woman, seducing me all over again."

She snorted. "Ah, yes. The ultimate seductress. That's me."

He pulled back and looked her in the eye. "Do you even know how beautiful you are?"

She blushed, and he didn't wait for an answer. He just ducked his head, whispering his lips over her breast. "I suppose I'll have to prove it to you all over again."

Not a hardship. His dragon grinned.

Within minutes, they were wrapped around each other, panting and groping all over again.

"I'm liking these perks," Natalie murmured, then arched at his next touch.

"So do I," he whispered, pulling her close. "So do I."

Chapter Twenty-Five

Two days later...

Natalie took a deep breath as she looked up at the imposing facade of Alaric's villa.

"We got this," Tristan murmured, squeezing her hand.

She forced a smile, though her stomach was full of butterflies. They had put off meeting the Guardians for a few days, but now, she just wanted to get it over with.

"On my own terms," she mumbled one of the lines she'd been rehearsing in her mind.

"Ready?" Liam asked from a few steps ahead.

Natalie pursed her lips. Was she ready? To start her new life — a life with Tristan, and as a Fire Maiden — yes. But ready to face Alaric?

Ready, her dragon side growled.

In the few days since Tristan had given her the mating bite, that inner voice had grown louder, and she'd grown more comfortable with it. The dragon wasn't a separate being. It was part of her and had been all her life.

Ready for anything, it insisted.

She straightened her shoulders. Slowly becoming a dragon shifter definitely boosted her confidence. Besides, she would never feel as secure as now, with Tristan and Liam backing her up. Liam had just received word of a new assignment in London, but he'd put off his departure to guard over the penthouse while she and Tristan recuperated. Of course, Liam had teased them mercilessly about all the — ahem — *resting* they'd done in that time. But he'd proven himself a true friend, giving them space and privacy — and somehow talking Madame Colette into doing the same.

An hour earlier, Natalie, Tristan, and Liam had gone out for a fortifying coffee, then taken the Metro to Pigalle. Liam had led the way, keeping her mind off the meeting with a constant stream of jokes and chatter.

"An Englishman, a Welshman, and a dragon walk into a pub..."

Most of his jokes started that way and ended with him laughing himself silly.

But that was an hour ago. Now, Liam hammered on the front door of Alaric's villa and called out, "Hello. Anybody home?"

Natalie tightened the scarf around her neck — the one concealing the tiny scars from her mating bite. She was dying to show them off, but she and Tristan had agreed not to flaunt that detail too much. If the others scented that they'd mated, fine, but they'd rather not complicate the meeting with their news, joyous as it was.

Jules, the bear shifter butler, opened the door with a sour look. But the moment he saw Natalie, he bowed deeply and motioned inside. *"Mademoiselle, s'il vous plaît."*

Natalie stepped past him with a smile and a sincere, *"Merci."* Jules was the only shifter in the place who didn't seem to have a hidden agenda of some kind.

Then she caught herself. Oops. A Fire Maiden was probably supposed to be aloof and regal. In other words, not too casual — and certainly not friendly — with staff. Then she snorted. She'd sworn to do this on her own terms, dammit, and she would. So she added a smile to go with her words, and miracle of miracles, Jules smiled back. Just a tiny one, but it was warm and genuine.

"Suivez-moi," he murmured, leading the way.

Tristan and Liam flanked Natalie, and their footsteps echoed over the marble floor. Jules turned a corner, then knocked on the double doors of Alaric's imposing den. A moment later, he pushed them open, and Natalie steeled herself for the worst.

Luckily, the first to greet her was Clara, who rushed up with a warm hug.

"Oh, my dear girl. So good to see that you're all right. And you, Tristan."

When Tristan nodded stoically, Clara rolled her eyes and thumped his arm. "Men. Always having to be such warriors. Are we not allowed to fuss over you from time to time?"

"Maybe from time to time," Tristan murmured, flashing a tiny grin.

Hugo came up beside Clara and winked. "Something tells me he's already had someone fuss over him."

Natalie blushed deeply. Obviously, her scent gave every steamy encounter away. But Hugo's eyes had already turned back to Clara, and they exchanged one of those secret looks that said, *Remember the time when...*

Then Hugo shook hands with Tristan and kissed Natalie on both cheeks. "I knew you could do it."

Natalie hadn't been sure of anything. But to have Clara and Hugo believe in her... That meant a lot.

"And I know you can do this, too," Clara whispered, tilting her chin toward the head of the room, where Alaric waited.

The dragon shifter appeared just as stern — and displeased — as ever. Marcel was nowhere to be seen — thank goodness — but Morfram stood in the shadows of the right side of the room, staring at her neck. Natalie forced herself to stare back until he dropped his gaze. Albiorix was beside him, following her with his beady eyes. But both men nodded deeply and shuffled back as if reminding each other, *Watch out for that woman. She kills vampires, you know.*

Not that Natalie ever wanted to kill anyone — or anything. Not even a vampire. But Morfram's reaction gave her the boost she needed to face Alaric, especially when Liam and Tristan dropped back, letting her take the last steps alone.

She clenched her fists. Once upon a time, each of those men had been summoned before Alaric, and each had proven his mettle. Now, it was her turn.

"Sir," she murmured with a tiny curtsy.

Alaric didn't say anything. He just sat on that throne of his, totally aloof. Then, ever so slowly, he reached for a newspaper, snapped it open, and began to read.

Well, it appeared as though he wanted to read. But his eyes glowed in frustration as he squinted at the small type. He turned the newspaper this way and that in the dim light, growing more furious by the second.

At first, Natalie thought the news was the source of his fury, and her stomach sank. Had there been a terrorist attack she hadn't heard about? Had new enemies staged an ambush? Had left-wing political parties made gains in the polls?

But then she spotted Alaric scowling at a pair of reading glasses on the far side of the table, and her pulse settled. Whew.

"Here, let me get them for you," she said, hurrying over for the glasses.

Which might have been a mistake, because Alaric looked madder than ever. But, heck. He couldn't be mad at her about his eyesight.

He grunted a begrudging *merci* and snapped the newspaper a second time, signaling his audience to listen and listen well.

"*Les catacombes vandalisées.*" He read the headline then scowled at Natalie over the top of the newspaper. *Catacombs vandalized.* Then his eyes flicked down, and he continued to read. "'Vandals strike the Catacombs. Jean-Marc Pourtaud, director of the catacombs, despaired as he reported fire damage to the historic Moine Ensemble, deep in the catacombs. The unique area, closed to the public, suffered significant burn damage. Although the artifacts of the ensemble escaped damage, it is clear they were tampered with by the incorrigible vandals. Have they no shame?'" Alaric flipped the newspaper down and glared at Natalie. "What do you have to say for yourself?"

Natalie gulped and looked at her feet, not quite sure what to say. Luckily, Liam piped up.

"The vampires started it, sir."

Natalie caught Hugo hiding a smile.

"Monsieur Bennett, my question was not directed at you," Alaric growled.

"No, sir. Sorry, sir," Liam murmured, taking a step back.

"We did our best to put the sword and dagger back into their original positions," Natalie tried.

Alaric didn't look impressed, but it was Morfram who replied. "Let us not forget it was a dragon shifter who orchestrated the attack."

"With the help of those vampires," Tristan pointed out.

"It was Jacqueline who initiated it all," Morfram shot back.

"Um..." Natalie interjected, seeing the makings of a fight.

"Jacqueline wouldn't have dared go so far without their assistance," Albiorix threw in.

"Gentlemen..." Natalie tried.

But Morfram spun on Albiorix, enraged. "Gargoyles did the reconnaissance for her."

"True," Tristan agreed. "Gargoyles were in on it from the very beginning."

Natalie looked to Alaric, then Hugo. Surely, they would say something to halt the escalating fight? But they just stood there without uttering a word.

Well, fine. She stepped forward, threw up her hands, and hollered a sharp, "Stop!"

Everyone stared, and she stuck her hands on her hips. "Listen to yourselves. Yes, vampires, gargoyles, and a dragon worked together to stage that attack. But if we don't cooperate now, we'll never beat them."

Morfram, Albiorix, and Tristan shot one another slitty-eyed looks, while Alaric and Hugo exchanged... Wait. Smiles?

Hugo winked at her. *I knew you could do it.*

Natalie took a deep breath, trying not to get intimidated. Then she stuck a finger at each of the men in turn. "Squabbling is always easier than finding common ground." She gulped, realizing that meant she had better lead by example and give Morfram a chance. "You have to be above that if you're going to succeed."

"You?" Hugo asked, raising his eyebrows in a way that asked, *Do you include yourself in that group?*

Natalie's heart hammered. She had already made up her mind to stay in Paris, but this was a stark reminder of exactly what that entailed. Paris wasn't all art galleries and pleasant walks in the park, and staying meant a lot more than spending time with the sexiest man alive. Accepting her role as a Fire Maiden came with great responsibility. There would be danger. Intrigue. Shifter-style politics. She chewed her lip, thinking it over one more time.

Alaric shot Hugo a worried look.

But the moment Natalie glanced at Tristan, she found herself replying without the slightest doubt.

"We," she said firmly. "We have to be above that if we're going to succeed."

Alaric still didn't look satisfied. "Succeed in what, exactly? Anyone can live in a fancy apartment and collect clothes."

Natalie saw red. She'd never been interested in such things. "That was Jacqueline, not me."

Thank goodness Clara came to the rescue then. "May I remind you Natalie never inquired about the perks?"

Alaric replied with a low, unhappy grunt, and Natalie tossed her hands impatiently.

"Look, you're the one who was searching for a Fire Maiden. You found one, though you didn't bother filling me in on all the details. Like this, for instance." She held up her crystal.

Alaric narrowed his eyes. "What do you mean?"

She shook it impatiently. "I know it comes from Liviana's treasure hoard, but what power does it have?"

Alaric looked blank. "It doesn't have any. It simply reflects whatever power the bearer possesses deep inside."

Natalie just about keeled over. That power... that determination... That had all come from her?

"But... but..."

Tristan stepped forward. "You placed Natalie in danger."

Alaric shrugged. "We had to be sure she was the one."

"You nearly made sure she was killed," Tristan muttered.

Natalie crossed her arms. "Tristan was nearly killed too. One of your own men. How could you?"

"Sometimes it is necessary to... shall we say, test a man for his virtues?"

Natalie's jaw dropped, and Tristan growled. "She could have died."

Alaric, damn him, simply nodded. "She would have, if she were not worthy. And yes, you would have died too. But as you can see, we are all here today."

Natalie put a hand on Tristan's arm, holding him back. Before she could snap at Alaric, Hugo stepped between them and spoke.

"I agree that Alaric's methods were risky." He shot the dragon a stern look. "But his heart lies in the right place. He only wants the best for the city."

"Would it be best if our Fire Maiden died?" Tristan growled.

Natalie was about to glare at Alaric, but a weary flicker passed over his eyes, and she reconsidered. Alaric had dedicated a lifetime to protecting the city. His methods were definitely old-school, but she didn't doubt he meant well. And, heck. She could only imagine what it was like to shoulder so much responsibility for so long — and all alone. For every loyal lieutenant, like Hugo, there had probably been a dozen Jacquelines, all plotting to overthrow him.

Natalie looked at Tristan. No matter what obstacles she faced, she could manage them with her mate's help. But Alaric had no one. Not a mate, at least.

"I came to Paris with another dream," she admitted. "And for a while, all I found was a nightmare. But now I have a different dream, and you helped me find it. A dream that will take a lot of work but can help a lot of people. Good people, like Philippe... Abdel... Yan..."

Alaric's blank expression asked, *Who the hell are they?* but Tristan nodded along. He'd met some of those homeless men and knew all about single moms struggling to make ends meet.

"Sometimes I think she knows the city better than we do," he pitched in.

Alaric's eyes darted between them, then finally rested on Natalie. "Do you really think you can do it? Can you live up to the measure of your ancestors?"

Natalie considered for a moment, then turned the question around, too tired to play games. "I don't know. What do you think?"

Alaric looked her over slowly and finally flapped a hand. "You'll do."

Hugo burst out laughing. "She'll do? My friend, when was the last time the Guardians were blessed with a woman of such grit and character? Other than my dear Clara, of course." He winked at his mate. "To have those qualities combined with royal blood is a rare gift, indeed."

Alaric sighed. "Fine. I agree on that count. But a Fire Maiden needs a suitable escort. Not this...this..." He waved at Tristan.

"Hero?" Natalie filled in.

"Lower-class warrior." Alaric frowned then shrugged at Tristan. "Nothing personal, of course."

"Of course," Tristan muttered.

But Natalie exploded. "Lower-class?"

Alaric merely shrugged. "Humans — especially you Americans — don't understand such things. But bloodlines are important. Your lineage is royal."

"So was Jacqueline's, correct?"

Alaric's face soured. "A drop of royal ancestry. Your blood is thick with it. And as a Fire Maiden, you have certain standards to uphold."

"Standards? Like Marcel?"

Alaric looked at Morfram, who looked at his feet. "I admit my nephew was an unfortunate choice, and I have reassigned him accordingly."

Natalie raised an eyebrow.

Hugo grinned. "Tunisia."

Tristan chuckled, while Liam burst out laughing. A moment later, they both covered up by coughing.

Alaric glowered at them then turned back to Natalie. "No need to preoccupy yourself, my dear. We will find you a suitable mate."

Obviously, Alaric wasn't the type to sniff out every nuance in a person's scent. Which left Natalie in a dilemma. Should she come out and let Alaric know she was already mated?

Nah, she decided, shooting Tristan a wink.

"Maybe I already found one."

"I said, suitable."

Natalie stepped closer. "I will be the one to choose my own mate, do you understand? One that's not just suitable, but the best."

Tristan stood a little straighter, and she could feel his inner dragon glow.

Alaric glared, and Natalie hoped he wouldn't stand up and shatter the confidence she'd mustered. But she was fighting for Tristan now, the way he had fought for her. So she dug deep and glared back.

"Tristan risked his life for me — not because of orders or royal blood." She made air quotes around the *royal* part. "Just because I'm me. Marcel, on the other hand, was only interested in power."

Alaric made a face. "If you had given him a chance..."

Natalie shook her head, standing her ground. This was it. Alaric might be scary as hell, but she had to set things straight, once and for all.

"No, I'm giving you one chance. You want me as your Fire Maiden? Fine. I accept — but on my own terms."

Alaric's glare said, *I'm the one who gives orders around here.*

She went on before he could protest. "I stay. I pick my own mate..." She glanced at Tristan in spite of herself. The second their eyes met, her heart leaped. "In my own time."

Never mind that she already had. Somehow, guarding that secret from Alaric made it even more special.

"In the meantime, I commit myself to helping your cause, but in my own way. If I want to work in a soup kitchen, I will. If I find a better way to serve the city, I will do so. My life. My choices. You got that?"

Alaric's face was red. "Fire Maidens do not mingle with commoners. They cannot be placed in danger."

She jerked a thumb toward Tristan. "You're forgetting about my bodyguard."

Tristan braced his legs and crossed his thick arms. He was trying to do that vacant, stare-into-the-distance thing the Queen's guards in London did, but Natalie caught the hint of a smile playing around his lips.

"I think our Fire Maiden has proven capable of protecting herself." Hugo grinned.

Natalie did too. Soon, she would be able to protect the city *and* protect herself, as Liviana's daughters had in their time. She could turn into a dragon and fly away from vampires.

Better yet, incinerate them, her inner beast rumbled.

Smiling, she imagined a long plume of fire. Of course, she still had to learn, but Tristan had promised to walk her through every step.

"And you never know," Clara added, winking at Natalie. "If she happens to find herself a nice dragon to mate with — by her own free will, of course — she'll become a dragon shifter. I'd like to see the vampire who would dare threaten her then."

Morfram shrank back, and Natalie hid a smile. If only they knew.

My mate, she whispered into Tristan's mind. *Forever.*

Forever. Tristan's eyes blazed.

Behind him, Liam grinned, and she could picture him joking, *And the sex is bloody amazing, or so I'm told.*

That, Natalie could attest to, but she bit her tongue. The idea of a vampire bite made her nauseous, but a mating bite from Tristan...

Her body heated all over again, and she struggled not to let it show.

But Alaric, the old curmudgeon, still frowned. "The ancient spell works best when the city is ruled by the strongest bloodlines."

Natalie cleared her throat and ran over the arguments she'd practiced. "Claudine d'Islay — she was one of the most powerful Fire Maidens, right? About two hundred years ago?"

Alaric stared, and Natalie did her best not to look smug.

"I read about her in one of your books. Her mate didn't come from noble stock. Breselan was a knight who proved himself in battle." She glanced at Tristan. That certainly fit. "Then there was Elizabeth Rhydderick — over in England in the seventeenth century, I think."

"Eighteenth," Alaric muttered.

Natalie nodded. "Her mate was a blacksmith, as another of your books pointed out."

Alaric frowned. "Your point is...?"

Natalie kept her cool. "The spell is at its strongest — and the city most peaceful — when the Fire Maiden isn't just in residence, but happy. Truly happy, in a way few people ever know."

Hugo and Clara nodded knowingly, and Natalie held her breath. Was it greedy to wish for that kind of happiness for herself?

It's not a wish. It's destiny, Tristan whispered into her mind.

Natalie resisted the urge to cuddle up to him — or better yet, to kiss him. But their kisses had a way of getting out of control, and she had a meeting to wrap up first. So she crossed her arms and faced Alaric.

"Those are my terms. Do you accept?"

Alaric's face was stony, but Hugo laughed. "My friend, you have your heart's desire. The city has a Fire Maiden again — a formidable one. What else could you wish for?"

Alaric grimaced. "A little more willingness to comply with orders."

"Then you'd be wishing for a weak Maiden and a dim-witted man at her side," Hugo pointed out. "That is not what Paris needs. Besides, a powerful Fire Maiden will allow you more time off."

Alaric's eyes brightened, though he cleared his throat gruffly a moment later. "We'll see about that." Then his face went stony. "Let us not forget that danger remains."

Everyone leaned forward, and Morfram uttered, "What now?"

The lines of Alaric's face deepened. "Jacqueline. We don't know where she's gone, but we know she was in contact with the Lombardi clan. They might not have dared enter the city on their own, but they have been waiting for an opportunity to stage a coup. They will be looking for our weaknesses."

"So we'd better not have any," Natalie said. "And we won't as long as we work together."

Tristan shot Morfram a suspicious look, while Morfram scowled at Albiorix. Alaric frowned at everyone. But Natalie made herself meet each person's gaze, and gradually, the suspicion gave way to determination.

"We work together," Morfram finally said, and everyone's head bobbed.

For the next few minutes, the air was thick with tension as each of the Guardians renewed their vows to protect the city. Then Alaric sighed and turned back to Natalie.

"I suppose you'll be moving in to the palace as soon as possible."

Natalie stood very still. Palace? Whoa. How much of an inheritance came with the job? "I prefer Tristan's apartment."

Alaric stared. "That inadequate little place?"

She resisted the urge to burst out laughing. "It's more than I ever dreamed of." Besides, it already felt like home.

Home, her heart sighed. *With Tristan.*

Alaric must have caught her blissful expression, because he heaved another theatrical sigh. "Any other demands?"

"No more demands," she said cheerily. "Oh, except maybe meeting with you weekly."

"I run this city," Alaric growled.

She stuck up her hands. "Believe me, I wouldn't want it any other way. But I need to know how I can help and what I have to be aware of. Would that be all right with you?"

Alaric pursed his lips and an agonizing minute passed. His gray eyes swept over her, taking stock in a whole new way. Finally, he gave a tiny nod and grunted, "Sundays. In the morning. Eight o'clock, sharp."

"Eight o'clock would be perfect."

Tristan groaned in her mind. Eight was sinfully early in his book — especially on a Sunday. But Natalie was sure it wouldn't last more than a few weeks. It was just another test — an easy one that didn't put her life at risk. Once Alaric understood she was truly committed, he would back off. Besides, she doubted he had any desire to start his Sundays early either.

"Perfect. Thank you." She bent into a little bow. "I guess we'll be going now."

Tristan nodded immediately, and Hugo grinned. "Yes, you'd better be going. You and your... bodyguard."

Natalie's blood warmed. She and Tristan had gone a whole two hours without having sex, and she was starting to feel the itch again. But, crap. Was it that obvious?

A moment later, she decided love was nothing to be ashamed of. So she hooked her elbow through Tristan's and smiled her goodbyes — including one for Morfram, though that one was a little forced.

"Thank you, everyone. I mean it." Her voice cracked when she looked at Clara. "Thank you."

"No, thank you," Hugo said, bowing his head.

Alaric maintained a grumpy silence, but Natalie figured she would take what she could get. Then she turned for the door, patting Tristan's hand. When they stepped into the sun-drenched courtyard outside, a weight fell from her shoulders.

"We did it," she whispered, striding away quickly.

Tristan brushed his lips over her knuckles. "You did it."

"That was a team effort, and you know it. But, whew. There were moments there..." She trailed off.

Tristan sighed. "I have to keep reminding myself Alaric means well."

Natalie chewed that one over. "He does. And I almost feel sorry for him, leading on his own for all that time."

Tristan made a face. "Almost."

She laughed. "Think about it. All those years without a mate..."

Tristan's arm slid from her back to her rear. "True. I've gone two hours without touching mine, and it's already driving me crazy. It's a miracle Alaric hasn't gone completely mad."

Natalie laughed, then went somber. "Maybe he never met his mate — the way I would never have met you if I hadn't come to Paris."

"We would have met. Destiny wanted us together. Even a lower-class warrior like me knows that."

Natalie put a finger to his scowl. "Lower-class? Don't get me started."

"But—"

She shook her head firmly. "Just hush."

"Hush? Are you ordering me around, woman?"

"No, I just need all my concentration to get to the end of the street without kissing you."

Her mind was already skipping ahead to all the fun they could have at home, but the sound of someone clearing his throat made her and Tristan both turn.

It was Liam, hurrying to catch up. He faked exasperation. "I know it's Paris, but still. Can we please limit public displays of affection?"

Natalie laughed. "Sorry."

"Not sorry," Tristan growled.

Liam ignored him, grinning from ear to ear. "I wish I'd had a camera to capture the look on Alaric's face when you laid out your terms."

Natalie's knees wobbled a little. "I'm just glad it's over."

Liam sighed. "Apropos, being over. It's time I said goodbye."

Her heart sank. Liam was a great friend and ally. It would be hard to see him go.

Tristan thumped his back. "Right. You've been given your own post. Finally," he teased.

It ought to have been an occasion to celebrate, but a man had never looked glummer than Liam just then. "Yes. I get a whole city to protect and my very own drafty castle to spend weekends in." He sighed. "Promise you'll visit soon."

Natalie laughed. "A castle, huh?"

Liam made a face. "It's not as glamorous as it sounds. Suits of armor, mothballs..."

Tristan grinned. "Duty calls. London needs you."

Liam nodded glumly. "Lord knows the city is a mess. I just wish it had a little more sun to bask in." Then he brightened and clapped, dismissing the thought. "Anyway, I'm off. Wish me *bon voyage* and all that."

Natalie hugged him. "Thanks for everything. And yes, I'd love to visit."

He winked. "Bring a friend, will you? And I don't just mean this guy." He turned to Tristan, and they edged into one of those man-hugs that involved a lot of backslapping and handshaking — anything to cover up the mistiness in their eyes.

A lump rose in Natalie's throat. Those two had spent most of the past decade together, and the depth of their friendship showed.

Then Tristan pushed Liam down the cobbled road. "Get going. See you in London."

"Ta-ta," Liam said and turned away.

They watched him saunter down the street and turn the corner. When he disappeared, Tristan sighed.

"Sad to see him go, huh?" Natalie whispered.

Tristan snorted. "That pain in the neck? No." Then he grinned. "Well, maybe a little. But I'm glad to have you to myself."

She ran a hand over his chest. "That reminds me — where were we? Oh, yes. I was trying to make it to the end of the street before kissing you."

"You might last that long, but I won't." He pulled her into the shade of a huge potted plant and backed her against the wall. "Permission for a kiss, Fire Maiden?"

She play-slapped him, then wound her arms around his shoulders. "None of that nonsense, not between us. But, yes. Kiss me. Please."

He leaned in slowly, and she breathed his oaky scent. A heartbeat later, his lips closed over hers, and she melted into his embrace. God, was she lucky.

Tristan shook his head, whispering between kisses, "Not luck. Destiny."

She nodded. "Destiny, my mate."

Epilogue

Two weeks later...

Natalie breathed deeply, inhaling the scent of lavender and sage. Then she shuffled from foot to foot and rubbed her arms, fighting off the night chill.

Shift, already. Let me out, a voice grumbled in her mind.

"You okay?" Tristan asked, hugging her from behind.

He was as naked as she was, and for a split second, she considered heading back to bed. Then again, they'd already spent most of the afternoon making love, and now that the sun had set, it was time to fly.

Or better put, to try to fly.

They were at a gorgeous vineyard in the south of France. *Her* vineyard, as it turned out. Apparently, being a Fire Maiden meant inheriting several properties and treasure hoards. The vineyard was just the tip of the iceberg of her fortunes, so to speak. Of course, that came with great responsibility. She wouldn't have to work a regular job for the rest of her life, but she would be fully committed to community projects. Lots of them, all the time. Her dream job, really.

On the other hand, she had a different set of worries now. Like flying. And not just flying, but breathing fire. Part of her job as a Fire Maiden would be to help Tristan patrol Paris, and she looked forward to that too. But, man. That all seemed so far in the future. Would she ever learn?

So far, she'd only shifted into dragon form a few times. When she had, she'd strutted around the back lawn of the sprawling farmhouse, nearly bashing pots of geraniums and an old-fashioned wine press with her tail. But she hadn't actually flown yet, because shifting had seemed like an adequate start. However, she'd promised herself — and Tristan — that the third time would be it, which meant...

She looked at the night sky and gulped.

"Ready?" Tristan asked.

Not really, no. But when he nuzzled her cheek, her resolve grew.

"Ready," she mumbled. *Sort of.*

The moon was rising over the hills in the east, casting pale light over rows of neatly tended grapes. Crickets chirped, and leaves rustled in the cool night breeze.

"You're going to love it. I promise." Tristan kissed her cheek, then stepped away and raised his arms. "On three. One..."

Natalie took a deep breath and mimicked Tristan, lifting her arms like wings.

"Two..." Tristan murmured.

Natalie tipped her head back and reached her chin skyward, feeling her neck stretch. Next, she pushed back her shoulders, closed her eyes, and—

"Three." Tristan's voice grew scratchy and deep.

Heat rushed through her body, and her skin prickled. Her blood seemed to double in volume, and a pull registered on the tips of her ears as they extended. Everything else extended, as well — her fingers, neck, and nose. A dozen scents hit her at once. Wafting lavender. The rich scent of the soil, and a pungent hint of fermentation from grapes that had fallen to the ground.

God, you're beautiful, Tristan's awed voice whispered in her mind.

She opened her eyes, about to correct him. But, wow. She really was beautiful. Her body was a dark coppery color that glinted in the moonlight, and her leathery hide was sleek yet tough at the same time. She held out her wings, admiring the delicate yet powerful curves.

Tristan's hide was a smooth, brownish-black, and together, they made quite the pair. Him all bulky and powerful, her leaner and more... well, feminine. Even glamorous, somehow.

A true Fire Maiden, Tristan added with pride.

Her tail lashed — a motion that had shocked the bejesus out of her the first time.

You're not looking too bad yourself.

He grinned, making her girl parts heat and her inner dragon purr. *Maybe we can practice more than flying.*

Natalie flapped her wings a little, trying to cool off. This was about flying, not mating.

Her dragon's head moved from side to side. *First flying, then mating. Okay?*

She smiled. A girl did need the occasional reward.

Tristan's grin grew. *Both are fun. But yes — flying first.*

He motioned, and she followed him to the top of a low mound. *So, the wind is coming from...*

She stuck out a wing. *That way.*

Exactly. Which means we should take off...

She pointed. *That way.*

He'd already explained the dynamics to her. Like planes, they would take off into the wind for the extra lift under their wings.

Not like planes, her dragon corrected. *Like dragons. We came first.*

Tristan made a sweeping motion with his wing. *Just a couple of quick steps, a few flaps of your wings, and you'll be airborne. Then we'll head that way...*

He went on for a minute or two, and she nodded, trying to memorize every word. But when she finally lined up for takeoff, her mind went blank. When Tristan took off ahead of her, all she felt was fear. Of taking off. Of flying. Most of all, of landing. She was scared of failing Tristan — and of failing everyone. What kind of Fire Maiden would that make her?

Oh, for goodness' sake, her dragon muttered.

And just like that, she was running down the slope, powered by a stubborn burst of courage. Leading with her nose and holding her tail straight, she picked up speed and beat her wings.

A few more steps, then up, Tristan called.

He'd explained that too — after hitting a certain speed, she simply had to lift her feet off the ground and trust her wings. So Natalie bared her teeth, promised herself she could do it— *Of course, I can do it,* her dragon snipped.

—and folded one foot against her belly. A moment later, she gingerly lifted the other, and—

Wheeee! her dragon cheered.

The first rows of vines rushed under her belly, and cool air flowed under her wings. She was airborne. She'd done it!

Okay, so she might have clipped a few vines on her way up. But, hey. She was flying! Soaring, even. Folding the back edge of her wings down, she shot upward. Before long, she was higher than the terra-cotta roof of the house. Higher than the barn. Higher than the hilltops, even, and it wasn't scary at all.

Tristan whooped. *Look at you go! Magnifique!*

It wasn't often that Natalie felt *magnifique*. But it was hard not to at a moment like that. Her wings were huge and steady, her tail straight, keeping her body streamlined. She was high, mighty, and totally in control.

Well, mostly in control. Every once in a while, she'd tip her wings too far and wobble. But with Tristan flying steadily by her side, she found her balance and flew on.

For the first few minutes, the exhilaration of flying made her cry out in joy. Then she started noticing the details of the landscape, too.

Wow, she breathed again and again.

The rows of vines below created a chevron pattern, following the contours of the hills. Meandering stone walls hemmed in the fields, and beyond them lay fields of lavender like so many purple blankets laid out to dry. Rows of sage sprang up between them, and she closed her eyes, savoring the rich aroma. In the distance, the spire of a village church pointed to the stars.

Bong... Bong... Bong...

The ring of church bells carried for miles, following the hilly landscape. It was a quarter to midnight, and she felt like Cinderella at a ball. Would the clock strike once more and wake her from a vivid dream, or was this all real?

I'm real, all right. Her dragon side flexed her claws and waggled her tail.

The wind whistled in her ears. The world was hushed, and the harvest moon was huge and orange.

Just like that vision, she thought, awed.

The first time Tristan had given her the mating bite, she'd pictured nearly the same scene. It was all there — the church bells, the vineyard, the scenery. Everything but fire crackling around her lips. But, heck. She was content to save that for a future lesson.

This way, Tristan called, dipping a wing.

He bore away to the south, then looked back to check that she was following. His eyes glowed softly in the darkness, so eager, her heart swelled.

This is amazing, she said.

It came out in coughy, guttural dragon talk that was strangely comprehensible to her ears.

It gets better. He grinned.

When she snorted, a tiny spark popped out of her mouth. Oops.

But Tristan just laughed. *No need to worry about anyone noticing that. But someday...*

His voice rose with pride, and Natalie pictured herself soaring through the air and spitting fire. She'd need a lot of practice, that was for sure. But once she learned that — well, let a vampire try to bother her then.

No one will dare, my Fire Maiden. Tristan's eyes flared in anger, then softened again.

For a few minutes, she flew with gritty determination. Gradually, the crisp evening air and sweet Provençal scents helped her relax again and simply enjoy.

Not long now, Tristan said as they glided along.

At first, she thought he might take her toward Nîmes, the historic town emitting a soft glow in the distance. But Tristan's course took them farther north, and soon, he dipped closer to the landscape. A silver line snaked between the folds of the hills, and Tristan took a sharp left, following it.

The river Gardon, Tristan murmured. *And up ahead...*

She looked forward, wondering what surprise lay around the next bend. A waterfall? A pool wide enough for a swim?

They banked right, then left, following the curves of the river. And when the river straightened again...

Wow, she breathed.

Le Pont du Gard, Tristan said. *The Romans built it.*

Natalie had seen the structure in postcards but never with her own eyes: three stories of delicate stone arches, forming a bridge that supported an aqueduct. The river flowed sedately underneath, creating a gorgeous scene that probably hadn't changed in two thousand years. Trees blanketed the hillsides on either side of the river, their leaves fluttering in the breeze.

Watch this, Tristan called, diving toward the lowest level of the aqueduct.

Wait. Natalie cried. Was he really going to—

She held her breath as he folded his wings and shot through the central arch. Then she yelped and twisted upward, barely clearing the top level in her moment of distraction.

Tristan zoomed through the arches then snapped open his wings and shot upward, grinning wildly.

Fun, huh? I haven't done that since I was a kid.

Fun? More like crazy. But Natalie couldn't bring herself to chastise her mate. Not when he seemed so free and happy.

You want to try? he asked.

She laughed. *No way. But maybe someday,* she hurried to add when his face fell. *I'll just watch for now.*

It's easy. You just fold your wings at exactly the right second—

And crash into the pillar, she nearly said.

But Tristan zoomed through effortlessly — once, skimming the water as he swept through the lowest level, and a second time through the central arch of the middle level. Natalie circled above, holding her breath.

See? Tristan grinned as he joined her.

She laughed. *Show-off.*

Maybe a little. But it is fun.

It did look fun. And the crazy thing was how natural it felt to be soaring over the ground.

We'll have to come back for a swim sometime, Tristan said, banking left. *But for now, let's go this way.*

For the next few minutes, they followed the line of the aqueduct over the countryside. Vineyards alternated with fields of herbs, and tiny towns clustered around hillsides, each crowned by a church. Natalie took it all in, awed. For years, she'd dreamed of a life like this. Now, she was living it, and in style. She had a penthouse apartment in Paris and her own country retreat. More importantly, she had a good man who'd proven his love for her again and again.

She exhaled deeply. How lucky could a girl get?

Maybe we can get even luckier, her dragon murmured, brushing up against Tristan.

He looked over, eyes aglow, making her body heat all over.

Oh, yes, her dragon purred.

His eyes were a rich, orange-red hue — the glow of passion. Natalie's eyes prickled, which probably meant they were glowing the same way. And who could blame her, what with the sultry images drifting through her mind? She imagined two dragons winding around each other, high in the sky. Coming closer and closer in a tight love knot, their wings and bodies pressed together. Their tails would whip the air beneath them, keeping them airborne just long enough to—

Natalie fanned herself with her right wing then cleared her throat.

How about we head home?

Tristan shot her a wicked grin. *So soon?*

She nodded firmly. Someday, she might be up to flying under bridges and enjoying aerial sex. But not on her first flight. On the other hand, the night was still young, and she knew just how she wanted to celebrate her first flight.

How? Tristan asked, reading her mind.

She licked her lips. The bed in the vineyard's farmhouse was nice, big, and solid. The sheets were soft, and the air would be tinged with the scent of the roses that climbed around the windows.

Oh, I may have a few ideas, she murmured.

Tristan drifted under her, brushing her belly as if warming up for what she had in mind.

I like your ideas, he murmured, making her heat all over again.

She snorted. In all seriousness, she had dozens of ideas for projects in Paris — and ways to finance them, as well as arguments to persuade Alaric of their worth. But tonight...

Tristan chuckled. *A good thing we have all night, my mate.*

Sneak Peek: Fire Maidens: London

"Rebel with a cause" Gemma Archer flees Boston one step ahead of the creep who insists she's his. Now she's in London, trying to build a new normal — and absolutely, positively, not getting involved with any men. That is, until an irresistible stranger prowls into her life. Liam is a sweet, sexy modern-day knight who sparks sizzling desires Gemma never even knew she had. The problem? He's as loony as some of her relatives. Dragons? Lion shifters? Werewolves? The poor man really seems to believe the tales he spins.

Liam Bennett is fresh out of the military and doing his best to adjust to civilian life. But fitting in was never his forte as a shifter of mixed blood. He's part lion — a member of London's most noble family — and part rogue, with "undesirable" dragon blood. When the Guardians of London hire him to help maintain law and order, Liam jumps at the chance to prove himself. Soon, he discovers nothing is as it seems — not among his allies, enemies, or even his own family. The only thing he can be sure of is the danger Gemma is in.

A deadly foe has stalked Gemma for thousands of miles, and Liam has no choice but to spirit his destined mate away to his ancestral dragon home — the remote castle in Wales he's been avoiding for years. But hiding out is not enough. To survive, Liam and Gemma must face cunning enemies — and the deceptions of the past.

Get your copy of *Fire Maidens: London* today!

Books by Anna Lowe

Fire Maidens - Billionaires & Bodyguards

Fire Maidens: Paris (Book 1)

Fire Maidens: London (Book 2)

Fire Maidens: Rome (Book 3)

Fire Maidens: Portugal (Book 4)

Fire Maidens: Ireland (Book 5)

Aloha Shifters - Jewels of the Heart

Lure of the Dragon (Book 1)

Lure of the Wolf (Book 2)

Lure of the Bear (Book 3)

Lure of the Tiger (Book 4)

Love of the Dragon (Book 5)

Lure of the Fox (Book 6)

Aloha Shifters - Pearls of Desire

Rebel Dragon (Book 1)

Rebel Bear (Book 2)

Rebel Lion (Book 3)

Rebel Wolf (Book 4)

Rebel Heart (A prequel to Book 5)

Rebel Alpha (Book 5)

The Wolves of Twin Moon Ranch

Desert Hunt (the Prequel)

Desert Moon (Book 1)

Desert Wolf: Complete Collection (Four short stories)

Desert Blood (Book 2)

Desert Fate (Book 3)

Desert Heart (Book 4)

Desert Yule (a short story)

Desert Rose (Book 5)

Desert Roots (Book 6)

Sasquatch Surprise (a Twin Moon spin-off story)

Blue Moon Saloon

Perfection (a short story prequel)

Damnation (Book 1)

Temptation (Book 2)

Redemption (Book 3)

Salvation (Book 4)

Deception (Book 5)

Celebration (a holiday treat)

Shifters in Vegas
Paranormal romance with a zany twist

Gambling on Trouble

Gambling on Her Dragon

Gambling on Her Bear

Serendipity Adventure Romance

Off the Charts

Uncharted

Entangled

Windswept

Adrift

Travel Romance

Veiled Fantasies

Island Fantasies

visit www.annalowebooks.com

About the Author

USA Today and Amazon bestselling author Anna Lowe loves putting the "hero" back into heroine and letting location ignite a passionate romance. She likes a heroine who is independent, intelligent, and imperfect – a woman who is doing just fine on her own. But give the heroine a good man – not to mention a chance to overcome her own inhibitions – and she'll never turn down the chance for adventure, nor shy away from danger.

Anna loves dogs, sports, and travel – and letting those inspire her fiction. On any given weekend, you might find her hiking in the mountains or hunched over her laptop, working on her latest story. Either way, the day will end with a chunk of dark chocolate and a good read.

Visit AnnaLoweBooks.com

Made in the USA
Columbia, SC
14 July 2022